Stewart Home  of
fiction and cult *nt
Pose, No Pity*, a *ke
Papers*. His novels, *Slow Death, Come Before Christ
and Murder Love*, and his edited collection, *Mind
Invaders: A Reader in Psychic Warfare, Cultural
Sabotage and Semiotic Terrorism*, are also published
by Serpent's Tail. He lives in London.

BLOW JOB

STEWART HOME

✢

Library of Congress Catalog Card Number: 97–068216

A complete catalogue record for this book can be
obtained from the British Library on request

First published in 1997 by Serpent's Tail,
4 Blackstock Mews, London N4, and
180 Varick Street, 10th floor, New York, NY 10014
website: www.serpentstail.com

Phototypeset in Garamond by Intype London Ltd.
Printed in Great Britain by Mackays of Chatham

✢ ONE ✢

THE MEMORIAL PARADE had lured several thousand demonstrators from warren-like council estates, decaying terraced houses and student halls of residence. Familiar faces were turning up like bad pennies. As Mike Armilus pushed his way past a group of punks, he caught a glimpse of Swift Nick Carter, who was making his way towards the cenotaph.

'Get back or I'll nick you,' a cop barked as Mike sidled up to the thin blue line that separated the massed ranks of antagonists.

Armilus melted back into the crowd. He'd been within gobbing distance of Genghis I-Hunn, head of an identity outfit known as the Church of Adolf Hitler.

'What's the matter, Mike?' Butcher demanded as Armilus stumbled into his former room-mate. 'I haven't seen you looking so miserable since you dropped a fifty-pence piece down a drain.'

'It was a pound coin!' Mike insisted before breaking into a grin.

'Seriously, Mike,' Butcher persisted, 'what's wrong?'

'I thought I saw Swift Nick weaving his way towards Jackboots Houghton.'

'You must have been mistaken,' Butcher hissed. 'Nick would never join up with the Anglo-Saxon Movement.'

'I don't . . .' Mike said and then broke off in mid-sentence, his attention distracted by two punks who'd steamed into the cops.

On the other side of this thin blue line, Swift Nick made the most of the disturbance. Unfortunately, he was surrounded by stewards within a matter of seconds of approaching the wreaths that were piled up against the cenotaph. Nick didn't have time to locate the bomb, let alone dispose of the device he knew nationalist provocateurs had planted amongst the flowers.

'What the fuck do you think you're doing?' a No Future Party steward demanded.

'I'm just admiring the tributes to Ian Stuart, our fallen nationalist martyr,' Nick replied.

Carter had to think on his feet. There was no point in fighting. If it came to a scrap, Nick would be carted off by the cops before he'd had a chance to find the bomb. He picked up a wreath and pretended to admire it.

'Don't touch the flowers!' the steward snarled. 'I'll let it pass this time, just stay away from the cenotaph.'

'Racial comrade!' Nick pleaded. 'I . . .'

'Shut up!' the steward fizzed. 'And don't argue. You're lucky you haven't had your head kicked in.

If it wasn't for the fact that I've seen you drinking in the Blade Bone, I'd suspect you were a Red! Now move!'

Split seconds later, the former leader of Class Justice was mingling with the main body of Nazi youth. Nick decided to bide his time. If the counter-demonstrators broke through the police line, the fascist stewards would be caught up in the fight and he would have another opportunity to locate the bomb.

The two punks who'd steamed into the cops succeeded in knocking a helmet from a constable's head before they were arrested. Four of their comrades were detained in an abortive attempt at a rescue. Armilus clocked Steve Drummond lurking close to the fray. The anarchist chief looked less than happy about the prospect of leading what remained of his forces against the Mets.

The mentality of the Class Justice membership made Mike sick. These cunts thought it was clever to get nicked for rucking the filth. They viewed the prospect of six months inside as a heaven-sent opportunity to raise their credibility rating. Class Justice were more interested in the possibility of porridge than cracking Met skulls. Doing time proved a soap-dodger's commitment to the cause and got the individual concerned a write-up in the press.

'I'd like to thank the police for turning up today,' a No Future Party steward bawled into a megaphone, 'and for the wonderful job they've done, despite the fact that parliamentary do-gooders have tied their hands with red-tape. I'd also like to assure everyone that an NF government would abolish all rights for criminals and provide the courts with sentences that would act as a proper deterrent to lawlessness.'

'Get your hair cut, you dirty bastard,' Swift Nick bawled at a posh squatter as the cunt was carted off by the cops.

Nick detested the left-wing wankers who preyed upon and exploited his class. They were as bad as the Nazis! In his book, a snake crawling through mud couldn't lower itself to the level of the public school leftists who formed the advanced guard whenever a part of inner London became ripe for gentrification.

From anger, Carter's mood swung to despair. It seemed unlikely that anyone would provide him with the type of diversion he needed. In those tense, ticking off moments, Nick felt he was losing control of the situation. Without an outbreak of mass violence to provide a suitable distraction, it was not within his power to prevent the fascist outrage.

Carter was disgusted by the mobs that had gathered on either side of the police line. Neither had the bottle to break through the wall of Mets and launch an all out attack on their political enemies. They were more likely to fight amongst themselves. Several members of the Violent Party were threatening Narcissus Brooke, leader of the White Seed of Christ. If it came to a punch-up, Brooke didn't stand a chance. His following amounted to perhaps a dozen teenage birds. Among the leftist groups to the north, feelings were running high between the Spartacist Workers Group and the Workers League.

However, if the Trotskyites could reach an agreement among themselves, it was more than likely that they'd team up to fight the anarchists.

'Harry Roberts is our friend!' the cry was coming from a group of anarchists who supported Class Justice.

'He kills coppers,' two dozen Anglo-Saxon Movement boneheads chanted by way of reply.

'No, no, no, no!' Jackboots Houghton bellowsed, 'We must support the police. You mustn't join in when the Reds sing unpatriotic songs!'

But Jackboots was incapable of suppressing the terrace culture his supporters imbibed every Saturday afternoon. Hundreds of youths who'd descended upon the cenotaph to fight each other were suddenly united by their hatred of the filth.

'Put him on the streets again, let him kill some others,' they thundered.

A thousand hearts beat as one during those fleeting moments of union as members of Class Justice, the No Future Party, the Regulated Activity Movement, The Violent Party, Invisible Banner and the Anglo-Saxon Movement, chanted their support for the Shepherds Bush cop killer. However, no Trotskyite voices joined in the song. Marxist-Leninism was a creed for college kids who lacked an education in the hard knocks of life. Having enjoyed a pampered existence, these cunts hadn't learnt to hate the law.

Fascist and Trotskyite stewards on either side of the police line were attempting to hold back kids who were surging towards the cops. The ideologues had lost their grip on the working and lower-middle class youth, who now realised they should unite against both the fuzz and their own political controllers.

Swift Nick Carter took advantage of this diversion to detach himself from the crowd and make his way towards the cenotaph. Split seconds later, a squad of fascist stewards fanned out ahead of him. Carter decided to beat a tactical retreat. Mike Armilus noted with pleasure that the pigs were shitting themselves. He caught sight of Nick as the former Class Justice leader hurried from the scene.

There was a lot of pushing and shoving going on but, as yet, there'd been no serious fighting on either side of the police line. Most of the blows being exchanged were between stewards and teenagers. Met involvement was more or less limited to snatching the odd kid from the crowd.

Having just emerged from an exhibition of avant-garde ceramics at the Institute of Contemporary Art, Patricia Good found herself on the fringes of the mêlée as she attempted to make her way towards Westminster tube station. Steve Drummond caught sight of the chick and liked what he saw. Being a bisexual, Steve rated skinny birds with long blond hair.

As Drummond was formulating a chat-up line, the bomb planted by fascist provocateurs exploded. A sheet of flame engulfed the cenotaph and a thunderous roar was followed by several seconds of shocked silence. Events had unfolded just as the leaders of the Nazi terrorist organisation AC Thor 33 had intended. Not even a conspiracy nut would think of blaming the far-Right for blowing up the cenotaph and simultaneously maiming scores of fascist youth. The Reds were sure to take the blame for this outrage and wishy-washy patriots would be transformed into hardline nationalists overnight! Even Tory wets would be baying for commie blood!

Teenagers with deluded Nazi views, who a few minutes earlier had been ready to take on the cops, joined forces with the Mets as they laid into anti-nationalist demonstrators. All the right-wingers were now of one mind, the destruction of the cenotaph had to be avenged! Old rivalries were temporarily forgotten as the forces of reaction sought to settle a more pressing score.

However, the united front of Nazis and cops began to lose its collective nerve when the anti-nationalist lines failed to crumble under the first wave of their assault. They'd expected the Reds to turn on their heels and flee. But if the leftists had lacked the audacity to smash through the police line earlier that afternoon, they demonstrated their resolve now that they'd actually come under attack. As the anti-fascists defended their ground with whatever improvised weaponry came to hand, the front ranks of the reactionary axis turned and charged back into the waves of racial comrades who'd been coming up behind them.

In the confusion that followed, those Nazis and cops who weren't clubbed down by the advancing ranks of leftists, began fighting amongst themselves as they vainly attempted to flee the savage retribution of the revolutionary forces. Many a thick skull was cracked open as the Nazis suffered yet another crushing defeat.

Steve Drummond didn't participate in the action that afternoon. He was giving his undivided attention to Patricia Good. The girl had been terribly shocked by the explosion. Steve took Patricia into the Institute of Contemporary Arts café, where he comforted her over a cup of tea.

'I'd never have guessed you were a journalist,' Steve sighed.

'It's not as glamorous a profession as most people imagine,' Good replied. 'I work for a Catholic paper, we're not interested in the smut that merits column inches in the popular press. We only cover news that is of interest to people who've committed themselves to the true religion.'

'I hate journalists and Christians,' Drummond spat.

'Gosh!' Patricia exclaimed. 'I hope that isn't going to stop us being friends.'

'It won't,' Steve said reassuringly, 'I like you, I really do.'

The Mall and Horse Guards Parade had been cleared of protesters. Most anarchists had enough sense to disappear once they'd dealt the forces of reaction a crushing blow. The few who'd failed to make tracks were soon rounded up by the filth. Police reinforcements were still pouring into the Mall because rumours were circulating of an imminent attack upon Buckingham Palace.

Martin Smith, head of the Spartacist Workers Group, was assisting the Mets with their investigations. Smith had volunteered to help the cops as a means of preventing the British public from confusing lawless anarchists with the true heirs of the Trotsky mantle. The filth were allowing Martin to work with them on the understanding that he'd defend the force against any criticisms of their conduct that might arise as a result of the cenotaph riot.

'I'm only going to ask you once more,' Smith bleated as a cop punched an anarchist nicknamed Dog in the kidneys. 'I want the names of the Class Justice members who planted the bomb at the cenotaph.'

'The bomb had nothing to do with Class Justice,' Dog spat through a mouthful of blood and broken teeth.

'Don't lie to me!' Martin mewed as he kicked the suspect in the groin. 'This time the anarchist movement has gone too far, I'm gonna see to it that your leaders are put away for a long time!'

Dog didn't reply, he'd blacked out, thereby bringing the interrogation to an abrupt end. Two constables carted his limp body down to the cells. As Smith lit a fag, the telephone rang.

'Yes,' the Spartacist barked into the receiver.

'Martin, it's Inspector Newman, we've got a positive identification on the bomber. Several No Future Party stewards caught him poking about among the wreaths that were piled up against the cenotaph. Unfortunately, they didn't recognise the cunt at the time. However, we've just identified him from a set of photographs in our files.'

'Yes, yes,' Smith squawked, 'who is he?'

'Nick Carter,' the inspector replied.

'Jesus!' Martin raved. 'I thought he'd retired from politics.'

'Obviously not,' Newman was stating the obvious. 'Presumably, he stepped down as leader of Class Justice to go underground.'

'How are you gonna describe him to the press?' the Trotskyist demanded.

'As the leader of Class Justice,' the cop crowed. 'It would simply confuse the public if we attempted to explain that he was no longer a member of the organisation. There's no point in being academic about this now that we've got an opportunity to get popular opinion lined up behind us. I'll have Swift Nick's head on a platter, I'm out to destroy the anarchist movement!'

'Good,' Smith interjected.

'I think we both agree that Britain must be protected from mad bombers and subversive political creeds,' the inspector pontificated.

'Yes, yes,' Martin shot back.

Similar sentiments were being expressed at a meeting of AC Thor 33, an organisation whose sole aim was to co-ordinate the activities of the No Future Party, the Anglo-Saxon Movement, the Brixton Black Separatists and the Violent Party. Membership of this secretive cabal was a privilege bestowed upon the handful of nationalist leaders ideologically flexible enough to bring their own views into line with the aims of the shadowy Industrial League.

'We've got to make sure this smear sticks!' Adam White thundered.

'There's no need to shout,' Nigel Devi tutted, 'I

think we're all agreed on this point. We know the Industrial League wants results – and is prepared to pay generously for them!'

'Listen ethnic, don't play the diplomat with me!' White regularly resorted to abuse as he desperately attempted to assert his authority.

'Don't insult me Adam, you know I'm Savitri Devi's son and that my father was a Brahmin, which makes me a thoroughbred Aryan.'

'The rank-and-file membership of the Violent Party might believe that but you can't fool me. I've never seen your birth certificate – and even if you can prove your immediate lineage, I'll never accept you as white. Brahmin or not, in my book you're an ethnic. Back in India you might cut it as a descendant of the Nordics who brought culture to the continent, but here in Britain you're just another immigrant.'

'My mother was half-British and has been widely recognised as a force for White Unity and the trans-cendence of cultural division among the Nordic peoples.'

'In other words,' Adam sparred, 'she was a race-mixer.'

'Bigot!' Nigel raged.

'Let's just get on with the business at hand,' Matt Dread put in. 'As the leader of the Brixton Black Separatists, I'm not interested in your sectarian in-fighting. What's the point of arguing? If we can't learn to work together, then we're all fucked as far as funding from the Industrial League is concerned.'

'Matt's right,' Jackboots Houghton concurred, 'let's get back to our agenda.'

'Have your stewards contacted the cops and identified Swift Nick Carter as the man who planted the bomb?' Dread asked the leader of the Violent Party.

'Yes, everything is proceeding according to plan,' Devi assured him.

'I hope we've done the right thing,' White popped, 'from my chats with Carter in the Blade Bone, I got the impression that with a little work he would have become a genuine convert to nationalism. He might have been a very valuable addition to the movement.'

'It's pure fantasy,' Devi bawled, 'to imagine he was anything but a mole. For a start, he never told us his real name. Secondly, after being allowed to overhear us discussing the bomb plot, the bastard attempted to locate the device.'

'He never went to the cops, did he!' Adam objected. 'Maybe he was simply concerned about the fact that rank-and-file nationalists were going to be injured.'

'Adam,' there was a note of condescension in Nigel's voice, 'he's an anarchist and as such doesn't believe in reporting anything to the police. Besides, if Carter had the moral fibre to become a patriot, he'd have understood that many a man and woman will have to be sacrificed before Britain can once again become Great.'

'That's rich, coming from an ethnic!'

'Liberal!' Devi squealed.

'For Chrissakes!' Dread rasped in exasperation. 'Let's get on with the meeting. Our instructions were to smear the left and the anarchists. The Industrial League wants the country swung to the right.

We've already discussed what happened at the cenotaph. We have yet to reach a decision on whether or
not it's necessary to plan another outrage.'

Bogroll Bates was looking forward to starting his
new job. He'd been out of work for more than two
years. Signing on the dole was a blow to his pride.
Bogroll had ten years of solid employment behind
him when he was made redundant. He'd been confident of finding a new job within a matter of weeks.
However, as the days slipped by, Bogroll's natural
optimism began to fade. At first, he found himself
being asked for interviews before receiving the
inevitable rejection letter. As the months went by,
the occasions on which Bates was called up before
a potential employer became increasingly rare.

Bogroll had applied for more than eight hundred
jobs before being offered a position in the warehouse
of Label Clothing Ltd. The thought of earning a fair
wage for an honest day's work had given Bates the
strength to throw away the pills he'd been taking
for depression. It was a stroke of luck that Alan
Jones was the personnel manager at the company.
He'd been a friend of Bogroll's back in the eighties,
when they'd both regularly attended acid house
raves. In fact, it was Alan who'd given Bates his
nickname. The first time Bogroll visited Jones, he'd
gone for a shit and was horrified to discover he was
expected to wipe his arse on old newspapers. Bates
rushed out and bought a twin-pack of Andrex. Alan
immediately dubbed him Bogroll and the name had
stuck.

'Mr Bates,' Jones said as his friend reported for

his first day at work, 'there's a bit of a problem. Could you come along to my office.'

'What's wrong?' Bogroll clamoured.

Bates didn't get a reply until he was seated in the personnel manager's office. Alan looked extremely uncomfortable as he sat down behind a desk.

'Look, Bogroll,' Jones sighed, 'I know we stopped seeing each other socially four or five years ago but I still consider you to be a friend. I'm going to tell you something you're not supposed to know. I'm putting myself on the line, so don't betray my trust by blathering to anyone about how you got the information. My company has withdrawn the job offer it made to you because you're on the Industrial League blacklist.'

'What?' Bates hooted. 'Are you telling me I can't work here? Christ, Alan, I've been unemployed for two years. I'd crawl on my hands and knees to get work. I'm that desperate, I've lost my dignity, don't kick me when I'm down. I'll do anything for that job in the warehouse.'

'I'm sorry, Bogroll,' Jones replied, 'there's nothing I can do about it. The company won't allow me to employ anyone who's on the Industrial League blacklist. It's out of my hands.'

'What the fuck is the Industrial League?' Bates blubbered.

'It's an organisation dedicated to improving relations between workers and captains of industry,' the personnel manager explained. 'It's working to raise industrial productivity, so the country can get back on its feet and take its rightful place as a first rank world power once again.'

'That sounds alright to me,' Bogroll confirmed. 'You know I've always been patriotic. I'd like to do my own bit to help the country, that's why I want a job, so that I can contribute something to society and get back a bit of dignity. What I don't understand is why I'm on this blacklist.'

'I don't understand it either,' Jones confessed. 'The Industrial League blacklist is supposed to be a roll-call of subversives, people who are out to wreck the country, communists, anarchists and nihilists.'

'But I've never had anything to do with politics!' Bates protested. 'Well, I always vote Tory at the elections but I've never been in a political party or nothing. I've never had anything to do with the Liberals or the Labour Party.'

'What about your mum and dad?' Alan asked. 'Sometimes the Industrial League puts people on the blacklist because they've got close relatives who are militants.'

'My folks run a newsagent's and vote Tory like me,' Bogroll sighed. 'I've not got any other close relatives, I've no brothers or sisters.'

'What about friends?' the personnel manager wanted to know. 'Have you got any mates who are commies?'

'No,' Bates lisped, 'I don't know nothing about politics. I wouldn't hang about with militant types, they'd put me down for being an ignorant pleb.'

'Well, as far as I can see,' Jones said, 'there's no reason for you being on the blacklist.'

'Take me on then,' Bogroll pleaded.

'I can't,' the personnel manager gestured helplessly, 'my superiors would sack me for ignoring

Industrial League advice. It wouldn't do you any good either. You'd be turfed out within a day or two.'

'Why don't you get onto this Industrial League and tell them they've made a mistake about me,' Bates suggested.

'Bogroll, you don't understand,' there was a note of despair readily evident in Alan's voice. 'If I questioned the directives of the Industrial League, they'd have me blacklisted as a trouble-maker. All I can do is advise you to go abroad, you'll never get a job in this country.'

Swift Nick Carter was a success with the birds. Nick was bisexual – but after quitting Class Justice and splitting up with his last boyfriend, he'd stuck to chicks. Immediately after making good his escape from the cenotaph, Carter had got onto the tube and chatted up a real stunna. He'd spent the night at her pad in Brixton. Now the bird was at work and Nick was sitting in a greasy spoon.

'News on the hour, every hour,' a radio blared as Carter waited for his breakfast. 'Police have identified the bomber responsible for yesterday's explosion at the cenotaph as Nick Carter, national leader of the anarchist Class Justice movement . . .'

Suddenly past incidents fell into place. Within a matter of seconds, Nick realised he'd been set up. It was sheer stupidity that led Carter to infiltrate neo-Nazi circles. While the average stormtrooper was unlikely to recognise Nick, it had been inevitable that some ideologue among the leadership would rumble him. If only the rank-and-file had sussed

Nick straight off and given him a kicking! Hospital-isation was nothing compared with the serious shit that would now be coming his way from the law.

A waitress placed an English Breakfast in front of Carter. A fried egg slithered about the plate as Nick attempted to cut it. Carter's mind wasn't on the food he was eating, he was too busy making plans. The anarchist thanked his lucky stars he'd not gone home the previous night. He would never go back to Hoxton. The filth would have his gaff staked out. Carter didn't like the fact – but he was now on the run. South London was well away from Nick's usual stomping grounds – all of which were north of the river, so he figured it was as good a place as any to hide. He went through the names of people he knew in the area and eventually hit upon Mike Armilus as the man most likely to put him up.

Armilus lived in a council flat on the Kennington Park Estate. It wasn't far from Brixton and it wasn't difficult to find. Twenty minutes after finishing his breakfast, Nick was banging on Mike's door.

'Alright?' Armilus boomed as he answered the knock. 'Christ, I wasn't expecting a national hero!'

Mike ushered Nick into his living room and then bustled about in the kitchen making tea. A few minutes later, Armilus handed Carter a cuppa and sat down opposite his guest.

'I saw you at the demo and at the time I wondered if you'd joined the opposition,' Mike confessed, then added: 'What you did was fuckin' brilliant!'

'I didn't do nothin',' Nick sputtered, 'I was set up by the Nazis.'

'What?' Armilus shrieked. 'Are you telling me you didn't plant the bomb?'

'That's right,' Carter replied, 'you see, I was attempting to infiltrate various fascist groups. They obviously figured out who I was before letting me overhear them plotting to blow up the cenotaph. The bastards knew I wouldn't go to the cops, that I'd attempt to deal with the bomb alone. They wanted Class Justice to get the blame for an outrage that would swing public opinion to the right. I'm the patsy who fell into their trap. I understand from radio reports that the Mets have photos of me poking about among the wreaths piled up beside the cenotaph.'

'Yeah,' Mike acceded, 'there's pictures in the papers and they've shown them on TV.'

'I have to assume the filth have got my drum staked out,' Nick explained. 'Since I can't go home, I've come to ask if I can stay with you for a while.'

'No problem,' Armilus assured his guest, 'but if you're gonna crash here, I want you to work on a project. I wanna set up my own Class Justice organisation. You're to edit the paper.'

'What?' Carter rustled in disbelief. 'This is crazy. Why the fuck do you wanna set yourself up as a rival to Steve Drummond?'

'Because,' Mike grinned, 'I get pissed off with all the bullshit that's written about Drummond. Taking the credit for blowing up the cenotaph has earned Class Justice a lot of media coverage. The membership is about to shoot up. Martin Smith has issued a statement saying he's assisting the cops with their investigations into those who're responsible for the violence at Horse Guards Parade. The cunt claims he's gonna hand the Mets the names of anyone he unearths who was connected with the trouble. The rank-and-file of the Spartacist Workers Group aren't gonna like that. Some of them will defect. They've got political skills which Class Justice needs, I want them in the official Class Justice Movement, not Drummond's breakaway group.'

'Hang on a minute!' Nick retorted. 'Drummond controls the official Class Justice.'

'No he doesn't!' Armilus insisted. 'You set up Class Justice, did the first issue of the paper on your tod. The media is saying you're still the leader of the movement. We're working together, which means we're the real Class Justice, Drummond is just an impostor.'

'But I quit Class Justice years ago!' Carter whinged. 'Since then, I've had no involvement with organised politics beyond attempting to infiltrate the odd fascist group.'

'Times change,' Mike exuded conviction, 'you've got to move with them, Nick. You're in the shit now, we've got to build you up, put you in a position where the government can't touch you. Revolution is your best bet for coming out on top of this predicament. Even if we don't succeed in overthrowing the state, we could make a fortune selling literature and soliciting donations. Christ, this cenotaph outrage will provide endless publicity, people will be showering us with money as they clamour to join the movement. Once we've got things up and running, there'll be enough dosh for you to go abroad and edit the paper in safety.'

'I dunno,' Nick mumbled.

'Come on!' Armilus enthused. 'You've got to think of the future. This is the easiest way for you to make money and that's what you need if you're gonna be on the run for a few years. Think of it, you'll be looking out for yourself and simultaneously furthering the revolutionary cause. Marx always said that as the first industrialised country, England was the most likely venue for the outbreak of world revolution.'

'I dunno,' Carter repeated lamely.

'You know what I'm saying makes sense,' Mike insisted, 'London is a microcosm of the world. The South is poor, the East heavily industrialised and the West affluent.'

'How come you live in the South if it's poor?' Nick wanted to know.

'I was born here,' Armilus announced proudly.

'You're fuckin' mad,' Nick muttered.

'You what?' Mike seethed.

'Nuffin',' Carter replied.

'Well, what about my proposal?' Armilus persisted. 'Will you lead a reborn Class Justice?'

'Oh, I suppose so,' Nick conceded.

Carter could see that if he didn't allow himself to be put up as a rival to Steve Drummond, he'd have to find somewhere else to stay. And perhaps Mike's proposal wasn't such a bad idea after all, since it provided Nick with a way of getting back at Drummond for wrecking what remained of Class Justice. Carter didn't like the thought of his former lieutenant deriving any advantages from the fact that a bunch of fascists had set him up as their fall-guy.

Nick figured that he could always change his mind about leading a new Class Justice at a later date – and stringing Armilus along would at least give him enough time to persuade someone else to safehouse him.

✥ TWO ✥

BOGROLL BATES WAS sick of listening to Jackboots Houghton rant and rave. Bates didn't give a shit about the evils of mixed marriages or how Eurocrats had set out to destroy the character of the Anglo-Saxon race. Anyone in the audience who was not a dedicated convert to Nazi cultism would have considered the speaker a crank.

'It is not the custom of our movement,' Jackboots concluded, 'to question its leader. We are not interested in pointless debates, our duty is the salvation of the White Race. However, I will talk to some of you informally before leaving this hall. Meeting closed.'

'Hail Houghton, Hail Houghton,' the party faithful bellowed as Jackboots raised his right arm in a Roman salute and clicked his heels.

Most of the thirty individuals present were still squealing their leader's name as he marched from the podium and into their midst. Houghton felt that his calling in life necessitated that he preserve a certain distance between himself and the Anglo-

Saxon Movement's street activists, and so what followed was one of those rare opportunities to
socialise with the 'great man'.

'I was very interested to hear you speak about
the spiritual aspects of our National Revolution,' a
follower buzzed, 'and I was wondering if you could
give me some advice concerning a personal matter.'

'Certainly,' Jackboots bombasted, 'I'm more than
qualified to speak on any subject and it goes without
saying that my advice will be a thousand times
sounder than that of some Judaeo-liberal commie
wanker.'

'Well,' the sycophant exhaled, 'my girlfriend is a
member of the Church of Adolf Hitler and she's
putting a lot of pressure on me to sign up with
Genghis I-Hunn. Do you think I should join his
congregation?'

'I'll be frank with you,' Houghton boomed, 'I
think you should find a new girlfriend. While the
Church of Adolf Hitler is not a proscribed organisation, I am still waiting for I-Hunn to respond to
my invitation to merge his operation with our own
and thereby bring his followers under my leadership. The Anglo-Saxon Movement is more than a
political party, it is a way of life, which means that
dedicated cadres will find spiritual as well as political
satisfaction from absolute commitment to our
cause.'

'I reckon the Church of Adolf Hitler are as nutty
as the White Seed of Christ,' a member of Houghton's honour guard piped up.

'No,' Jackboots insisted, 'you've got it completely
wrong. Our only argument with Genghis I-Hunn is

over his failure to recognise my leadership. Politically we are in agreement. On the other hand, Narcissus Brooke and the White Seed of Christ are a bunch of sectarian bigots who stir up hatred among Aryan brothers. The Church of Adolf Hitler is a manifestation of the true Identity Creed, which recognises the twelve nations of Europe as the lost tribes of Israel. Brooke reckons that only the British people are the true Israelites, he's a chauvinist who opposes white solidarity and the divine authority of our saviour Adolf Hitler, the late-born Child of Light.'

'You're right, commander,' the stormtrooper admitted humbly, 'and I thank Adolf Hitler that I have a great leader to set me straight whenever I err on doctrinal matters.'

'Hail Houghton, Hail Houghton,' the assembled believers chanted in unison as their right arms shot into the air.

'What I wanna know,' Bogroll Bates put in, 'is about your policies on unemployment.'

'An Anglo-Saxon Movement government would provide work for everyone,' Jackboots prated. 'The work-shy will be cured of their illness in camps where they'll be driven back to freedom by a relentless programme of forced labour. Those who will not work should not eat!'

'But what about me?' Bogroll demanded. 'I'm desperate for a job but I've been blacklisted and now no one will employ me. What can you do for me?'

'We'll find you work,' Houghton insisted, 'there's dignity in labour and if the communist unions have blacklisted you, as has happened to many of our comrades in the past, we'll find you a job in a factory that's not under their control.'

'It's the fuckin' Industrial League that's black-listed me!' Bates heaved. 'Let's get a mob up and storm their offices!'

'We can't do that!' Jackboots prattled. 'The Industrial League is a fine patriotic organisation. You're confused, we've got to deal with the bankers and the Reds, then every man who deserves a job will be able to find work.'

'I'm tellin' you the fuckin' truth when I say that the Industrial League is an enemy of the working man!' Bates howled. 'A mate of mine showed me your paper, he said you helped the unemployed!'

'You're a puppet of the sub-men, a stooge of the mud-races!' Houghton screeched. 'Honour guard, teach this man a lesson, beat him senseless and then remove him from my sight.'

Strong arms grabbed Bates. He was punched repeatedly in the face. A Nazi thug landed a hay-maker in his stomach. Blood welled up from deep inside Bogroll's guts and spurted out through his lips. Bates was hurled to the floor and split seconds later, a dozen boots were beating a tattoo against his heaving bulk. Bogroll was only semi-conscious as he was frog-marched out of the hall and dumped in a back alley.

'Fuck off and die, commie scum!' were the last words Bates heard before he blacked out.

Steve Drummond had intended to have a quiet pint in the Tanners before hopping a bus to the West

End. He had a date with Patricia Good. The girl was a fucking tease! Although Steve had been seeing her for weeks, he'd yet to get into her knickers. Bleedin' papist, getting him all steamed up and then refusing to do anything whatsoever. Patricia would sleep with Drummond and had even given him the odd hand-job – but her twat was a no-go area. She wouldn't play with herself, let alone allow someone else to get their hands on her bits. Steve wondered why he bothered with the chick and figured he must be getting old, he'd never had problems getting laid until now.

''Ere Steve,' Dog honked as he sat down beside his leader and spread a paper on the table in front of them, ''ave you seen this?'

'Jesus fuck! What the hell are you showing me?' Drummond scolded as he took in the Class Justice masthead and the headline *Hang British War Criminals* beneath a picture of squaddies on patrol in Canterbury.

'There's a geezer sellin' 'em on the High Street,' Dog explained. ''Ee says it's the first genuine issue of *Class Justice* in years. It seems that Swift Nick Carter is taking advantage of his notoriety as the cenotaph bomber, and has launched a rival group with our name.'

'This is serious!' Drummond fumed. 'It could confuse the recruits who've been pouring in since *Class Justice* showed the workers how to deal with the reactionaries responsible for the Ian Stuart Memorial Parade. What with that and Martin Smith mouthing off about how he'd provide the cops with a list of those who'd caused trouble at the demo, we've picked up scores of disillusioned members of the Spartacist Workers Group. Class Justice is a viable organisation for the first time in years and Swift Nick is fuckin' us about by setting up a rival group!'

'What are we gonna do?' Dog demanded.

'We've got to find the bastard, make him see sense!' Steve asserted.

'Some of the comrades are complaining that Nick's paper is better than ours, that he's returned to the roots,' Dog put in.

'Christ!' Drummond swore as he flicked through Carter's paper. 'This is garbage. It's the sort of stuff we were running ten years ago, before we decided to compete with the organised left. This isn't a threat to us, it's for lumpens, it won't appeal to comrades who've developed political skills in the Trot organisations, it'll alienate those men and wimmin we need to recruit if our movement is to grow!'

'We might as well forget Carter then,' Dog said as he folded up the paper.

'Give that to me!' Steve belched as he snatched the copy of *Class Justice* from Dog's hand.

'It's mine,' Dog whined.

'I need it,' Drummond burbled, 'I must study it and work out our movement's position on this upstart.'

'But you just said it wasn't a threat to us!' Dog protested.

'Not politically,' Steve explained, 'Carter doesn't have my theoretical coherence. Nevertheless, it's a bloody nuisance if someone with his credentials is claiming to run the real Class Justice. He's in hiding and the media are putting it about that he's the leader of our movement. We need to persuade Nick to work with us. He'll have to change the name of his organisation, we can't allow the kind of confusion he's generating to go unchecked – but I can see real possibilities in what's happened. Officially, we'd have to pretend that Carter's mob are our political enemies – but if we could clinch a deal to co-operate secretly, then we could perform a pincher movement on the rest of the left. Nick would clean up on the lumpen elements, he knows how to deal with them, while we concentrate on recruiting the bulk of the respectable working-class.'

'You're a fucking genius!' Dog pealed.

'Of course I am, that's why I'm your leader!' Drummond boxed.

'But I thought anarchists didn't have leaders,' Dog parried.

'Shut up!' his chief retorted.

Narcissus Brooke eyed up the three girls who stood before him. As he ogled them, Narcissus felt that in appreciating the artistry that had gone into fashioning woman from Adam's spare rib, he was communing with the Godhead. Unlike the kosher Christians who rejected his Identity Creed, Brooke did not consider sex to be sinful. Indeed, he fervently believed that every erotic encounter between two pure-blooded Anglo-Saxons was an act of the highest moral standing. Procreation was necessary if the White Seed of Christ was to vanquish the forces of darkness and see God's purpose realised here on planet earth.

'If the Kingdom of Heaven is to prevail over the Legions of the Anti-Christ,' Narcissus announced, 'then a new generation of White Warriors must spring from the womb of Aryan Womanhood!'

'Yes, master,' the three girls replied in unison.

'Every race-conscious patriot must plant his seed in the belly of a British woman before taking up the sword to do battle with the Satanic spawn we know as the mud-races!'

'Yes, master,' the girls shot back.

'Eve Parry, Liz Jones, Linda Cort,' Brooke said after looking each girl in the eye, 'I'm entrusting you with a special task. As you know, Nick Carter committed an outrage against our nationalist movement. While it is clear that his mind has been warped by liberal creeds and a multicultural education, Carter is nevertheless a fine specimen of Anglo-Saxon manhood. I want you to save his seed for Christ before this race-traitor is punished for desecrating the cenotaph. The White Race can't afford to squander its genetic wealth. This particular container is worthless – but as you well know, what it contains is the most precious thing in the world, the DNA codes of a pure-blooded Aryan.'

'Yes, master.' The girls were a picture of submission.

'I am certain,' Narcissus snuffled, 'that you can discover Carter's whereabouts without any great difficulty. It's simply a case of being prepared to suck a lot of anarchist cock. You must question these bastards as the endorphins flow through their brains.

That's the time when repressed racial instincts are most effectively exploited. Make sure you go no further than blow jobs. I don't want any of you knocked up before you get to Carter. I've picked you because of the even spacing between your menstrual cycles, your wombs must be empty, ever ready to preserve Carter's issue.'

'Master, I understand that most anarchists expect to go all the way when they lie with a woman,' Eve blushed. 'It might make our mission easier if we were allowed to use contraceptives.'

'Never!' Brooke sparred as he slapped Parry's face. 'That is the road to racial suicide! You should know by now that protected sex is a crime against God. We are the chosen people, the lost tribes of Israel. No matter what difficulties we may face, as free-born English men and women, we must never violate the commandments God has laid down for our benefit.'

'We are British,' the girls looked as if they were about to break into a dance routine. 'Brit meaning covenant, to remind us of the promise which binds us to God.'

'That's right!' Narcissus piped. 'No wooden shoes! No rest for the wicked! Shout it loud, we're White and Proud, fighting for our Race and Nation – Britain, the Kingdom of God.'

'We are ready,' the girls replied, 'ready to do battle with the mud-races who gather beneath the banners of the Anti-Christ. We are ready to fight the sub-men who direct this mongrel horde. We're ready to do God's will here on earth, to conquer the world for our Lord Jesus Christ.'

'We'll regain the British Empire!' Brooke hollered. 'We'll rebuild everything the Anti-Christ has
attempted to destroy. God's chosen people, the
British Israelites will once again rule the world! It
will come to pass just as has been prophesised in the
Bible!'

Martin Smith wanted the world to see that he could
act decisively. He would not allow the rank-and-file
membership of the Spartacist Workers Group to
desert the Trotskyite cause and join up with Class
Justice. Smith had made a serious miscalculation
when he announced to the press that he'd assist
the police in tracking down those responsible for the
violence at the cenotaph. As a result, Class Justice
had taken the credit for the outrage and SWG activists were not only accusing him of being a
reactionary opportunist – but actually resigning
from the movement so that they could sign up with
the anarchists! Worse still, public opinion had not
been swayed by Martin's actions, the masses
remained unconvinced that the Spartacist Workers
Group was a party of moderates seeking the overthrow of capitalism by means of the legal revolution.
    To date, ninety-seven activists had returned their
membership cards with covering letters citing
Smith's collaboration with the cops as their reason
for breaking with the movement. This was an
extremely serious matter, the party ranks were deci-
mated with forty per cent of the cadre having
resigned. The most serious loss was in Surrey, where
the entire branch had decided to regroup as a Class

Justice cell. Martin was accompanying the task force he'd organised to deal with these recalcitrants.

'How much further is it?' Smith demanded.

'Two miles,' the driver replied.

'Right,' Martin woofed as he turned around and addressed the teenagers in the back of the van, 'we've nearly reached Redhill. I want you to remember that this is a surgical operation. We're gonna call at the homes of the five former members of the Surrey branch. If the bastards are in, we beat them senseless and smash up their pads. If they're out, we break in and do as much damage as possible.'

'Okay,' the task force chimed.

Smith turned his back on the kids and focused his eyes on the road ahead. Redhill appeared to be a complete dump. Like Aldershot, Crawley, Croydon and Woking, it was one of those dreary concrete towns which blighted the otherwise affluent appearance of the London commuter belt. The citizens of neighbouring Reigate looked down on Redhill residents as uncultured proles whose very existence was an affront to everything the British hold dear.

'Here we go!' the driver saluted as he pulled up in front of a crumbling terrace on a nondescript street. 'Three of the bastards live 'ere, including George Sanders, the man who led the Surrey Branch prior to its defection.'

Some of the task force were wearing knuckle dusters, others were tooled up with knives and clubs. Smith sat in the van and watched as his men positioned themselves around the front door of number thirty-six. Someone rang the bell. Sanders answered the door and was immediately beaten senseless by three youths wielding baseball bats. As George crumpled in a bloody heap, his former comrades swarmed over his body and into the house. Pipes were torn from walls. Furniture and windows were smashed. A teenager who shared the house with three of the former members of the Surrey Branch was caught as he attempted to bolt through the back door.

'Cunt!' a militant shouted as his knuckle duster cracked the kid's jaw. 'That'll teach you to fuck with the rightful representatives of the proletariat.'

The hands that had been restraining the teenager released their grip on his shoulders and wrists, the kid collapsed like a punctured balloon. As he lay unconscious, the boy was subjected to a savage kicking.

'Retreat! Everybody out!' someone commanded and within two minutes the task force was back in the van.

No one was in when the militants called at the next address, so they used sledge-hammers to break down the front door, before proceeding to smash the toilet and a top-flight hi-fi system. Their final victim pulled a shotgun on his former comrades and the task force fled in terror.

'Go back and get the cunt!' Smith commanded his followers as they piled into the van.

'We're not gonna charge some idiot with a gun!' they protested.

Martin was outraged. This was a direct challenge to his leadership. The cadre were refusing to obey orders! He was about to reiterate this instruction when a bullet shattered the windscreen and embedded itself in metal mere inches from the commander's head.

'Let's get outta here!' Smith yelped at the driver.

The van careered out of Redhill, the militants having more or less accomplished their task. Hitting two out of three targets with deadly accuracy wasn't a bad score! However, Martin resolved not to accompany his followers the next time he assigned them a special mission. It was wrong of him to risk life and limb when the fate of the movement rested on his shoulders. Smith calmly accepted the fact that he must make the ultimate sacrifice and check his impulses towards recklessness. The proletarian masses were depending upon him to provide them with the political leadership necessary for their communist victory. For their sake, Smith was dutybound to do everything he could to preserve his own life!

Steve Drummond and Patricia Good sat gazing at each other over cups of coffee and Big Macs. Even an Oxford Street McDonald's could become a romantic setting to a couple who were in love.

'What do you fancy doing?' Steve asked before biting into his burger.

'Oh, I don't know,' Patricia sighed. 'Anything, really, as long as I'm with you.'

'There's a John Waters double bill on in King's Cross,' Drummond announced. 'I quite fancy going to that.'

'Okay,' Good agreed, 'we'll go to the movies. But first I want you to finish your Big Mac. I've also brought you some chocolates. I love watching you eat sweets, it seems to make you so happy, just like a little child.'

'You're always buying me sweets,' Drummond expostulated. 'It's mad when you won't eat any yourself.'

'I don't like sugar, you do,' Patricia demurred. 'There's nothing wrong with enjoying yourself.'

'Alright,' Steve cut in. 'I'm not complaining. I'm just a bit worried that if we go on like this I'll get fat.'

'What time do the films end?' Good asked diplomatically changing the subject. 'I don't want to stay up too late.'

'They'll be over by midnight,' Drummond assured her. 'Afterwards we can get a cab back to your place. Those old Divine films always make me feel horny.'

'I want you to understand this, Steve,' Patricia said firmly, 'I'm a good Catholic girl. I know I've let you stay overnight a couple of times – but that doesn't mean that I'll go all the way. I don't intend to sacrifice my virginity until I get married.'

Drummond suppressed a groan. Why the hell did he have to get involved with a Catholic girl when he'd already fallen out with his own family over the issue of faith? His mother would love Patricia, if the pair ever met. It was the anarchist's mum who'd blessed him with Irish blood. Steve's dad was an English convert to the creed. Drummond thanked his lucky stars he'd been born in London, where it had been relatively easy for him to break free from the baleful influence of popery. Steve's mum had appealed to his sense of family loyalty when he'd first refused to attend mass. When Drummond let it be known that he didn't give a toss about the Kevins and Micks back in Kildare, the family insisted he'd later regret these words. Blood ran thicker than water, so it was said – but in Steve's case it seemed that the mighty Thames, rather than Roman Catholicism, coursed through his veins. Nationalism be damned! Drummond was an anarchist, he knew that the working-class had no country. Nevertheless, Steve loved London, it was more than the world's greatest city – it was the only place someone with the refined sensibilities of the Class Justice leader would even consider living!

Vicki Douglas had proven more adept at infiltrating nationalist circles than Swift Nick Carter. Before embracing lesbian separatism, she'd had several run-ins with the Class Justice leader. The very first time Vicki heard Carter speak, she'd concluded he was a misogynist. The standing ovation Nick received from male activists whenever he spoke at a Class Justice meeting, had prompted Douglas to quit anarchism for the wimmin's lib scene. In Vicki's book, Carter was a prick whose interest in overthrowing capitalism stemmed from the realisation that patriarchy had a better chance of survival if the male sex could transcend the class differences that divided it. Liberating the species had nothing to do with the former Class Justice leader's brand of anarcho-radicalism, his politics were simply self-interest served up with a thin veneer of altruism!

It was Vicki who'd been the first to identify Carter as a security threat when he began hanging out in nationalist circles. Douglas was not surprised that Nick had turned to fascism in his middle age. It was common for men to express their reactionary views more openly as they grew old. Vicki had never played a prominent role in the anarchist scene – nevertheless, she'd had to protect herself by exposing Carter as a mole before he had the opportunity to rat on her. Although Douglas had the advantage of deep cover, she couldn't afford to take risks when her plans were so close to fruition.

It had taken Vicki the best part of three years to get really close to Genghis I-Hunn. Douglas had known from the outset that Hunn was a masochist. However, it took a great deal of effort on Vicki's part before the high priest of the Church of Adolf Hitler trusted her enough to give expression to his perverted lusts when she was actually around to witness the spectacle. Nevertheless, Douglas hadn't needed much insight to see how things really stood with Genghis. Vicki knew that all men were passive bores who loved to cross-dress and be spanked with bundles of thorns. However, because men were afraid of their own desires, they set out to prove that they were active – and in attempting to prove an error, they were compulsively driven to abuse wimmin. It was this fact that accounted for all the cruelty and violence the anti-sex had perpetrated down the ages.

After several years of hard work, Douglas had Hunn exactly where she wanted him – on his knees as she towered above this pathetic example of male mediocrity. Although Genghis was dressed in a skimpy French maid's uniform, the outfit didn't do much for him. In fact, he looked fucking awful because the seams on his stockings weren't straight and the make-up that was plastered across his face had smudged.

'Read this!' Vicki instructed as she handed Hunn a sheet of paper with a sentence scrawled across it.

'I am a turd,' Genghis intoned, 'a lowly, abject, turd.'

'Say it with conviction!' Douglas retched as she ground the heel of a Doctor Marten boot into Hunn's groin.

Genghis yelped and then repeated the sentence he'd fluffed, this time proclaiming it with great feeling. Suddenly, he could see Vicki's point, coming as they did from the warped perspective of a patriarchal society, his politics were seriously fucked up. The key conflict in the modern world was based on gender rather than race. Hunn resolved to call together the whole of his congregation and inform them that he was resigning as leader of the Church of Adolf Hitler. Douglas would take his place and immediately dissolve the organisation so that it could be relaunched as the Church of Valerie Solanas. In return for his compliance, Genghis would be allowed to join the Men's Auxiliary. After that, he could sit back, relax, enjoy the show and ride the waves to the demise of the male sex.

The Jute Unity Action Group was holding a meeting at Hackney town hall and once again the ranks of the far-left and ultra-Right faced each other with only a thin blue line of cops acting as a brake on some really serious violence. However, the number of demonstrators on each side had been greatly depleted by the hundreds of injuries sustained a few weeks earlier at the cenotaph. In addition, the East End was an anarcho-squatting stronghold and the crusties would not be drawn into supporting any form of nationalism.

'No Popery! No wooden shoes!' howled the fifty fascist activists who'd assembled to protest against British soldiers being shot in the back by Kent separatist cowards.

'Red, white and blue, we shit on you!' a hundred or so supporters of the Spartacist Workers Group and the Workers League trilled in unison.

It looked like it would be a good night of rowdy chants with a swift pint or two in the pub before going home. The Nazis were outnumbered at least two to one but they felt secure in the knowledge that the cops would protect them from the numerically superior leftists. Both sides felt confident about claiming a victory, knowing full well that their supporters were unlikely to question the completely biased reporting of events that would soon be published in each party's street paper.

However, neither the fascists nor the Trots had counted on the intervention of a reborn Class Justice. This was not Steve Drummond's mob whose watered-down programme was simply a pale imitation of anarchism's original outrageous aims. Instead, Mike Armilus marched at the head of a motley crew of squatters, scumbags and two-time losers – a representative sample of the street trash that flooded into London's Giro Borough from all over Europe, North America and the Antipodes.

The smartly dressed honour guard who marched in step with Armilus were in sharp contrast to the faceless mass that followed in their wake. King Anarchy had donned his shit-smeared purple robes and not a single Nazi or Red knew what to make of a banner proclaiming NEITHER NATIONALISM NOR TRILATERALISM that was borne irresistibly forward with this flood. The lumpen mass frothed against the sides of shops and houses – and for a few seconds it was unclear whether it would inundate the Jute or the British nationalists.

Then a crustie handed Mike Armilus a black flag. If his satellites looked wild, Armilus looked a great deal wilder – not, it should be added, due to his clothes or hair, for he was a smartly dressed skinhead; but because he was shouting to those around him like a polymorph in the full throes of an orgasm, while waving the black flag in the direction of the fascist demonstrators. Mike's eyes flickered with the penetrating gleam of a man who had transcended the petty limitations of bourgeois normalcy.

The anarchist horde advanced and within seconds the fascist demonstrators were reduced to a bloody pulp, fifty bags of twisted and broken bones left festering in the gutter. Seeing their opponents utterly crushed, the Reds let out a cheer which instantly died in a hundred separate throats. Armilus had pointed his black flag at the student activists who stood guarding the entrance to the town hall. The police lines parted, the Mets would not risk life and limb to protect a gaggle of Trots from the wrath of an insurgent anarchist mass.

The Class Justice crew swarmed up the steps and

into the town hall. The first wave knocked the Trots to the ground, while those comrades following in their wake had to content themselves with trampling the Reds underfoot. Inside the town hall, a Jute Unity Action Group speaker was in the process of soliciting donations for the Kent Freedom Fighters, the outlawed paramilitary wing of the organisation he was representing. Mike Armilus and his honour guard stormed through the hall and onto the stage. The speaker was unceremoniously thrown into the front row of the audience.

'Fuck nationalism!' Armilus roared. 'I'm all for shitting on the Union Jack but let's shit on Wat Tyler too, he's not a working-class hero, he was an asset of the Knights' Templar, as everyone here ought to know!'

As Mike spoke, members of his honour guard set fire to both Jute and British flags. Meanwhile, the great mass of crusties made sure that every last nationalist remained in their seat as Armilus delivered a devastating critique of every statist ideology. When Mike had finished his speech, a femail comrade took his place.

'You talk about Jute liberation,' she raged, 'but what about wimmin's liberation? Most of you aren't even from Kent, you're London lefties. You wouldn't support a British organisation that was opposed to contraception and abortion on demand, so why support reaction in Kent?'

Having delivered these speeches, the anarchists trashed the auditorium, then swarmed out of the building and laid into the cops.

✦ THREE ✦

STEVE DRUMMOND HAD been neglecting Class Justice. For some months, Patricia Good had overtaken the revolutionary project as Steve's primary concern. In many ways, Steve had a right to feel complacent. He'd patched things up with Swift Nick and Mike Armilus. Class Justice was now working as Drummond had always intended it to function. The organisation was acting as a pole of regroupment for the class. Although the stable membership was only around twenty – the original hardcore in Stoke Newington plus the Redhill branch of the Spartacist Workers Group who'd defected to Class Justice – large numbers of former Trots were passing through the group as they moved from dogmatic Marxism to freewheeling libertarianism. While the vast majority went on to find permanent political homes in organisations such as Liberty, Invisible Banner and the Regulated Activity Movement, it was Class Justice that provided them with a stepping-stone between statism and anarchy.

No one could doubt that Steve had come out on

top during the negotiations between the rival Class Justice groups. Steve had retained control of the name and with this, he was able to maintain the circulation of his paper at thirty-five thousand. Carter and Armilus had renamed their outfit the Nihilist Alliance and were cleaning up on the lumpen elements, whose support Drummond did not covet. In terms of membership, the Nihilists far outstripped Class Justice but this had to be counterbalanced against the fact that they'd failed to publish more than a pilot issue of their paper, whereas Steve's mob were putting out an issue of *CJ* every six weeks!

Drummond had spent the afternoon with Good. He still hadn't fathomed the girl's hold over him, if he ever did, it would probably mark the end of a beautiful relationship! Patricia would kiss and cuddle but absolutely refused to give Steve what he wanted – penetrative sex. Although the two lovebirds had been petting in bed for the best part of an hour, Drummond hadn't succeeded in getting his hand down Good's knickers. Patricia allowed her tits to be fondled but her twat was a no go area.

Steve was thinking about getting up, there was a Class Justice meeting he didn't want to miss. As a concession to Carter and Armilus, Drummond had agreed that either they, or one of their representatives, could attend Class Justice meetings to recruit any lumpen elements who showed more interest in violence than competing with the organised left. Drummond felt obliged to put in a personal appearance at these chin-wags just in case Armilus attempted recruiting individuals who were, by rights, the property of his own organisation, for example, students or skilled manual labourers.

Patricia had fallen asleep. Steve seized the opportunity to slide his hand beneath the elastic waistband of her knickers. As Drummond's middle finger slipped through Good's pubic thatch and got to within millimetres of her clit, his girlfriend awoke with a start.

'No, no, no, no, no!' Patricia gusted as she pulled Steve's hand from her panties.

'Why not?' Drummond wanted to know.

'Because,' Good replied, 'it's not my scene. I'm a Catholic girl and you'll have to wait until we're married before you get any hanky-panky.'

'Will you wank me off instead?' Steve whimpered.

'Okay,' his girlfriend conceded, 'but don't expect me to do this every time I see you. You've got an abnormal sex drive and we both need to work at getting it under control.'

Drummond didn't bother arguing with Good's ridiculous assessment of his sexuality, instead he threw the bedclothes to the floor so that his girlfriend would have more room to manoeuvre as she tossed him off. By the time Patricia grabbed hold of Steve's dick, it was rock hard.

'Loosen up, baby!' Drummond's voice was several octaves higher than usual.

Good hadn't yet mastered the art of the hand job, she'd a tendency to hold her boyfriend's love muscle so hard that when she jerked it up and down, he worried that the skin would split.

'Keep a nice easy rhythm, fast and smooth,' Steve

instructed. 'That's it, make your movements flow and whatever you do, don't slow down!'

Once Patricia hit her stride, it wasn't long before Steve could feel love juice boiling inside his groin. It would be a matter of seconds before he shot his load.

'Oh, baby, that feels so good, I'm gonna cum!' he moaned.

Good let Drummond's genetic pump slip from her hand.

'Don't stop now!' Steve ejaculated.

'I don't want to get your sperm all over me!' Patricia stormed. 'It's dirty, and besides, you've got to learn to control your sex drive.'

Good slapped Drummond's hand as he reached down to finish himself off.

'I've got to cum!' Steve sobbed.

'You've got to learn to control yourself!' Patricia caterwauled. 'Here, I've some chocolates in my bag, have one of those instead.'

Split seconds later, Good had unwrapped a Mars Bar and shoved the sweetie into Drummond's mouth. Simultaneously, she'd sat on her boyfriend's crotch, to prevent the over-sexed anarchist from bringing himself off. Steve's attempt to complain about this treatment proved futile, his mouth was filled with chocolate and the words he spluttered could not be understood.

Genghis I-Hunn enjoyed the demeaning treatment that was dished out to all members of the Men's Auxiliary. It gave him a hard-on just thinking about what Vicki Douglas was likely to do when she returned to deal with the slaves who'd been trussed up and abandoned in a locked room. Hunn fantasised about being selected to clean Vicki's funky twat with his tongue, and after performing the duty with such enthusiasm that he caused his mistress to have an orgasm, being flayed with a horse whip for failing to carry out the task with suitable decorum. He'd been barking mad devoting twenty years of his life to Hitler worship, when that time would have been better spent on his knees in front of Douglas or some other, equally stern, Amazon.

Douglas was Hunn's idea of the perfect mistress, she had the grace of an angel and a temper that would have shocked Satan. For her part, Vicki was less than thrilled by the antics of the Men's Auxiliary. Every last one of these pricks had pledged unswerving support to the Society For Cutting Up Men, but it was patently obvious that they were more interested in licking out toilet bowls and being whipped senseless, than in playing a useful supporting role in the destruction of the male sex.

'Sisters!' Vicki erupted at the minions who were gathered around her. 'The male is a biological accident, a walking abortion, an incomplete femail. It is time to strike against the sub-wimmin, the anti-gender, the unresponsive pricks who are incapable of relating to the world around them! We must show no mercy now that we're about to embark on the elimination of the male sex!'

'Yes, yes!' the assembled congregation of the Church of Valerie Solanas yelled enthusiastically.

'Sisters,' Douglas trumpeted, 'the enemy is in our midst! The Men's Auxiliary we sanctioned is actually a threat to the success of our project. Its members are more interested in having us pander to their masochistic inclinations than assisting thrill-seeking femails stamp out the Legions of the Anti-Sex!'

'Shame, shame!' the sisters roared. 'Kill them, kill them!'

'That's right,' Vicki screeched, 'they must die, horribly! I've got them all tied up in a back room of the farmhouse. I'll take them one by one onto the roof and throw them off, you're all to stand in the garden and attempt to catch the bastards on your bayonets!'

'Hurrah!' the sisters whooped.

Douglas selected Genghis I-Hunn as her first victim. As she frog-marched him upstairs, each sister armed herself with a Czech 7.62 Model 52 Rifle. These had originally been acquired by AC Thor 33 and were then sold to the Church of Adolf Hitler after the highly secretive neo-Nazi cadre organisation had updated its armoury. The gun was somewhat unusual in that it featured a tipping bolt with frontal locking lugs. It was also the first Czechoslovakian rifle which, under Soviet influence, incorporated a non-detachable bayonet. Otherwise, despite extensive use of stampings, the overall design was not particularly remarkable for a weapon first manufactured in 1952, and so by the early seventies, it had ceased to be standard issue in the Czech army. Nevertheless, when wielded with iron determination by militants from the Church of Valerie Solanas, the sisters were convinced the rifle would prove potent enough to destroy the male sex.

Vicki waited until the sisters had arranged themselves on the lawn, and then pushed Hunn off the edge of the roof. Tina Lea ran forward with her rifle held upwards. As his stomach was pierced by Lea's bayonet, Genghis reflected that he considered the body a surface that ought to be preserved. In S/M sex-play, consenting adults should be allowed to do anything to that surface except puncture it. Hunn didn't like to see blood, particularly his own blood, spilled during sex.

Tina staggered under Hunn's body weight, and split seconds later, collapsed. The sisters screeched, whistled, clapped and stamped their feet. Lea crawled out from under Hunn's corpse, cursing because her khaki uniform was covered in blood. Vicki went to fetch another man as two sisters picked up Hunn's remains and carried them to the compost heap.

Janet Skinner broke ranks with the intention of impaling the second sacrificial victim, but she didn't act fast enough and he hit the grass in front of her with a dull thud. She was then joined by Sharon Taylor and the pair of them used their rifle butts to break every bone belonging to this bloated example of the Anti-Sex. While Janet and Sharon were having their fun, Vicki went to fetch another doomed member from the fast-dwindling ranks of the Men's Auxiliary.

The material unfolding of those historical forces that would lead to the destruction of capitalism were mirrored by the class consciousness Bogroll Bates was fast developing. Now that he knew of his black-listing by the Industrial League and had suffered a beating at the hands of the Anglo-Saxon Movement, this formerly apolitical worker had moved decisively to the left. Since Class Justice were acting as the pole of regroupment for proletarian forces, it was hardly surprising that Bogroll should make his first contact with the organised workers movement at a meeting of this notorious anarcho-communist sect.

Bogroll arrived on the dot at seven-thirty, which was when the meeting had been advertised as starting. Not being a thoroughly politicised animal, Bates hadn't realised that anarchist events never start on time – adherents to this creed consider punctuality an authoritarian trait. Bogroll naturally gravitated towards Steve Drummond, spending the best part of an hour drinking and chatting with the Class Justice supremo.

Drummond quickly concluded that Bates was a lumpen. Bogroll lacked any kind of political or theoretical skill. His conversation was extremely repetitive. He was obsessed with rucking Nazis and wrecking the Industrial League. Worse still, Bates appeared to be unaware of the fact that Drummond was his intellectual and organisational superior. He'd failed to grasp Steve's political standing and as a consequence did not treat the Class Justice leader with the deference that the head of this sect had come to expect.

Mike Armilus cut a dramatic figure, within seconds of the Nihilist Alliance leader entering the Approach, all attention was focused on the proletarian superman. Armilus ordered a pint and then sat down beside Drummond and Bates. An awed hush fell over the pub since those present realised that a conversation of supreme consequence was about to commence.

'I couldn't help overhearing your conversation,' Mike said as he fixed his gaze on Bogroll Bates, 'and you're quite right about the necessity of fuckin' the Nazis. We've got to smash the cunts! It's all very well talking about revolution, but unless we're prepared to actually go out and do the business, all the fine sentiments we express to each other don't mean a bleedin' thing. There's no point talking to our enemies, whether they're fascists, cops or rich bastards. The only language these pricks understand is that of the fist and the boot. All the yellow-bellied cowards who aren't prepared to face up to the fact that violence is the most effective form of communication should just fuck off and die, we've no use for them in the revolutionary movement!'

'Yeah!' Bogroll rumbled. 'That's the most sound idea I've heard all evening. Endless talk about organisation won't get us anywhere!'

'Now we've sorted out our priorities,' Armilus said, addressing this statement to the fifteen or so Class Justice supporters present, 'why don't we get on with the meeting?'

Steve Drummond's crew followed Mike to an upstairs room and seated themselves around a large table. While Drummond did not like the way Armilus usurped his authority, he remained confident that his followers were sufficiently committed to the Class Justice brand of armchair revolution not to be permanently swayed by inflammatory rhetoric. Like their leader, these individuals would always opt for personal safety rather than the reality of revolutionary warfare.

'Okay,' Steve croaked in an attempt to reassert his authority, 'let's start the meeting. Whose gonna take the minutes?'

'I'll do 'em,' Dog volunteered, 'if someone'll give me a pen and paper.'

'Right then,' Drummond announced as Tiny handed Dog the implements he needed to minute the meeting, 'I'll go through the agenda: 1) Minutes of the last meeting; 2) distributing the paper through newsagents; 3) discount for bulk paper sales; 4) cover for next issue of the paper; 5) any other business.'

'What about getting a crew together so that we can go and ruck the Anglo-Saxon Movement?' Bogroll Bates demanded.

'We'll put that under any other business,' Steve was determined that the meeting should run smoothly. 'Right, minutes of the last meeting: one, it was agreed that we'd retain the Bronstein Press as our printer because they were prepared to give us ninety days credit on every job, whereas the two firms that gave slightly lower quotes required cash on delivery; two, it was agreed . . .'

'Hold on,' Butcher put in, 'I'd like it noted in the minutes that I objected to the decision to use the Bronstein Press and felt that we should use an anarchist printer such as the Bakunin Press. While this might prove slightly more expensive in the short term, it makes more sense to plough money back into our own movement rather than giving hard cash to our political enemies.'

'Okay,' Drummond assented, 'objection noted.

Point two, it was agreed that the minimum number of copies of the paper that fully paid-up members of the organisation were expected to sell would be raised from twenty-five to forty per issue.'

'What about getting a ruckin' crew together and fuckin' the Nazis?' Bogroll Bates was becoming increasingly exasperated.

'We'll come to that later,' Steve responded, 'it's down under item five, any other business, at the moment we're going through the minutes of the last meeting. Point three, it was agreed that we should decrease the time between the production of each issue of the paper from six to four weeks while retaining the same format and number of pages. Point four, following enquiries from Hendon Police College and the Industrial League, it was agreed that libraries and academic institutes should be allowed to subscribe to the paper . . .'

'You shouldn't sell your paper to the Industrial League, they're a bunch of fascists,' Bogroll Bates bayed. 'I know, I've been blacklisted by them and haven't been able to get a job for the past two years!'

'If you wanted to discuss institutional subscriptions, you should have come to the last meeting!' Drummond growled as he simultaneously thumped his fist against the table.

'I want to get a wrecking crew together so that we can do the Nazis and the Industrial League!' Bates railed.

'I've already got that down under any other business,' Steve said wearily. 'Now, to go back to the minutes of the last meeting: point four, it was agreed that libraries and academic institutes should be

allowed to subscribe to the paper. Institutional subscription rates were set at double the rates for
individuals. Right, that's the minutes for the last
meeting, are there any other objections or
amendments?'

'Minutes agreed!' came the unanimous reply from
the Class Justice cadre.

'Item two,' Drummond announced, 'distributing
the paper through newsagents. It's felt that if every
member can find six newsagents who'll stock the
paper then we could greatly increase the circulation,
which would in turn increase membership.'

'Look,' Bogroll Bates snarled, 'I didn't come here
to prattle about selling newspapers, I wanna get a
ruckin' crew together to fuck the Nazis!'

'I know!' Drummond admonished. 'And I've put
it down under any other business. We'll discuss it
later, if you can't wait until we've got through the
rest of our agenda then I suggest you leave the
meeting.'

'I'm going,' Bates bickered, 'I thought you were
a revolutionary group but now I can see I was
wrong. I'm not interested in becoming an unpaid
lackey to a publishing house!'

Mike Armilus followed Bogroll down to the bar,
where he insisted on paying for the pint Bates had
just ordered. Moments later, the pair were seated at
a table and getting down to a serious discussion
about revolutionary activity.

'Don't get put off politics by Class Justice,' Mike
was saying to his new friend. 'I know they're just a
talking shop for armchair revolutionaries, but I
belong to a group that's seriously into doing the

business, it's called the Nihilist Alliance. We don't hold many meetings, we prefer to go out and do a bit of violence.'

'It sounds good,' Bogroll hedged. 'But would you help me ruck Nazis?'

'I most certainly would,' Armilus yelled, 'whenever there's a fascist demonstration, the Nihilist Alliance is there clobbering the bastards.'

'What about doing the Industrial League, how could you help me with that?'

'That's a different kind of target,' Mike said knowledgeably, 'more elusive. The best way of destroying the League would be to knock off the people who run it one by one.'

'Do you think I should murder the lot of them?'

'Sure,' Armilus replied easily, 'and I can help you too. The Nihilist Alliance has compiled a list of the Industrial League hierarchy that includes home addresses. I can give you a copy.'

'Brilliant!' Bates enthused. 'I like the sound of your organisation, I might even join it!'

'Don't take my word about how good it is,' Mike said softly, 'come along on a few of our actions and see how the reality of organised class violence grabs you.'

'I will!' Bogroll affirmed with great conviction.

Since he'd moved to South London, Swift Nick Carter had been seeing a few chicks regularly and a redhead had taken precedence over all the other birds he was screwing. Tina Lea lived in a tower block named Stirling House. It took less than ten minutes to cover the distance between Lea's flat and

Carter's pad. Tina had admitted to Nick that she was a member of the Church of Valerie Solanas. But she'd managed to keep her love affair a secret from the sisters, who'd have shot her if they'd known she was sleeping with the enemy. Vicki Douglas' use of femino-communism as an ideological substitute for Nazi occultism among members of what was formerly the Church of Adolf Hitler, had not been entirely successful in Tina's case. Lea now abhorred all forms of racism and felt that Vicki's femail supremacist beliefs smacked of a similar biological reductionism. However, Tina's friendship networks were so closely intertwined with the Church of Valerie Solanas hardcore, that she'd not yet worked up the courage to break with the group.

Nick had popped out to buy a pint of milk when he was stopped by Narcissus Brooke. Fortunately, Carter had grown his hair and a beard since going underground, and so the head of the White Seed of Christ did not recognise his arch-enemy. Nick, however, recognised Brooke instantly.

'I'm a bit lost,' Narcissus gushed, 'could you tell me how to get to Stirling House?'

'I was going there myself,' Nick lied, instantly suspicious and wondering if the Nazi guru was perhaps planning to pay Tina a visit. 'I'll take you to the flats, this way.'

As they hurried to the tower block, Carter got nothing more than pleasantries out of Brooke. When Nick and Narcissus got into the lift and the fascist wanted to go to Tina's floor, the titular head of the Nihilist Alliance knew exactly what to do. He needed more time with Brooke in order to draw information out of the prick. The elevator was not in particularly good working order, as the door was clanging shut, Carter kicked it. The door jammed, with only an inch of space left between it and the frame and so, not even a slip of a man could have squeezed out of the lift, let alone Narcissus Brooke, who was overweight!

'Fuck,' Nick swore, 'the lift's jammed again!'

'What d'ya mean the lift's jammed?' Narcissus looked as if he was about to burst a blood vessel.

'I mean,' Carter explained patiently, 'that it's broken and we're stuck in 'ere unless we can force open the door.'

'Well get to it, man!' Brooke decreed, 'I haven't got all day! I might get claustrophobia! Put your back into it!'

Nick tried pitting all his strength against the door but to no avail. It was easy enough jamming the elevator, but getting the door to open again was a different matter.

'It's no good,' Carter panted, 'it won't move. We're stuck in 'ere until we can get somebody to call the fire brigade.'

'How long will that take?' Narcissus remonstrated.

'Well,' Nick paused to weigh his thoughts. 'I was trapped in this lift for the best part of three hours last week. The first person to come along said they'd get the emergency services but they didn't bother, in the meantime I'd told everyone else who came by that somebody had called assistance. Eventually, I realised that the guy who said he'd get help hadn't bothered, so I got someone else to make an emergency call. Once the fire brigade got here, they had me out in no time at all.'

'It must have been hell!' Brooke blurted.

'It wasn't so bad,' Carter replied. 'I'd just been to the offie, so I had eight cans of Tennants with me. I just sat down, relaxed and drank myself stupid. I was pissed out of me brains by the time I got out.'

'Let me have a go at forcing that door,' Narcissus said as he elbowed Nick out of the way.

Brooke didn't have half of Carter's strength and his efforts to free himself from the elevator were utterly futile. They simply left him dripping with sweat and looking as if he was going to throw a fit.

'Don't just stand there, doing nothing!' Narcissus screamed. 'Give me a bloody hand, I'm not gonna be able to budge it on my own.'

Nick edged in beside the big man and they both pitted their strength against the door, but to no avail! However, Brooke managed to press his crotch against Carter's rump and the bastard had a hard-on. Narcissus had never indulged in anything that could be described as an unnatural act, and was at a loss to explain the urges he sometimes felt when he was in the company of other men. After all, he was not a pervert!

'It's no use,' Nick sighed, 'we'll just have to wait until someone comes along and get them to call the fire brigade.'

'But that might be an hour or more!' Brooke raged.

'Well, what other suggestions have you got?' Carter kept his cool.

'Isn't there an alarm bell or something?'

'Yeah,' Nick said pressing the button, 'and it doesn't work, it's not making any noise.'

'Let me have a go,' Narcissus coughed as he pushed Carter out of the way and jabbed his finger against the button.

'It wasn't working when I got trapped in here last week,' Nick observed caustically.

'That's disgusting,' Brooke heaved, 'the council isn't doing its job. It's bloody dangerous failing to keep these lifts properly serviced.'

'Write a letter to *The Times* about it,' Carter sneered. 'No, they wouldn't print it, wouldn't mean anything to their readers, you'd be better off trying the *Guardian!*'

'HELP! HELP!' Narcissus hollered, 'SOME-BODY HELP ME! I'M STUCK IN THE LIFT! WILL SOMEBODY PLEASE HELP ME!'

'Shut up!' a voice blustered from a tenth-storey flat, 'can't a man enjoy a bit of peace and quiet in his own home. If you don't keep quiet, I'll call the police!'

'PLEASE DO THAT!' Brooke yelled.

'You're bloody mad!' the voice replied. There was the sound of a door slamming and then silence.

Nick sat down, resting his back against the lift door. He took a packet of Polo mints from a shirt pocket, removed one of the sweeties and popped it into his mouth. He offered the packet to Narcissus, who shook his head, so Carter put the remaining mints back in his shirt pocket.

'I could do with a drink,' Nick sighed.

'It's attitudes like that which have ruined this country!' Brooke screeched.

'Are you a man of strong political convictions?' Carter enquired.

'I,' Narcissus proclaimed, 'am a National Socialist disciple of Christ!'

'What's that when it's at home then?' Nick retorted, feigning ignorance.

'A doctrine elaborated by the great leaders of the Nordic Nations, originally invented by our saviour the Lord Jesus Christ, its spirit has been kept alive by the likes of George Lincoln Rockwell, Adolf Hitler and Arnold Leese!'

'I see,' Carter lowed, 'it's some kind of Christian Nazism, or pan-German mysticism.'

'It's more than that,' Brooke proclaimed, 'it is a religion designed to save the Aryan people from racial suicide!'

'But I thought Jesus was a rabbi,' Nick put in.

'Fool,' Narcissus cried, 'you've been duped, brainwashed by the Zionists. Jesus was British, after his death, the British people left Palestine and came here to England from where they colonised Northern Europe, North America and the Antipodes! We are the Chosen People!'

'In that case,' Carter demanded, 'why are you trapped in a lift, in a block of council flats, in Kennington?'

'It's all part of the divine plan!' Brooke explained. 'You see, Jesus has sent me to save you. I'm the head of a church called the White Seed of Christ. If you join, various female members will be obliged to offer themselves to you, so that you may plant your seed in their bellies and thereby preserve your racial heritage! After that, you'll become a warrior for Christ and Country, venturing forth to do battle with the evil forces of multiracialism!'

'Fair enough,' Nick admitted, 'but why did you come to this block of flats?'

'Well,' Narcissus said and then paused, 'as well as fulfilling God's plan to save you, I'm also here to rescue a woman called Tina Lea from the clutches of evil. Tina is a racially conscious believer who belongs to an organisation that has been subverted by Satanic feminists. I'm making unannounced visits on all members of her group, in the hope of bringing them back into the arms of the Lord.'

'I see,' Nick said before lapsing into silence.

Having extracted the information he wanted from Brooke, Carter had nothing more to say to the Nazi moron. He felt like beating the bastard to a bloody pulp but refrained from this course of action because it would probably land him in trouble. When the fire brigade were finally called and released him from the lift, they'd be a bit suspicious if, after forcing open the door, they found the nihilist sitting next to a corpse.

'What are you thinking about?' Brooke asked, hoping to get the conversation going again. Time was dragging and the previous ten minutes had seemed like an eternity.

'Being in 'ere's a bit like Waiting For Godot, innit,' Carter droned.

'What?' Narcissus chirped.

'Well, if you take my Polos as a substitute for the turnips and radishes, it's a bit like Beckett's play.'

'What?' Brooke repeated, failing to recognise this allusion to the Theatre of the Absurd.

'Forget it.'

There was silence until a resident who attempted to use the lift was prevailed upon to call the fire brigade. After that, the emergency services were on the scene in less than five minutes.

'Are you alright in there?' a voice enquired.

'Yes,' Nick affirmed.

'No,' Narcissus yowled.

'Either way, there's not a lot we can do about it until we've got the door open,' a second voice observed.

'Stand back in there,' the first voice commanded.

Brooke pressed himself into a far corner, Carter got up and stood in the middle of the lift. There followed a series of metallic crunches and squeaks.

'Can you get a bit more pressure on over there, Darren,' the first voice said.

'Okay,' his mate replied.

The lift door inched backwards and a few seconds later, Nick stepped out into the hallway. The two firemen were already packing up their tools.

'Thanks,' Carter said.

'Bloody hell,' Narcissus swore as he took in his two rescuers, 'there's millions of white men who've been thrown out of work and they give fire brigade jobs to ethnics!'

Nick spun around and his fist cracked against Brooke's fat mouth. There was the sickening crunch of splintering bone and the bastard staggered backwards, spitting out gouts of blood and the occasional piece of broken tooth. After a blow to the stomach, Narcissus doubled up and split seconds later, Carter's boot slammed into his face. The two firemen helped Nick give the fascist the kicking he so richly deserved. After a few minutes of this sport, one of the firemen picked Brooke up and threw him down a rubbish shoot.

Carter shook hands with his two new friends and then climbed the stairs to Lea's flat. After Nick had recounted his recent escapade, Tina agreed it would be a good idea if she moved out of her pad. The address was well-known within fascist circles and it made her an easy target. During the course of their discussion, it was agreed that Lea would move in with Carter until they could sort out a more permanent arrangement. They spent the afternoon packing up boxes. After loading Tina's possessions into her car, they cruised up to Kennington Park Estate.

'Jesus!' Nick exclaimed, 'the place is crawling with cops.'

'Look up there,' Tina added, 'the filth are raiding your pad!'

'Let's get outta here!' Carter bawled.

Tina didn't need any further encouragement. A few minutes later, they were speeding through Brixton and down towards the South Coast.

FOUR

BEING A HOT-HEADED youth, Bogroll Bates dismissed the suggestion that he knock off members of the Industrial League one by one. Instead of accepting Mike Armilus' counsel, Bates decided to bomb the League's London HQ and thereby inflict maximum damage with a single blow against the forces of bourgeois reaction! The Industrial League offices were tucked away on Bride Lane, just off Ludgate Circus. Bogroll didn't have any real plan of attack, he just wanted to steam into the place. Above the entry phone were the words *Listing and Black Ltd, Est. 1926.* The bastards running the operation had a sick sense of humour, while they didn't want to advertise their whereabouts, there was no real attempt made to hide the nature of the operation.

Bogroll loitered in the doorway. He couldn't really ring the bell and ask to be let in, if he did then the element of surprise would be lost. Dave Brown, the Industrial League's security expert, stepped out onto the street and pulled the door firmly shut behind him. Brown looked Bates up and down. There was something familiar about the boy. Suspecting a connection with his youngest sister, the security expert decided not to challenge Bogroll, although his instincts told him the youth was up to no good.

A few minutes after Brown had sped off to snatch a late lunch, a motorcycle courier was admitted into the building. Bogroll slipped into the hallway behind the messenger, who disappeared up a flight of stairs as the door clicked shut behind Bates. A minute later, the courier came back down the stairs, marched past Bogroll and onto the street. Bates correctly deduced that the Industrial League reception was at the top of the first flight. He took off his rucksack and removed two Molotov cocktails before slinging the bag back over his shoulders. Bogroll lit the petrol bombs before charging up the stairs.

'Bolshevist attack! Bolshevist attack!' an ageing receptionist screamed as Bogroll lobbed one of the Molotovs through an open doorway.

A sheet of flame engulfed the room and the fire had a firm hold within seconds. The Industrial League's files, which were maintained on a card system to prevent those blacklisted seeking redress under the Data Protection Act, were soon reduced to ashes.

'I hate the rich!' the sound of Bates' voice echoed around the cavernous office as he chucked the other bomb into a conference room.

Bogroll ran back down the stairs and into the street. An assortment of besuited bastards were pouring into the reception. The secretary manning this post, who'd been cowering under her desk, was helped to her feet and led down a fire escape. Two of the younger Industrial League employees decided to chase the bomber. As they reached the street, a motorcycle backfired. Thinking they'd come under attack from armed militants who'd been stationed to ambush the League workforce, these would-be heroes charged back up the stairs and then down the fire escape, so that they could join their colleagues who'd assembled in a courtyard situated to the rear of the building.

'They've got guns!' one of the pair yelled.

'We're lucky we weren't killed,' shouted the other, 'if we hadn't reacted so quickly, we'd have been mown down in a hail of bullets. God only knows how we managed to dodge the first volley!'

'There must have been a dozen of the scoundrels!' his colleague elaborated.

Mike Armilus was roused from unconsciousness by a bucket of cold water that had been thrown over his head. He felt as if he was dying. His stomach had been pummelled by Met fists and the nihilist leader could taste blood trickling into his mouth from a split lip. A strong light had been directed into Mike's eyes and all he could see beyond it were white walls that were bathed in the same brilliance. Armilus tried to collect his thoughts. He'd not told the cops anything. The less he said, the better. Strong hands shook the nihilist as an authoritarian voice demanded that he answer the questions that were being fired at him.

'Lawyer?' Mike mumbled.

'Don't pull that bullshit on me,' Inspector

Newman grunted, 'just forget all about your legal rights. Answer my questions and rather than getting a lawyer, I'd strongly advise you to seek medical aid once you've been released. However, if you don't co-operate, you won't be needing a doctor, you'll be seeing an undertaker instead.'

'Telephone call,' Armilus croaked.

A searing pain shot through Mike's body as a police boot slammed into his groin. Then both Armilus and the chair to which he was handcuffed were thrown against the nearest wall. Mike was still conscious but pretended that he'd blacked out.

'Set him upright!' Newman whooped at two constables.

'Yes sir!' the men answered and then did as they'd been told.

'Where's Swift Nick Carter hiding?' the inspector demanded as he threw a bucket of cold water over Armilus. 'What was your role in the cenotaph outrage? What do you know about the bomb attack on the Industrial League?'

'You'll get nowhere questioning an unconscious suspect,' Martin Smith informed Newman. 'You might as well save your breath until he comes around. Anyway, what's all this about a bomb attack on the Industrial League?'

'I had word while I was questioning Armilus that a group of terrorists petrol-bombed the Industrial League HQ in Bride Lane. It's obviously the anarchists who did it, they're the only sect seriously into taking direct action against establishment targets!'

'Do we really need to worry about attacks upon the Industrial League?' Smith asked rhetorically.

'After all, they've got their own security operation and plenty of cash behind it. I'm sure they'll track down the bastards responsible for this latest outrage.'

'You're right!' the inspector admitted. 'What we've got to do is find Carter!'

'I know where the cunt's been hiding since he blew up the cenotaph!' Martin crowed.

'Where?' Newman demanded.

'With Armilus, I've just been through the flat with some of your men and it's fuckin' obvious Carter's been living there.'

'That's crazy!' was the inspector's riposte. 'We could have raided the flat at any time. It should have been obvious to both Carter and Armilus that once we decided to put the screws on the Nihilist Alliance, it would be the first place to be turned over.'

'Maybe they were banking on the fact that all the media attention is focused on Steve Drummond's Class Justice and figured you'd never get around to harassing a rival organisation.'

'Christ!' Newman swore, 'I never thought of that!'

'That's why you're a cop and I'm a politician,' Smith replied.

'So what do we do now?' the policeman enquired.

'Let Armilus go,' the SWG leader instructed, 'you've got nothing on him. He may have been harbouring a terrorist but we can't prove that yet. Give the bastard enough rope to hang himself. In the meantime, let's concentrate on capturing Carter and smashing Class Justice.'

Mike groaned and pretended that he was regaining consciousness. He'd faked the blackout to gain a respite from the beatings he'd been suffering. This successful manoeuvre had also yielded him some very valuable information. Inspector Newman seemed to take Smith's judgements at face value, whereas Armilus recognised that while despising the Nihilist Alliance as a political organisation, the Trotskyite had a tactical interest in protecting it as far as possible from the Mets. If the Nihilists could be used as an instrument to split the anarchist movement, there was a good chance of stemming the flow of members quitting the Spartacist Workers Group for Class Justice.

Tina Lea parked her mini in the multi-storey car park on Worthing High Street. As Tina snapped a steering lock into place, Swift Nick got out of the motor and stretched his six-foot frame. The oldest parts of Worthing had been built around 1800 but the modern town centre immediately to their west was a much more recent development. Tina and Nick wandered past the closed shops before drifting down to the sea front.

'You got any money?' Carter asked.

'Not much,' Lea replied, 'but if we can find a Halifax cashpoint, I've got nearly seven hundred quid in my account.'

'That'll keep us going until we've sorted out some other way of getting dosh,' Nick observed. 'As long as Armilus doesn't get put away, he'll be a good source of income. I've done alright from the Nihilist

Alliance so far, I don't see why they shouldn't continue supplying me with cash.'

'Do you think the cops arrested Mike?' Tina asked anxiously.

'I reckon so,' Carter sighed, 'coz if they know I was living in the flat, they'll do Armilus for harbouring me, and if they don't know I was staying in Mike's pad, then they were out to fit him up for his activities with the Nihilist Alliance. Either way you look at it, Armilus is knee-deep in shit.'

'Poor Mike!' Lea cried.

Nick and Tina walked the length of Worthing's decrepit pier. This particular Victorian relic needed far more than the odd lick of paint to set it right. For a start, it was too short and something needed to be done about the smell given off by the sea, a stink which gave visitors the impression they were standing above an open sewer.

'It ain't exactly romantic!' Carter observed.

'I don't know,' Lea drawled, 'if you hold your nose, there's a wonderful crashing of waves and squawking of seagulls. And I'm pretty much sold on the way the sun's going down as well.'

'Pah,' Nick spat, 'until you can conjure up a mental picture of the entire royal family swinging from a scaffold, you don't know the meaning of beauty!'

'That's easy,' Tina rejoined, 'see, I've just done it!'

'I didn't see anything,' Carter insisted.

'In that case,' Lea teased, 'you're the one with a deficient appreciation of the sublime.'

Nick conceded the point by wrapping his arms around Tina's neck and forcing his tongue into her mouth. Lea melted in Carter's embrace and for a few, fleeting seconds her heart beat out the primitive rhythm of the swamps. Then the kiss was over and the two lovers gazed across the waves to the sun sinking beneath the western horizon.

Tina took Nick's hand and led him back down the pier. The two of them looked more like a respectable couple enjoying a traditional seaside break than fugitives from police oppression and fascist hit squads. A pair of young trendies were walking towards them as they stepped back onto the esplanade.

'Excuse me,' Tina asked the trendies, 'but is there anywhere to go for a bit of excitement in this town?'

'Not unless your idea of action extends to attending a pensioners' bingo night!' the girl sulked.

'But if you wanna come back to Portslade with us,' the boy said, 'I'm sure we could all get something on.'

'Where the fuck is Portslade?' Nick demanded.

'Between Shoreham and Hove,' the girl smiled at the stranger's ignorance of the local geography.

'Just down the road really,' her boyfriend added, 'it's only . . .'

'Will we be able to get a bed and breakfast out that way?' Lea cut in.

'I was suggesting the type of action that would require you staying the night,' the boy giggled coyly.

'You want group sex!' Tina exclaimed, thinking that she'd grasped the situation.

'Tim doesn't want group sex,' the girl said flatly, 'he's a masochist, he just wants to be humiliated and forced to watch your boyfriend poke me.'

'Oh shut up, Fiona,' Tim groaned, 'you'll spoil all the fun before it even gets started.'

'I've got a better idea,' Carter bullied, 'you two chicks can rub pussies while I make Tim suck my cock. You'd like that Tim, wouldn't you!'

Tim didn't reply, he didn't need to, he was blushing from head to toe and his prick was bulging against his flies. Nick wasn't in the least bit surprised, this wasn't the first het masochist he'd come across whose deepest longing was to be fucked stupid by a member of his own sex.

After a brief discussion, the four polymorphs decided they'd all travel to Portslade in Tina's mini. Fiona and Tim had sold their car the previous day to raise extra money for a six-month jaunt to the States. They'd been hoping to find someone who'd rent out their flat, but with only a couple of days until they left, there didn't seem much chance of locating a tenant. Flogging the motor meant they wouldn't need to skimp while they were away.

'Yeah,' Tim was elaborating, 'we'd be grateful if someone would live in the flat rent free, just to look after the place while we're gone.'

'I wouldn't mind giving it a go,' Nick offered.

'That's marvellous!' Tim enthused. 'It'll keep the old place safe from squatters.'

Everything was agreed. Tim couldn't wait to get home and phone up his parents. He'd made the trip to Worthing to persuade them to look after his pad while he was in the States. His mum and dad had reluctantly agreed to this, and they'd be very pleased to be freed of the responsibility. Although retired, Tim's parents had very little free time because they devoted all their energy to promoting the interests of the Christian Anti-Communist Crusade.

'Just park anywhere down here,' Fiona told Tina and then pointing at a building said, 'we live above the newsagent's over there.'

Boundary Road was the main drag in Portslade, with most of the shops running in two long rows from the railway station down to the coast. The seaward end was blighted by a series of industrial premises, at one time there'd even been a gas works, although that had been scrapped when the country switched to the natural supplies in the North Sea. If Portslade attracted any tourists whatsoever, they had to be those possessed by the most perverse aesthetic sensibilities. Beyond a Norman church and the manor house, even the old town several miles to the north was bereft of historic interest. As the name suggests, Boundary Road divided East and West Sussex, and this fact was reflected in the area's psychogeography. It was most definitely a place on the periphery, a town where fragments of the human refuse torn loose from the masses of modern society could pass their lives in anonymity.

Tim phoned his parents while Fiona made tea. The flat had been decorated and refurnished very recently, with trendy black fittings which provided a strong counterpoint to the white walls. The main room was large enough to house a chrome and black leather three-piece suite, a black desk pushed against a window, a large TV, expensive hi-fi system and an extensive collection of books and CDs stacked on black shelving. The bedroom was poky, with a double bed dominating the cramped space.

'Milk? Sugar?' Fiona enquired.

'Just milk,' Nick and Tina replied in unison.

Fiona doled out cuppas and seconds later, they were all contentedly slurping the brew. Carter, who'd sunk back into the sofa, drained his mug of tea in three gulps and then stood up.

'Okay, Tim,' Nick boomed, 'I reckon it's about time I sampled your cock-sucking technique. I want you to kneel in front of me.'

Tim did as he was told and once Nick had given him the word, he reached up with shaking hands to unzip Carter's fly. His efforts were rewarded by eight inches of erect manhood that sprang from Nick's briefs. Tim clasped Carter's love muscle with his right hand and shook it vigorously.

'Hold on, hold on,' Nick moaned, 'before you bring me off, I want you to unbuckle my belt, so that my sta-pres fall down around my ankles.'

Tim took the tip of Carter's prick into his mouth and licked it. Keeping his lips around Nick's genetic pump, Tim released his grip on the fuck stick and fumbled with Carter's belt. Split seconds later, the top's trousers were lying in a rumpled heap at his feet.

Fiona thought that watching Tim give head beat fucking the louts they'd picked up since getting into group sex. It was the first time Tina had seen Nick in action with another man, and Lea found the scene so exciting that she literally wet her knickers! As he worked Nick's love stick with his mouth and his hand, Tim could feel his own prick straining against the cotton briefs he'd put on that morning. Million-year-old genetic codes were scrambled and unscrambled across the two men's bodies as narcotic endorphins seized control of their brains. Both blokes had left Portslade and modern society behind them. They were writhing on the mudflats of prehistory where the sexual impulse that had driven billions of species through the evolutionary process, first crawled out of the waves and thrust its way towards life on dry land.

Tim increased the speed with which he was working Nick's genetic pump and his frenzy was rewarded by the spurts of love juice that shot into his throat. The draught was strong and salty. The taste of it so excited the masochist that he spilt his own seed. With orgasmic groans, Nick and Tim fell to the floor, so that they might rest after their sexual exertions.

'Well done, well done!' Fiona and Tina applauded. 'What a show, very entertaining!'

The two girls clapped for a couple of minutes, then lifted their skirts and dropped their knickers. Fiona sat on Nick's face, while Tina pressed her twat against Tim's mouth. The two chicks were not prepared to remain mere spectators, they insisted on physically participating in the oral action!

After months of deliberating over the most effective means of unifying the ranks of the far-Right, Adam White had concluded that the diverse grouplets who vied to lead the forces of Anglo-German nationalism could never be brought together by peaceful negotiation. If Adam was to rise to his rightful position of Führer lording it over a European Nazi movement that had been born again in flames, those traitors who refused to recognise his leadership had to be crushed mercilessly! One by one all rival sects and heresies had to be smashed until everyone on the far-Right had lined up behind White.

Adam was convinced that a series of audacious moves would enable him to reunite the divided German tribes and restore to this abused people their native Saxon language. Germany, Austria, Scandinavia, Switzerland, the Netherlands and the UK would once again become the single Fatherland from whose dear soil our pagan ancestors had sprung! One Race, One Language, One Destiny, were the watchwords that had guided the No Future Party since White had first launched his crusade for a return to the traditional Nordic values of rape, pillage and plunder.

White swung round in his seat and gazed lovingly at the troops who were sitting cross-legged in the back of his Ford transit van. Adam had mustered fifteen shock troops to take part in the raid on the White Seed of Christ's Epping commune. Narcissus Brooke would be made to pay for his heresies and deviations. White did not understand the Identity Preacher, for a start, there was something extremely perverse about an avowed National Socialist who preferred an exclusively femail following to an entourage of gorgeous blond-haired boys dressed in smart paramilitary uniforms!

'Okay, men!' Adam yapped as the transit pulled up on a gravel driveway, 'we're here, everyone out of the van.'

White's troops lined up two abreast, with their Führer and the boy who'd sat next to him in the transit at the head of this column. Instead of rifles, Adam's troops held baseball bats against their shoulders. White shouted an order and the troops goose-stepped to the entrance of the old vicarage that Narcissus Brooke had transformed into his communal HQ.

'Stormtrooper Two and Stormtrooper Three,' Adam whistled, 'break the door down with your baseball bats!'

The wood soon splintered beneath the blows of the Nazi fanatics. The NF activists marched into a hallway that was lined with portraits of men who'd devoted their lives to the ideal of the British Empire, Milner, Rhodes and numerous members of the Cliveden set. Once inside, they were met by the vast majority of the wimmin who made up the membership of the White Seed of Christ. At their head was Sarah Pratt, Brooke's deputy.

'There was no need to break down the door, I'd have opened it for you if you'd knocked,' Pratt scolded.

'Stormtroopers Four, Five and Six, punish that woman for insulting me!' the Führer snivelled.

Stormtroopers Five and Six grabbed hold of Sarah. Number Four raised his baseball bat above his shoulders. White stroked the hair of the blond boy who'd been sitting next to him in the van. The only sound to be heard was a slight whooshing as the bat sailed through the air. Then there was the sickening crunch of splintering bone as it slammed into Pratt's left knee.

'Aaaaagggggghhhhh!' Sarah squealed, barely taking in the fact that her leg had been broken as she gave vocal expression to the excruciating pain that flooded her body.

'And the other one,' Adam blubbered.

The operation was repeated, the only difference being that this time it was Pratt's right leg that was broken. The two Troopers who'd been restraining Sarah released their grip and she fell to the floor in a crumpled heap.

'That's what happens to people who fail to respect my natural authority,' White spat as he simultaneously shook his fist, 'their legs get broken, or they get killed, or worse! Do you understand?'

'Ja wohl, mein Führer!' the assembled members of the commune shot back as they simultaneously clicked their heels.

'That's better,' Adam meowed, 'that's much, much, better. Just what I like, a bit of discipline! Now, tell me where I can find Brooke.'

'He's out,' several of the wimmin chimed, 'should have been back hours ago. We don't know where he is.'

'That's unfortunate!' White mooed. 'Most unfortunate, it means I'll have to hang around until he gets back. Stormtroopers Seven and Eight, make the building uninhabitable.'

'Ja wohl, mein Führer!' the two soldiers lisped as their right arms shot forward to give the fascist salute, then they marched down the hall intent on carrying out their mission of destruction.

'Now girls,' Adam minced, 'I want you to provide me with the names of any members of your commune who aren't present, along with whatever

information you have concerning their whereabouts.'

'Eve Parry, Liz Jones and Linda Cort,' the
wimmin replied in unison, 'have been sent out from
our community to liberate the seed of the anarchist
leader Swift Nick Carter. Narcissus ordered them
not to return until one of their bellies was swollen
with Carter's child. Our leader is of the opinion that
Carter is a degenerate but his issue is still worth
saving for the White Race!'

The sound of china, glass and metal being shattered, mangled and otherwise destroyed, was coming
from the kitchen. Stormtroopers Seven and Eight
were evidently carrying out their assigned task of
destruction with considerable aplomb. The Führer,
while aware of this cacophony, paid it no heed.

'Listen girls,' White flared, 'there's gonna be a
realignment of forces on the far-Right. Brooke's day
has passed, when he returns, I'll crush him like a
bug! I'm giving you a choice, either you march to
victory under my banner, or else you get your legs
broken with a baseball bat. Everyone who wants to
join the No Future Party stay where you are, anyone
who wants their legs broken can step forward.'

The Führer stroked the blond hair of his boy
mascot. He was pleased to see that nobody moved
but was rather at a loss about what to do next. If
only Brooke would show up, then the men could
beat him to a bloody pulp before clambering back
into the van and speeding off to their destiny.

'Does anyone know where Brooke is?' Adam was
desperately racking his brain about what to do next.

'Nein, mein Führer,' White's new disciples chirped.

Adam checked his Timex. It was getting late. Stormtroopers Seven and Eight had completed their demolition of the kitchen and were wrecking another room. White wondered if Brooke was going to come back that night. Perhaps the Identity Preacher had got word of Adam's plans and gone into hiding. Maybe the bastard was even planning a counter-attack! Adam would have to watch his back. There was no telling what might happen! While no impartial observer could doubt that he was a charismatic leader of the first rank, the membership of the White Seed of Christ had been converted to his cause too easily. There was a distinct possibility that a trap was about to be sprung! If White transported the girls to his headquarters, once he'd retired to his bed, these foxy vixens might murder him in his sleep.

'Girls,' the Führer brayed, 'wait here. Men, follow me outside.'

The troops marched two abreast behind White, who led them back to his van. The Führer took up his customary position on the front seat, between the blond driver and his favourite. He stroked the mascot's hair for a few seconds and then focused his attention on the matter in hand.

'Right men,' Adam announced, 'we're going to drive away and enjoy a swift pint in the first boozer we find. What I'm trying to do is ascertain whether the membership of the White Seed of Christ have really come over to our side. If they are sincere about marching to victory under my banner, then they'll still be standing in the hallway when we get back. If they're simply laying a trap to be sprung on us at a later date, they'll probably attack Stormtroopers Seven and Eight. Should they have shown any signs of disobedience by the time we return, we'll know that every last one of them is a piece of vermin polluting both Mother Earth and our glorious nationalist movement.'

'But my Führer!' Stormtrooper Ten protested, 'what if Seven and Eight are murdered by these vixens?'

'Number Ten,' White admonished, 'get a grip on yourself! I know you are emotionally attached to Seven but if he is unable to defend himself against a bunch of girls, then he's not a worthy foot soldier of our future Reich. If your boyfriend fails to live up to the arduous standards of our National Revolution, then I will order my favourite to comfort you for the remainder of the night.'

'You are too kind, my Führer!' Ten cried as he threw his right arm forward in a Nazi salute.

The assembled troops then fell into a spontaneous chant of 'White, White, White, White!' Adam stroked the blond hair of his favourite and gazed benignly on his men. Each, in turn, was sucked into the black pits of their leader's eyes. There they found themselves reborn with all the dross of a materialist society wiped from their minds. Or put another way, these bozos had allowed themselves to be conned by the same bullshit that had made wo/mankind's existence a misery for aeons, they'd fallen for the religious trip. The spirit lived, not until the end of time, but on the blood and misery of those individuals deluded into believing in any reality beyond the pleasurable functionings of the body. Completely lacking in talent, taste or sense, White's coterie preferred the paltry pickings of Nazi Myth to the global ebb and flow of polysexual transnationalism.

✣ FIVE ✣

Swift NICK CARTER had really enjoyed his first few days on the South Coast. He'd needed a break from London, and falling on his feet, with a free pad, had put the anarchist in an exceptionally good mood. However, a man cannot live on the joys of sea air alone and since Portslade failed to offer the distractions of life in London, Carter had set to work on a number of texts. He was rapidly completing a series of articles on the history of urban guerrilla warfare for *DYNAMITE!*, the street paper of the Nihilist Alliance.

In a day or two, Tina would attempt to deliver these to Mike Armilus in London, along with some news stories and a revised version of the Nihilist Platform. Nick felt it was important to produce a flood of Nihilist propaganda, although Tina had found herself a job as a typist, Carter did not consider her salary sufficient to keep the two of them in the style to which he was accustomed. He was therefore banking on Armilus supplying him with dosh and he'd rightly concluded that his comrade would be more generous with the Alliance's loot if the organisation was getting something in return for its money.

Having worked with Armilus on the production of a business plan for the Nihilist Alliance, Nick knew the organisation was generating enough money to pay him for his work at half the NUJ rate. Mike was also drawing a salary but otherwise there were no paid employees. The Nihilist Alliance had been founded on a much sounder financial footing than Class Justice. Whereas Drummond's mob prioritised circulation over profit in the production of their street paper, the Nihilist Alliance was not interested in recruiting a mass membership.

Nick and Mike had opted for a niche market where they could count on a steady income from a wide range of books, pamphlets, magazines, newspapers, tapes, CDs, T-shirts, badges and posters that were sold almost exclusively by mail order to a few thousand dedicated activists. Class Justice boasted that the circulation of their street paper was now thirty-five thousand, but Carter knew for a fact that this figure actually represented its print run and that nearly half the copies of any given issue remained unsold by the time the follow-up appeared. Class Justice was unprofitable because in the hope of boosting circulation, the number of pages had been increased without raising the cover price, and national distributors were given huge discounts as an incentive to take on the paper.

Besides, there was a strict mathematical relationship between falling circulation and increases in the frequency with which issues of Class Justice were produced, as the casual sales that had failed to increase from year to year were spread between more and more issues of the paper. It was regular donations from the membership, in terms of both time and money, that subsidised this farce. Both Armilus and Carter were vehemently opposed to frittering away the revolutionary will of the masses in this way, and should the revolution fail to materialise, they would at least have a profitable business!

However, it would be wrong of the reader to conclude from this description that the Nihilist Alliance was solely geared towards turning a profit. As a dedicated and lucid revolutionary, Swift Nick Carter recognised that while any viable political organisation must adapt itself to the conditions prevailing in the capitalist economy, the Nihilist Alliance was free to act according to the principles of potlatch within the cultural realm. It was for this reason that he was working on two pamphlets which would be mailed out anonymously to members of fascist organisations.

Nick took a situational approach to politics and believed that the most effective way of dealing with Nazis was to push the internal contradictions of fascist ideology to their logical conclusion. He sincerely believed that exercises of this type were more debilitating to the morale of the nationalist movement than countering the false consciousness of these wankers with the theoretico-practical tasks of revolutionary organisation. And so, while Carter abhorred all forms of anti-semitism, he recognised that anti-semitic beliefs could be rationally employed to destroy the fascist movement.

The first pamphlet Nick was working upon was provisionally entitled *For A Few Shekels More: The Ku Klux Klan Exposed!* In producing this text, Carter was drawing upon genuine historical data, Nazi conspiracy theory and his own fertile imagination to 'prove' that rather than being the spontaneous creation of 'good ol' boys', the Klan was actually a puppet of sinister cosmopolitan forces! As is well-known, the Klan was revived by a showman called William Simmons who milked money from the organisation to make himself rich. Royalties from his book *The Kloran* soared after a pair of unscrupulous public relations experts were hired to promote the movement. Simmons was simply cashing in on the box-office success of D. W. Griffith's film *Birth Of A Nation*. The movie had, in turn, been based on a novel by Thomas Dixon called *The Clansman: An Historical Romance of the Ku Klux Klan*. Dixon numbered among his friends John D. Rockefeller and President Woodrow Wilson. These easily verifiable historical facts should have been enough to make any right-thinking Nazi deeply suspicious of the Klan, and the inventions Nick was adding to this data would have the fascist movement baying for KKK blood!

The second pamphlet, entitled *National Socialism Is Jewish!*, pulled even fewer punches. In Carter's outline, the text was broken down into three major sections. The first, *Nationalism*, would demonstrate that nationalist ideas were ultimately derived from the Jewish conception of a 'chosen people'. The next part, *Socialism*, would explore the Jewish roots of

socialism by plagiarising and paraphrasing reactionary conspiracy theories, in particular those
dealing with either the Russian Revolution or the
racial origins of Marx, Trotsky and other top-flight
communists. The third part, *National Socialism*,
would show that the German NSDAP and earlier
Thule Society had developed their interrelated occult
and political doctrines by drawing on an ancient
tradition of Jewish mysticism.

With so much work ahead of him, Nick was
pleased that Tina had found herself a full-time job,
he'd need plenty of peace and quiet during the day
so that he could get on with his writing. There was
a world to win and Carter knew that it was his
revolutionary duty to play a central role in clarifying
the tasks facing Nihilists, while simultaneously
aiming to demoralise and confuse every opposing
tendency!

Adam White deeply regretted his attempts to unify
the far-Right by the use of force. It had backfired
so badly! Narcissus Brooke's decomposing body
had been found jammed into the rubbish chute of a
block of council flats, and the No Future Party's
attack on the White Seed of Christ's Epping
commune had quite wrongly led to Adam's impli-
cation in this murder.

'I'm sorry,' Inspector Newman apologised to his
old friend Adam White, 'but the police have no
choice in this matter. The Home Secretary will ban
the No Future Party later this afternoon. You'll have
to go underground, otherwise you'll be arrested
within a matter of hours!'

'But James!' White protested. 'What about the fact that neither I nor my party had anything to do with the Brooke murder? Whatever happened to our Anglo-Saxon liberty? The proscription of my movement is a monstrous travesty of the democratic process which is the birthright of every freeborn Englishman!'

'What is this nonsense you're spouting?' Newman demanded. 'I've always supported you on the basis that you'd suspend parliamentary democracy once you came to power!'

'But James, don't you see?' Adam wailed. 'That's precisely my point, the No Future Party has yet to achieve power! Until that glorious day, when flanked by blond-haired bodyguards, I assume full dictatorial powers as the Führer of Westminster, we're depending on the maintenance of the democratic system so that we can realise our bold plan for the seizure of power!'

'You're succumbing to voluntarist illusions,' the police chief warned the Nazi leader. 'As we all know, fascism and democracy are the two political forms that capitalism assumes according to the needs of the historic moment. If you are not ready to assume power when the fascist expedient of rule by decree becomes a historical necessity, then there will always be alternative candidates ready to take on the leadership function that you, perhaps understandably, consider to be rightfully yours.'

'But,' White countered, 'I am the man of destiny! I am the Unique One, He who returns whenever He is needed!'

'That's all well and good,' Newman replied, 'but if you're not ready to assume power then you aren't needed.'

'Marxist cant!' White quacked. 'I will always be needed! The nation has to be disciplined, we've got to purge the country of liberal filth and provide youngsters with something to respect! How could young people look up to a buffoon like Jackboots Houghton or that lunatic Nigel Devi? I am the only man with the charisma to cut it as a British Führer while simultaneously bringing our kith and kin in the White Commonwealth back under British dominion!'

'Okay, okay! I believe you,' the inspector conceded, 'but what I want to know is how you're going to go about conquering political power in this country?'

'Well,' Adam hedged, unable to meet this challenge, 'what do you suggest?'

'What I'd do,' Newman elaborated, 'is go into hiding with your most trusted militants and use these men as a guerrilla force. What you must do is destabilise the country, and once this has been achieved, come forward as a force for National Salvation!'

'Yes, that's what I'll do!' White replied dogmatically.

'So you're gonna go underground?'

'Of course I'm gonna go underground!' White was emphatic on the point. 'You should know me well enough by now to understand that my belief in the National Socialist faith is unwavering! I will always take whatever steps are necessary for our forces to win because Victory Is Our Destiny!'

Steve Drummond was proud of the way he'd succeeded in building the movement's paper. *Class Justice* was widely recognised as a soaraway workerist read! The opposition might consider it to be an insult when they described *CJ* as the anarchist equivalent of the *Sun*, but in Steve's opinion, such a comparison demonstrated that his group had mastered the art of political agitation. Whereas Trot groups wasted the energy and enthusiasm of their cadre by sending them onto the streets to sell leftie drivel which no one in their right mind wanted to read, *Class Justice* was such a good crack that people were clamouring to buy it, with the result that the experience of paper-selling actually boosted the morale of the rank-and-file.

A couple sliding into the seats immediately in front of Drummond disturbed the anarchist's train of thought. Where the hell was Patricia? It didn't take ten minutes to have a slash. The second movie of the afternoon would be starting soon and Steve didn't want his attention distracted once the Chow Yun Fat flick began. Just as Drummond was despairing of his bird ever showing her face again, she reappeared laden down with enough junk food to cure even the most severe attack of the munchies.

'I thought you might be hungry,' Patricia said as she flopped down beside her boyfriend.

'I'm always hungry,' Steve fulminated, 'but I'm getting seriously worried that I'll end up fat thanks to all those sweeties you buy me!'

'Nonsense!' Good protested.

'I've put on seven pounds since we've been going out, give it another couple of months and I'll have a pot belly and multiple chins.'

'There's only one way to stop your moaning,' Patricia gushed. 'And that's to stuff your mouth with food. What do you want first, a can of coke, crisps, chocolate, smarties or pop corn?'

'I'll have the smarties,' Drummond replied.

'That's better,' Good warbled.

Split seconds later, she popped several of the candies into her boyfriend's open mouth. The anarchist chewed and then swallowed the sweeties. The instant he opened his mush for a refill, Patricia shovelled more in. Good loved playing this game, which she hoped would wean Drummond off sex and onto types of physical indulgence that did not endanger his immortal soul. Since she'd learnt that Steve was a Catholic, Patricia had been determined to bring her boyfriend back into the One True Faith before marrying him.

'You're so greedy!' the journalist giggled.

Steve didn't reply, he simply opened his gob so that Patricia could shovel in a third helping of smarties. Drummond's hand had been resting on his girlfriend's thigh. He slid his digits across Good's crotch. Patricia let out a soft moan as she tipped several smarties out of the tube and into her boyfriend's mouth. Steve tugged on the zipper that held Good's jeans in place and the fly opened with promises of ecstasies soon to come.

'Naughty boy!' Patricia hissed as she slapped

Steve hard on the wrist.

'This is ridiculous,' Drummond whispered as his girlfriend rezipped her fly, 'what's wrong with you, why won't you let me touch your cunt?'

'I'm not ready to do that kind of thing yet,' Good snapped. Then, after a moment's pause, added, 'We haven't known each other very long, you've got to give me time to learn to trust you.'

'So when are you gonna learn to trust me?' Steve demanded.

'Once we're married,' Patricia cooed.

'Then we might as well forget the whole thing!' Drummond barked. Lowering his voice, he continued: 'Let's just split up now, I'll find myself another chick. It's madness marrying someone without knowing whether they generate the right kind of sexual energy in the sack.'

Good was in two minds about what to do. She didn't want to commit herself to a sexual relationship, but on the other hand, she couldn't bear to lose Steve's love. After a few seconds, during which Patricia felt as if she was being torn apart, love won the day.

'Okay,' Good mumbled in Drummond's ear, 'I'll have sex with you on my birthday, it's only a few weeks away.'

'You won't regret it,' Steve replied and then kissed his girlfriend on the cheek. 'I'll show you a good time.'

Patricia imagined that several pairs of eyes were focused on her back. She was saved any further embarrassment by the start of the film, it made her insignificant, everyone was giving their full attention to the dashing figure cut by the *God Of Gamblers*.

Forgotten comrades were turning up like bad pennies. The Nihilist Alliance's *Old Price* protest march had lured several hundred demonstrators from warren-like council estates, decaying terraced houses and student halls of residence. As Mike Armilus pushed his way past a group of skins, he ran into Bogroll Bates who was searching for a familiar face.

'Alright, Bogroll!' Mike boomed. 'Glad you could make it. We've attracted a good turnout today!'

'Yeah,' Bogroll shot back, 'great issue, it appeals to everybody, no one wants to pay over the odds for their shopping.'

'The Nihilist Alliance is a populist organisation,' Armilus elaborated. 'And we've got a strong grasp of history too. In the eighteenth century there were riots in London as the mob attempted to get the old prices restored immediately after inflationary hikes on goods and services. Things got so serious that the government actually nicked people for wearing bits of clothing marked with the initials O.P., standing for Old Price.'

'You're joking!' Bates exclaimed. 'That's totalitarian.'

'Straight up, I can assure you it's true,' Mike was vehement on the issue. 'If you don't believe me, you can read it up in history books.'

'Do you think it could happen again?' Bogroll wanted to know.

'Well, many cultures view history as essentially

cyclical, there's even a significant minority of individuals in our society who share this view,' Armilus prattled. 'I can see a lot of parallels between our time and two hundred years ago. There's whole classes of wo/men who are excluded from the production process and the only way in which they can give expression to their political aspirations is as consumers.'

'Blimey!' Bates swore, 'what you're saying does my head in. Where the fuck did you learn to speak like a dictionary?'

'I've been in and out of political groups since I was fifteen,' Armilus confessed, 'I briefly belonged to a Leninist group when I was a teenager, but I soon concluded that they were a bunch of reactionaries who were incapable of conceiving of any form of political struggle occurring outside the workplace.'

'I suppose I'm what you'd call a few sandwiches short of a hamper when it comes to political knowledge,' Bogroll sighed. 'I just never had any interest in how things was run until I found out about the Industrial League blacklisting me.'

'Don't put yourself down,' Mike told his friend, 'I saw the stories in the papers about the Industrial League HQ being burnt out, that's first class work. You really put yourself on the line.'

'But I didn't succeed in killing any of the bastards,' Bates seethed.

'There's always next time!' Armilus observed.

'Now there's a thought!' Bogroll chirped.

'Make them pay for what they've done to you!' Mike's voice was tinged with fanaticism. 'But in the meantime, let's get this march off and moving. Are you coming with me to form the head of the parade?'

'Yeah!'

The march had been legally organised. The Tower Hamlets and Hackney cops hadn't heard of the Nihilist Alliance and considered the theme of the demonstration to be ridiculously archaic. They figured the protest would attract no more than a handful of cranks and so assigned just ten officers to police the event. The cops had made a terrible miscalculation, as the marchers shuffled out of Bethnal Green Gardens and into Cambridge Heath Road, their ranks were swelled by late-comers spilling from the tube station.

'What do we want?' one section of the marchers chanted.

'Old Price!' the rest replied.

'When do we want it?' the first group demanded.

'Now!' was the resounding response.

'Ten pence for a tin of beans!' everyone bellowsed, 'Ten pence for peeled plum tomatoes! And onions at a penny a pound!'

At the head of the march, there were a handful of smartly dressed activists. They carried a banner bearing a guillotine logo and the legend *Nihilist Alliance*. Behind them stretched a ragged column of lumpens, a disintegrated mass made up from a combination of the sub-proletariat and ruined elements of the bourgeois class: tramps, postal workers, discharged soldiers, freelance graphic designers, jailbirds, aspiring rock musicians, pick-pockets, poets, brothel keepers, community artists, lavatory attendants, beggars, unemployed youths and even the odd rag-picker.

Attracted by the noise and demands for price reductions, legions of shoppers joined the demonstration. A group of pensioners fell in at the rear of the march – thereby bringing the number of protesters close to the four figure mark. Rather than calling to mind May '68, or even 1848, the demonstrators looked more like a bank holiday crowd letting their hair down at a seedy south coast resort.

'Bring back shillings and sovereigns!' the pensioners yelled. 'Abolish decimal currency!'

'Bring back capital punishment, let's behead every last member of parliament!' the activists leading the march responded.

Before long everyone had returned to the original rallying cry: 'What do we want? Old Price! When do we want it? Now! Ten pence for a tin of beans! Ten pence for peeled plum tomatoes! Onions at a penny a pound!'

It has been observed elsewhere that in revolution, the resurrection of the past can serve to exalt new struggles. Rather than simply parodying the past, such appeals to historical precedent exaggerate given tasks in the imagination. Instead of fleeing the present, the Old Price demonstrators were solving it in reality and recovering the spirit of revolution. Such were the forces that the Nihilist Alliance had set in motion. The original idea had been to march to Hackney Downs and then hold a rally, but the material unfolding of events led instead to a far more radical denouement.

As the marchers lumbered past Hackney town

hall, a good number of them broke away from the demonstration to attack this symbol of municipal oppression. The masses had seized the initiative, and so to catch up with their own followers, the leadership had no choice but to attack their police escort. POW! Nihilist fists and boots thudded into Met bodies. ZOWIE! Several of the bastards staggered backwards spitting out gouts of blood and the occasional piece of broken tooth. KERRANG! The cops were beaten senseless. While his comrades were being pounded into the ground, PC Philip Dixon got down on his knees and begged for mercy.

'Be reasonable boys, don't hurt me,' Dixon winged. 'I'll do anything you want, you can have my arse or my mouth. I'll suck everybody's cock!'

'Okay bozo,' Mike Armilus said as he whipped out his love muscle, 'I want you to gag on this!'

'Yes, boss,' Philip whimpered.

'Hold on cocksucker,' Mike snapped as Dixon puckered his lips around the pecker, 'are you sure that what we're about to do is ideologically sound?'

'What do you mean?' was Dixon's puzzled reply.

'Are you one hundred per cent certain that you've freely consented to giving me a blow job?' Armilus exhorted. 'Are you sure in your own mind that there's no element of coercion involved in your decision to give me oral sex?'

'Of course there's an element of coercion,' the PC replied indignantly, 'if I don't give head then I'm gonna be beaten to a bloody pulp!'

'In that case,' Mike avowed, 'I just can't go through with this scene. I believe that any sexual activity between consenting partners is acceptable, but I find it deeply offensive whenever someone is forced into doing something they don't wanna do.'

Mike pulled a hammer from beneath his jacket and used it to strike the cop's head. The pig collapsed like a bellows that had been punctured by a pin, then the boots went in – HARD!

Bogroll Bates couldn't believe what was going on around him. First, the filth was beaten senseless and now hundreds of shop windows were being smashed. The *Old Price* demonstration had been transformed into a riot, all around him, militants were helping themselves to consumer goods and setting fire to rubbish bins!

'Let me suck your cock,' begged a final year art student who'd run up to Mike Armilus.

'Okay,' the nihilist assented.

The member was limp as the kid popped it into his mouth.

'Swallow it right down,' Mike instructed. 'Quick, get my plonker down your throat before it starts to swell.'

The art student did as he was told. He tugged on Mike's balls and wondered whether he was gonna gag as the genetic pump swelled up inside him. It made the boy feel ten feet tall to be on his knees sucking cock in the middle of a riot. Already, in his mind's eye, he was working upon a series of paintings based around the halcyon days of the Hackney Rebellion.

Bogroll Bates wandered into a newsagent's and helped himself to a bottle of Lucozade. A gang of teenagers had formed themselves into a human chain and were stuffing sweets into carrier bags and then passing them to a crowd of kids who'd gathered on the pavement outside.

'I'll be ruined, ruined,' the proprietor muttered as he stood by helplessly.

'If the price you charge for a Mars Bar is anything to go by, you deserve to be shot,' one of the youths observed laconically, 'so just shut up or we'll do ya!'

The art student pumped up the volume and was rewarded by the taste of liquid genetics as Mike Armilus shot a great wad of the stuff into his throat. The kid swallowed the cum. Mike's dick was still stiff when he removed it from the boy's mouth.

'Oh, that felt so good!' the student gasped. 'I want more! I want more! Can you piss in my mouth? I wanna drink your pee!'

Armilus obliged. He shoved his cock back into the kid's gob and within seconds, urine was splashing around the orifice. The student swallowed whole mouthfuls of the golden fluid but he wasn't able to drink as quickly as the torrent of piss came pouring out of Mike's prick. Urine was frothing over the kid's lips and splashing down his chin. Mike pulled his cock from the student's mush and took a step backwards, he was a self-respecting nihilist and didn't want piss stains on his sta-pres. Armilus directed his piss over the cocksucker's face, and the kid succeeded in catching a fair amount of this golden shower in his gob.

Several cars were burning, smoke was pouring from looted shops, the rioters were moving on to hit new targets. It was a fine afternoon for looting, arson and other forms of wanton destruction. The purpose of the demonstration had been completely forgotten in a glorious orgy of violence! The demand for price cuts had served its purpose by providing a spark to ignite the anger of the dispossessed. Now that this force had been set in motion, the rioters wanted far more than a slice of the bourgeois cake, they were demanding the entire fucking bakery!

✢ SIX ✢

DAVE BROWN IDENTIFIED Bogroll Bates as the per-
petrator of the attack on the Industrial League HQ
within seconds of learning of the outrage, and this
knowledge left the security expert in a quandary.
Brown was now fully conscious of why he'd recognised Bates when he passed the youth on his way
out of the Bride Lane premises. The private detective
had altered a set of records the Industrial League
was preparing about his brother-in-law, who shared
the same name as Bates, so that this innocent youth
would shield Brown from the nefarious activities of
this relative who, for reasons Dave had never been
able to fathom, was a card-carrying member of the
Spartacist Workers Group.

While the original file doctored by Brown had
been destroyed as a result of Bogroll's petrol bomb
attack, a xeroxed duplicate undoubtedly existed at
the Central Records and Research Department
complex in Croydon. It would not be safe to finger
Bates until this record had been destroyed. And even
if the incriminating evidence was removed, there

remained the possibility of some nosy parker linking Bates and the security man's brother-in-law. This left Brown with little option but to frame someone else for the crime, as well as a strong desire to do something about his sister's choice of marriage partner.

As a result of this train of thought the gumshoe had decided to visit his sister in Luton. He would explain to Paula that she was married to a potential terrorist, and that for her own safety, not to mention for the sake of his position at the Industrial League, she should divorce the bastard immediately. Paula had always been a sensible girl and Dave was sure that once the facts had been laid before her, she'd see things from his point of view. However, Brown had to be careful, he was worried about being trailed. Since the bomb attack, the Industrial League had brought in several security experts who were working completely autonomously of him. Dave resented these outsiders being given free access to the results of his work, he was also convinced that the real reason they'd been called in was to check out his recent activities.

Brown parked his car in Soho Square. He cut across Oxford Street and into the Virgin Megastore. He walked smartly through the shop and then out of the Tottenham Court Road exit. If any one had been tailing his car, he should have lost them by now. Dave marched up to Goodge Street tube. He stood on the southbound platform and then, at the last possible moment, ran across the station to catch a northbound train. The door clanged shut split seconds after the security expert darted through it.

No one had followed him! However, to make sure he'd eluded any tail, Dave took a flat cap from his bag and pulled it down over his eyes. Brown also made use of his reversible bomber jacket, so that to all intents and purposes, the garment was now black rather than white. He then took a Tesco carrier from the back pocket of his jeans and tipped the contents of his Victoria Wine bag into it.

'Are you trying to hide from someone?' the man sitting next to Dave enquired.

'No!' Dave insisted. 'Why do you ask?'

'I was a copper all my working life,' the pensioner replied, 'I've got a nose for suspicious behaviour.'

'I've got to go,' Brown lisped as the train pulled into Warren Street, 'this is my stop.'

'Come back here you bloody criminal!' the ex-cop harangued as Dave vaulted through the carriage doors.

The gumshoe ran across to the Victoria Line, he was sweating profusely as he jumped onto a Walthamstow train. Still, if the pensioner had been travelling on the Northern Line in an attempt to tail him, Brown had successfully eluded the bastard. To be extra safe, Dave took off his cap, reversed his jacket and tipped the contents of his Tesco carrier into a Woolworths bag.

Brown alighted at King's Cross and followed the subway to the Thameslink section of the station. He bought a cheap day return to Luton, then walked to the platform. Dave didn't like the Thameslink service. Things had been much better when he was a kid. Back in the old days, the Luton to London train service had terminated at St Pancras Station, a masterpiece of Victorian architecture designed by Sir George Gilbert Scott, whose visionary work fused an early Gothic treatment with a tinge of Byzantine.

Almost as bad as the Thameslink section of King's Cross Station, which in Brown's view anyone but a philistine would admit was an architectural abortion, was the fact that the trains ran from either Gatwick or Brighton through to Bedford. This meant that rather than getting onto a clean and empty train, anyone heading for Luton from London found themselves packed into carriages filled with tourists who were in transit between two of the airports that serviced the British capital.

Dave knew from bitter experience that there wasn't anything worth seeing through the train windows, so he pulled a Martin Amis novel from his bag. Brown had no taste whatsoever – it didn't matter what area of the arts he was confronted with, his natural gravitation was towards the middlebrow, the mediocre and moderation. Since Dave's favourite band was Dire Straits, it's hardly surprising that when it came to reading matter, he also opted for complete shit. Amis, who is the literary equivalent of warm and very flat lager, had naturally been hailed as a genius by the braindead majority of the London literati. After reading a chapter of the book, Brown slipped the novel back into his carrier and instead focused his attention on a copy of the *Daily Mail*.

'Would you like a tea or coffee, sir?' a spotty youth operating a TrackSnax trolley enquired. 'Or perhaps you want something stronger?'

'No thanks,' Dave replied.

'A sandwich or a packet of crisps perhaps?' the boy persisted.

'I've already told you,' Brown snapped, 'I don't want anything!'

'I'm sorry, sir,' the kid was almost in tears, 'it's just that sales have been so bad, I'm worried that if they don't improve, I'll lose my job.'

'Listen, boy,' Dave drawled, 'forget about being a waiter, find yourself a career, something with prospects and a bit of excitement. I'm a private detective, I might be able to offer you some real work. If you're interested, give me your name, address, phone number and date of birth.'

Brown had no intention of helping the boy, he was simply pulling a stunt that he'd perfected many years ago. Dave made a point of obtaining the name of every individual who annoyed him because he firmly believed that revenge is indeed sweet. Given the nature of his job, the security man was in a position where he could wreck almost anyone's life. Brown simply added the name of every bastard who rubbed him the wrong way to the Industrial League blacklist! He personally saw to it that whingers such as the TrackSnax operator didn't fuck up the economy, by making it impossible for them to find paid work.

Dave folded his copy of the *Daily Mail* and put it into his carrier. He'd soon be in Luton. The familiar vista that spread before him as he gazed through the train window made Brown grateful his parents were dead. There wasn't a single town or village between their graves and the Smoke that could be described as anything other than a dump. Before his mother croaked it, Dave had felt obliged to make regular visits back home. Now it was a rare occasion indeed when he hooked up with his sisters, neither of whom had got it together to move out of Luton. Dave would never understand why they'd not followed his example and escaped to London before settling down to raise their families.

After getting off the train, Brown decided he wanted a slash, so he made his way to the station bogs. As he stood at a urinal, Dave couldn't help gazing at the pecker of the well-hung man standing a foot or so away from him. The only other individual in the toilet was a teenager who hurried out to catch a train after relieving himself. The handsome stranger – who was dressed in a freshly laundered white shirt, black slacks and Doctor Marten shoes, turned towards Brown.

'Kiss it!' the man said as he shook his plonker.

Dave got down on his knees. He felt the stranger's dick swell in his mouth as he slavered over the fine specimen of uncut meat. Brown reached up with both hands to feel the man's stomach, as he did so, the stranger pulled a pair of handcuffs from under his shirt and snapped them over the security expert's wrists.

'I'm a police officer, cocksucker! You're under arrest.'

Dave nearly choked on the cop's love muscle and his life passed before his eyes as the bobby shot an enormous wad of liquid DNA into his quaking throat. Dave's career was in ruins, the Industrial League would never keep him on after he'd been done for a sexual offence. He was in two minds about what to do next. If he bit hard on the bobby's dick, he might be able to incapacitate the bastard and make a run for it. That way he'd have a fighting chance, but if the plan failed he'd find himself in even deeper shit. It was odds on that if the cops were out to catch cruisers, there'd be dozens of fuzz swarming all over the railway station. In such circumstances, attempting a getaway would amount to a futile gesture. In any case, the opportunity had been missed. The cop removed his prick from Brown's mouth and zipped himself up. Dave didn't understand what happened next, the police officer unlocked the handcuffs and slipped them into a trouser pocket. He then turned around and began to walk away.

'What's happening?' Dave demanded. 'Am I under arrest?'

'No,' the bobby assured him, 'it was just a bit of S&M role-playing, it gets me excited.'

'Are you a cop?' Brown asked.

'Sure,' the constable replied, 'I'm a cop and I also like to have my dick sucked. Have you got a problem with that?'

'No,' Dave whimpered as the bobby departed.

Brown could feel his breakfast churning up through his guts. He staggered into a cubicle, where he retched half-digested bacon and eggs into a welcoming toilet bowl. Almost immediately, he began to feel better. After cleaning himself up, Dave headed for his sister's house. Brown decided to leave it until later to deal with the cop who'd taken such sadistic delight in threatening him with arrest. Instead, Dave mentally rehearsed the arguments that would win

Paula over to his point of view. He'd come to the conclusion that the best approach was to deliver a well-rehearsed pack of lies as if they were a spontaneous outburst. Brown was still reviewing the mechanics of his polemic as his sister answered her front door.

'David!' Paula exclaimed. 'What a lovely surprise!'

'How's tricks?' the security expert asked as he leaned forward and kissed his sister.

'Let me get you sat down with a cuppa and I'll tell you my news,' she demurred.

Brown suppressed a groan as he was led into the sitting room. A portrait of Karl Marx hung above the gas fire and a poster of Trotsky decorated another wall. Dave sat on an overstuffed sofa and listened to his sister rattling around in the kitchen as she made tea.

'We'll just give it a minute to brew,' Paula muttered as she carried in a tray laden with cups, saucers, spoons, milk, sugar and a teapot that was covered with a cosy.

'Look, Paula,' Dave said abruptly, 'I don't really know how to broach the subject, so I'll get straight down to it. It's about Nigel.'

'You've never liked Nigel, have you!'

'Let's not argue,' Brown hedged. 'As you know, I couldn't give a damn about a bloody Red like Nigel, but your personal safety does concern me.'

'I'm much obliged, I'm sure,' Paula batted back.

'Don't be sarcastic,' was Dave's rejoinder, 'what I've got to say is deadly serious. As you know, Nigel is a member of the Spartacist Workers Group . . .'

'How do you know that?' Paula rallied. 'I've never told you anything like that and you won't even speak to Nigel.'

'Paula,' Brown was trying very hard not to lose his temper, 'I've been a private detective most of my working life, the Industrial League has been employing me as a full-time security expert for the last five years. Unearthing subversives is my occupation. However, it doesn't require professional know-how to work out your husband's political affiliations, for Chrissakes, you've got a portrait of Trotsky hanging on your living room wall!'

'Nigel is a very good social worker!' Paula was on the defensive. 'Anyway, how do you know the poster isn't just a souvenir from his student days?'

'I know, just believe me, I know all about Nigel,' Dave sighed.

'So what if my husband is a member of the Spartacist Workers Group, it isn't illegal, is it!'

'Not yet.'

'What do you mean, not yet?' Paula rounded. 'Are you planning on setting up a police state?'

'Certainly not!' Brown cried. 'It's a full-time occupation defending our democratic traditions. I believe in freedom, which is more than can be said for your husband!'

'I think you ought to apologise for that remark,' Paula huffed as she poured the tea.

'I'd rather explain it,' Dave smarmed as his sister passed him a cuppa. 'You see, the Industrial League has very strong evidence to suggest that the Spartacist Workers Group is about to embark on a campaign of armed terror. We know for a fact that the leadership have been stock-piling guns and bombs at sites around the country. A list of targets has come into my possession and it makes horrible reading, the mad bastards want to kill off the government, high court judges, industrialists, the entire backbone of the nation!'

'Nigel wouldn't get involved in anything like that,' Paula replied thoughtfully.

'Possibly not through choice,' Brown whispered, 'but these Reds are fanatics, they'll force Nigel into some compromising situation and then he'll have no choice but to take part in their murderous activities.'

'But it all sounds so unlikely!' Paula chimed. 'Nigel's been really depressed lately because so many members of his party have defected to Class Justice. He's now the only member of the Luton group, both the teenagers who belonged to the branch have signed up with the anarchists! If the SWG only has fifty members nationally, how on earth could they stage a revolution?'

'You've got to think about the issue dialectically, which means irrationally,' Dave explained. 'You see, these Reds, they're completely crazy, their ideas weren't invented by Marx, he just popularised the thought of a mad German philosopher called Bagel. Anyway, once you've grasped the fact that the Spartacist Workers Group look at the world through the prism of Bagel's dialectical method, then it's possible to understand their way of thinking although it still doesn't make any sense. Mad as it sounds, they believe that if you launch armed attacks against the state, then that's a contradiction, because most British people are in favour of democratic government. It's an article of faith with them that once you have a contradiction, it must inevitably lead to communism. I've never been able to fathom the logic of this last bit but then I'm not a pinko!'

'Where did you learn all this?' Paula enquired.

'A couple of years ago the Industrial League paid for me to attend a day course on *The Irrational Origins of Communist Thought*.'

'Well, you seem to have forgotten most of what you learnt because the German philosopher you were talking about isn't called Bagel, his name is Hegel.'

'How do you know?'

'Don't get cross! Nigel has a complete set of Hegel. I once tried to read a translation of the *Phenomenology* but I couldn't understand a word of it.'

'Well, then, you know that I'm right, even if I got Bagel's name wrong, the geezer was bonkers!'

'Nigel thinks his writing is very profound.'

'Nigel's a pinko and a social worker to boot! Anyway, surely you can see that Nigel being involved in this terrorist campaign places you in considerable danger. I think you should leave him.'

'I can't do that,' Paula disputed. 'I married him for better or for worse.'

Brown spent two hours arguing with his sister but all to no avail. She wouldn't dream of leaving the man who'd fathered David's niece. In the end, Brown made his excuses and left, he still had an emergency plan for dealing with the bitch.

It was Tina's day off from her work as a typist, Swift

Nick had sent her to London where she was to make contact with Steve Drummond. Lea had been instructed to deliver an assortment of texts and messages to the Class Justice leader, with a covering note explaining that these were to be passed on to Mike Armilus. The cops didn't know about the secret accord between the Nihilist Alliance and Class Justice, therefore, it was unlikely they'd pay too much attention to a pretty chick who happened to call on Steve Drummond. The filth were likely to be more vigilant in checking out anyone who contacted Armilus.

Nick was pleased he'd got Tina out of the way. She would not approve of how he was spending the day. Admittedly, there was an element of risk involved but Carter figured he had more than enough front to pull off this particular act of derring-do. Nick disguised himself, then travelled to Worthing where he succeeded in entering the Anglo-Saxon Movement HQ without being recognised. A suitably doctored water board identity card was accepted as genuine by two inefficient ASM security men who spent five minutes gazing at the document without thinking to ask why a rubber stamp and signature were smudged.

'What's it all about then?' one of the heavies demanded.

'My department has received a number of reports which suggest that the water in this street has become contaminated. It's nothing serious but it's likely to give kiddies the runs. I've got to check everything out and track down the source of the germs.'

'How long is that likely to take?' the heavy who'd already spoken enquired.

'That depends upon how many sources of contamination there are and where they happen to be located,' Nick explained. 'It's gonna take me all of today just to check out this building.'

'Jackboots won't like that!' the first heavy declared.

'He won't like it one bit,' the second security man confirmed.

'Our leader,' the first heavy informed Carter, 'will be furious if there's workmen getting in the way when he arrives to deliver a dignified but devastating riposte to the Red provocateurs who are planning to hold a demonstration in front of this building for the best part of the afternoon. Couldn't you come back and do your work another day?'

'I'll have to speak to my boss about it. Can I use your telephone?'

'Alright,' the heavy assented.

Nick dialled a number at random. He was taking a chance on the possibility that the ASM might have someone listening in to the conversation on an extension line. As it happened, Houghton's outfit didn't own a second phone, and so Carter's gamble paid dividends.

'Hello, Gee – six – two – seven – seven reporting in, sir.'

'You must have the wrong number mate,' a voice that was inaudible to the heavies spluttered.

'Occupants of the building scheduled for examination today report that timing is most inconvenient. I'm therefore requesting permission to change my schedule and deal with this building later in the week.'

'You're winding me up, I've already told you that you've got the wrong bleeding number!' the voice spewed before the receiver was slammed down.

'Okay, sir, I'll tell them that.'

'What's the news?' the first heavy wanted to know.

'Not a chance of moving the inspections around,' Carter apologised. 'I don't like being pushy, but I've been told to inform you that you're legally required to provide me with access to all the plumbing in this building and that if you should obstruct me in my work then the water board will have no choice but to take out a court summons against you.'

'I thought I was meant to be living in a bloomin' democracy!' the heavy complained. 'Whatever happened to individual freedom?'

'Went by the boards sometime after the war,' Nick appeared vehement on the issue, 'the trendies haven't got any use for traditional values such as freedom and patriotism.'

'Are you a patriot yourself?' the heavy wanted to know.

'I certainly am!' Nick ratified. 'I still believe in my Queen and Country, even if the government haven't got any time for them.'

'Do you know about the Jews?' the heavy asked.

'You've lost me there,' Carter drawled.

'I won't go into it now, come along to one of our meetings and it will all be explained to you. Anyway, since you're a patriot and you tried to reschedule your visit, we'll help you in whatever way we can.'

Amhurst Road will live forever in the anarchist hall of fame because it's where the Stoke Newington Eight, the class comrades accused of the Angry Brigade bombings, were busted in the early seventies. As a recent convert to the libertarian creed, Tina Lea knew nothing of this. She saw the street as providing just another example of endless North London flats and terraces. When Tina knocked on Steve Drummond's front door she didn't know that she was less than a hundred yards away from British anarchism's number one shrine.

'What can I do for you darlin'?' Butcher crowed after answering Tina's knock and taking in her svelte figure.

'I'm looking for Steve Drummond.'

'He ain't around,' the skinhead informed her, 'but you can come in and wait for 'im if you want.'

'Do you know where I might find him?' Lea persisted. 'It's quite urgent and I haven't got all day.'

'Hang on a minute,' Butcher said as he turned his head and hollered down the hall. 'TINY! TINY!'

A few seconds later, a scruffy punk appeared from behind a door. His dishevelled appearance was in stark contrast to the razor-sharp creases in Butcher's sta-pres.

'Yeah?' Tiny mumbled. 'What is it?'

'Do you know where Steve is?'

'Yeah, down the boozer!'

''Ee's in the Tanners,' Butcher told Tina, 'it's only a couple of minutes walk away on the High Street.

I'll take you up there if you promise to stop and
have a drink with me.'

'Okay,' Lea agreed.

'I'm off out with this bird,' the skin shouted down
the hall to his mate.

'You're what?' the punk probed.

'Jealous?' Butcher whooped before slamming the
front door behind him.

The Tanners Hall attracted its fair share of day-
time drinkers. However, the pub was big enough to
make the gathering look modest. Steve Drummond
was deep in conversation with George Sanders, a
recent recruit to the Class Justice movement, whose
energy and commitment had made him an indispens-
able addition to the group within the space of a few
weeks. Lea seated herself next to Drummond, while
Butcher ambled over to the bar. She exchanged a
few words with Steve and then handed him a pile
of documents with instructions to pass them on to
Mike Armilus. Drummond read the covering letter,
then folded the sheet of paper and slipped it into
the back pocket of his sta-pres. The gesture made
George Sanders think of the proletarian hero, Terry
Blake. According to legend, Terry, who'd been a big
hit with the birds, stored the telephone numbers of
his numerous conquests in this way.

'It's lucky Nick is such a devious bastard,' Steve
laughed, 'and that you brought this stuff to me.
Armilus was beaten up by the cops and as a result
he's a bit paranoid. He's moved out of his own pad
and is living in a squat up by Clapton Pond. You'd
never 'ave found 'im if you'd gone looking for the
cunt!'

'What about the cops?' Tina demanded. 'Do they know where he is?'

'Search me!' Drummond shrugged.

Butcher placed pints in front of Tina and Steve, then went back to the bar to collect two more.

'Fuckin' bar staff!' the skin complained when he returned. 'There's meant to be three on duty but two of the bastards followed some chicks into the bogs after the slags promised to give them blow jobs if they pointed out any anarchists who were drinking in 'ere. It took a fuckin' eternity to get served.'

'Look over there,' Sanders said as he nodded his head in the direction of the loo, 'they're just coming out and the barmen are pointing them in our direction. Here's to blow jobs!'

'BJ's!' Steve and Butcher toasted as they raised their pint glasses.

Eve Parry, Liz Jones and Linda Cort had heard about their leader's death but nevertheless resolved to stay true to the ideals of the White Seed of Christ. As they saw it, there could be no more fitting monument to the memory of Narcissus Brooke than if they secured the genetic wealth of Swift Nick Carter for the White Race. The girls introduced themselves to the anarchists and sat down.

'We really like sucking Class Justice cock,' Eve, Liz and Linda announced together.

'Ooooohhhhhh!' Drummond moaned, his affair with Patricia Good was proving to be a series of prolonged frustrations that left him in desperate need of sexual release.

'But,' Eve put in, 'licking dicks is thirsty work,

so before we give any head, you'll have to get some drinks in.'

Steve was up and ordering pints of lager within a matter of seconds. Saliva was dribbling down his chin and the bloke who served him could see exactly what was on the Class Justice supremo's mind.

'Those girls give the best head I've ever had,' the barman said as he handed Steve his change.

Tina was downing the remains of her pint as Steve placed lagers in front of Linda, Eve and Liz. Lea got more than her fair share of sexual kicks from Swift Nick, she didn't have any need of sordid encounters in a pub toilet.

'I'm off,' she announced.

'Away so soon!' Butcher chided.

'You've got substitutes,' Tina said as she nodded at the three girls who were still seated.

'I could still do with a bit of what you've got,' the skin leered.

'Some other time,' Lea said politely before leaving the boozer.

'Do you know everything about the anarchist scene?' Eve tittered at the boys.

'Steve does,' Butcher assured this borderline nymphomaniac.

'Do you know Swift Nick Carter?' Liz asked.

'Sure do,' Drummond said with pride.

'Where is he hiding?' Linda enquired.

'I might tell you,' Steve equivocated, 'but not until you've given me a plating.'

'Let's all go to the ladies,' Liz implored.

'Good idea!' the three boys approved.

As Drummond disappeared into the loo, Patricia

Good walked into the pub. She'd been sent to Stoke Newington to cover a story and decided that as she was in the area, she would track Steve down. Good made a bee-line for the bogs, she was determined to prevent Drummond from compromising himself.

Liz Jones was rubbing Steve's stomach with one hand, while she unzipped the anarchist's flies and pulled out his plonker with the other. The cock was hardening in her palm, and Liz was about to pop it into her mouth, when Patricia burst into the toilet.

'Leave him alone you filthy beast!' Good thundered as she beat Jones about the head with her fists. 'He's my boyfriend, mine! Leave him alone!'

Drummond zipped himself up and hauled Patricia out of the loo. What a fuckin' embarrassment! They walked onto the street in silence, then Steve had to nip back into the pub to collect the documents he was to deliver to Mike Armilus.

'Men, men!' Good fumed. 'They'll go with any woman who'll have them.'

'What do you expect if you won't let me fuck you?' Drummond prevaricated.

'I've told you, we'll make love on my birthday,' Patricia hissed as a tear rolled down her cheek. 'Can't you even wait a couple of weeks instead of accepting the first hussy who offers you a quick tumble in a pub toilet? You've got to learn self-control. Come on, let me buy you some chocolate, hopefully that'll take your mind off sex.'

Swift Nick Carter had worked hard and very fast. After telling various Anglo-Saxon Movement activists that under no circumstances were they to use the water, he'd drained every last pipe in the building. Nick refilled the empty system with petrol, making the most of a garden hose and a pump at the garage two hundred yards down the road in order to do so. Fortunately, all the party workers in the building were too busy preparing for their Führer's imminent arrival to notice what Carter was up to. Next, Nick checked that the smoke detectors and automatic fire extinguishing system were switched on. The Anglo-Saxon Movement was very concerned that the opposition might attempt to burn them out and had taken numerous precautions in a futile effort to prevent this from happening. When Carter's bomb went off, rather than spraying the resulting blaze with water, the sprinklers would douse it with petrol!

Demonstrators who supported the Christian Love and Understanding Crusade were gathering outside the building. In response, the Anglo-Saxon Movement had strung three banners from the upstairs windows of its HQ: THE CHRISTIAN 'OTHER WORLD' IS AS UNREAL AS AN LSD TRIP, CHRISTIANITY AFFECTS THE MIND NOT UNLIKE HALLUCINATORY DRUGS and CREATIVITY IS THE WHITE MAN'S RELIGION. All three slogans were taken from strap-line aphorisms featured in Ben Klassen's book *Nature's Eternal Religion*.

'Let Jesus into your heart!' the demonstrators were chanting.

Jackboots Houghton was standing in an upstairs room and watching this effeminate rabble from behind steel-grilled windows. Soon his troops would be arriving, and then he'd be able to watch from safety as the Christians got a real pasting.

Nick's bomb was an extremely crude but nevertheless deadly device. Basically, it consisted of two plastic bottles filled with paraffin and sponges lightly soaked in petrol. The bottles were taped together with the sponges jammed between them. A box of matches with a firework fuse protruding from it had been shoved into the sponges. Nick placed the bomb beneath the kitchen sink, lit the fuse and left the building. In the course of an hour, the fuse would burn down to the box of matches and the petrol-soaked sponges, which would catch fire, generating enough heat to melt the bottles. Not long after, the Anglo-Saxon Movement HQ would be burnt to the ground.

Carter was heading back to Portslade when Houghton's supporters arrived and began to rough up the Christian demonstrators. The police stood by and watched. There was no love lost between the cops and supporters of the Christian Love and Understanding Crusade. The leaders of this rabble claimed that Jesus had been a rebel who overthrew the existing world order. This was not an article of faith to which the local Chief Constable, a deeply religious man, subscribed.

The fifty Anglo-Saxon Movement activists who'd turned up to harass the Christians were having a field day, because their foes believed in turning the other cheek. Those on the edges of the five-hundred strong demonstration were soon battered and bruised. Nevertheless, the Christians either stood their ground or fainted on the spot, which given their tactics of passive resistance, more or less amounted to the same thing. The Nazis made periodic forays into the crowd, before stopping to regain their breath, regroup and charge again.

'Let Jesus into your heart!' the Christians intoned.

'The Christian philosophy is suicidal!' the Nazis jeered.

The set-piece confrontation had been going on for the best part of fifty minutes when Nick's incendiary device finally ignited. The kitchen was soon in flames, the smoke detectors activated the sprinklers which, thanks to Carter's intervention, spat petrol. Within seconds, the entire building was ablaze!

Doused with petrol and trapped upstairs by the fire, Jackboots Houghton's first instinct was to risk the odd broken limb by jumping from a first-floor window. Unfortunately, these were barred by grilles that were extremely difficult to remove. Houghton ordered his minions to batter the bars with a chair but while the steel buckled, it did not break. Guzzling petroleum, the fire shot through the room.

'I don't believe this is happening to me!' Houghton shrieked as he was embraced by the hot red fingers of flame.

'Nooooooo!' a minder trilled.

The few seconds during which the Nazi leadership disintegrated under the onslaught of the flames seemed like an eternity to the fascist cranks. Death would have been a welcome relief from the agony of dying if those consumed had been conscious of the transition between these two states. Seeing their party HQ in flames sent the activists outside into a frenzy of insanity and hatred. They charged the

Christians with a mad roar. Ten members of the God Squad were killed and scores injured before the fuzz armed themselves with shooters from a van parked on a back street. The cops shot every last Nazi and accidentally killed thirty-seven supporters of the Christian Love and Understanding Crusade. There was no other course of action that could have been taken without endangering police lives. The deaths were an unfortunate necessity if public order was to be maintained.

❖ SEVEN ❖

HACKNEY'S ANARCHISTS WERE cock-a-hoop, the cenotaph outrage and *Old Price* riot had put their demands back on the political agenda. Libertarian ideas were being discussed on the radio and TV, while the press was full of stories about this particular menace to democracy! Sales of anarchist literature were soaring and the majority of those who adhered to the creed seemed to think there was fuck all the state could do about this situation.

Despite a bizarrely warped view of the world derived from a lifetime's adherence to the Trotskyite cause, Martin Smith was neither naive nor particularly gullible. Although the Spartacist Workers Group were a minuscule sect, cunning is still required to exercise authority over even the most outlandish coterie of cranks.

Smith's interminable intriguing had led to a collaboration with the Metropolitan Police that worked almost exclusively to the SWG's benefit. Martin had persuaded the cops to ignore the Nihilist Alliance and instead concentrate on destroying Class Justice.

In his conversations with Inspector Newman, Smith maintained that Mike Armilus was fronting a paper organisation entirely devoid of members, support and resources. In fact, Martin realised that the Nihilist Alliance posed a greater long-term threat to the state than Class Justice, his attention was focused on the latter organisation because it was a more immediate danger to Trotskyism.

Steve Drummond was competing with the SWG for the support of the skilled working-class, whereas the Nihilist Alliance were drawing the great mass of the lumpen proletariat into a single organisation. This was a constituency that Smith would never reach by his own efforts. Martin wanted the Nihilist Alliance to grow, so that at a later date, he could enter into a tactical accord with a single group monopolising the support of the most revolutionary elements outside his own vanguard party. After capitalism had been overthrown, Smith planned to seize control of the Nihilist Alliance, and if this proved unfeasible, to destroy it with the same ruthless efficiency that Hitler had exhibited when purging the NSDAP of the SA.

The dawn raids should not have come as a surprise to any anarchist who believed the propaganda disseminated by Class Justice. Unfortunately, most libertarians were more interested in their image as intransigent militants than coherent political thought. Therefore, discovering the repressive nature of the state came as a rude awakening to the scores of anarchists who were hauled from their beds as cops armed with guns and sledge hammers smashed through numerous rotting doors.

The suspects were transported to nicks dotted all over North and East London. Martin Smith and Inspector Newman exchanged banalities in Stoke Newington police station as they waited for officers to bring Steve Drummond in for questioning. The building echoed with thuds and screams, as libertarians were subjected to interrogations and beatings.

'You can't do this to me!' a youth mewed as a copper punched him in the kidneys. 'This is a democratic country, I've got human rights you know!'

'You fuckin' pinko scumbag,' the constable retorted, 'you forfeited your democratic rights when you joined the anarchists. If you had your way, half the fuckin' population would be killed off while the rest were put to work in camps. You make me sick!'

The cop then kicked the kid hard in the balls and the youngster mercifully blacked out. Similar scenes were taking place in a dozen other rooms. The filth took great pleasure in extracting their revenge for the beatings they'd received at the cenotaph and during the *Old Price* riot. However, from the cop's point of view, the score would not be completely settled until hundreds of libertarians were permanently locked away. And to that end, they'd already spent weeks fabricating evidence!

'Bad news Inspector,' a sergeant informed James Newman, 'we raided Drummond's gaff but the bastard wasn't home.'

'Goats and monkeys!' Martin Smith vomited, 'Are you telling me that I got up at 4 a.m. for no reason?'

'I'm very sorry,' the sergeant mumbled.

'Get the bastard, get him!' the inspector fumed.

Drummond had been lucky. He'd spent the night at Patricia Good's pad. Despite a great deal of effort, he'd not actually succeeded in screwing the Catholic journalist, but he had at least avoided arrest and an inevitable beating at the hands of the metropolitan police.

Mike Armilus was happy with the way his plans were progressing. The only hiccup had been the police raid on his old pad. Now that he'd moved to Cotesbach Road in Clapton, Mike was keeping his new address a closely guarded secret. Armilus was determined to avoid the scrutiny of the cops! Luck had been on the side of the Nihilist Alliance when Swift Nick evaded Met clutches during the Kennington Park Estate raid, but from now on, Mike was determined to apply a scientific rigour to his security measures and thereby avoid leaving any hostages to fortune.

It was good that Carter was back in contact with his comrades. The texts that had been forwarded via Steve Drummond were already being rushed into print. Steve needed as much written material as he could lay his hands on, so that both the movement's paper and its book service could be expanded. Because Mike recognised the wisdom of restricting himself to short runs with higher cover prices than those charged by groups such as Class Justice, his publishing enterprise was operating on a sound financial footing and he was already enjoying a steady income from it.

Armilus had agreed to provide Swift Nick with a modest allowance in exchange for a minimum of sixty thousand words of political analysis every month. Some of this would be used in the Nihilist Alliance paper, some of it in a theoretical journal, while the remainder would be issued as pamphlets or in anthologies of revolutionary thought. What with the contributions of several articulate supporters and the fruits of shameless plagiarism, a vast bulk of theoretical literature was being accumulated with remarkable speed.

However, words alone were insufficient to feed the flames of nihilistic 'disbelief'. The prose of thought had to be transformed into the poetry of deeds. It was for this reason that a hardcore of Nihilist Alliance supporters had gathered outside All Saints Church in Poplar. Ten militants stormed into the building and hurled petrol bombs at a lunch-time congregation. There were screams as the vicar's vestments went up in flames after a Molotov cocktail shattered on the bastard's bonce.

'May God forgive you!' a verger erupted.

'You fuckin' wanker!' a nihilist retorted as he punched this pillock on the nose.

The All Saints action was simply the first of many attacks that would be directed against institutions which opposed the basic tenets of nihilist materialism! Christianity was the dominant religion in the country and would thus receive the brunt of the revolutionary onslaught, but this did not mean that mosques and synagogues would escape the wrath of the un(wo)man. Armilus had already targeted cemeteries of every denomination for destruction –

gravestones would be smashed, corpses disinterred and suitable walls sprayed with slogans proclaiming that DEATH IS A PRODUCT OF HUMANIST IDEOLOGY and HEROIN IS THE OPIATE OF THE PEOPLE.

Patricia Good had taken the day off work. Although she was virtually thirty, Good still lived with her parents in their swanky Kensington pad. Since her father's retirement, the old dears spent at least six months of each year abroad, and these jaunts provided ample opportunities for having her boyfriend stay overnight. Steve and Patricia had slept late. It was one o'clock when Drummond woke. He ran his hand down Good's thigh, which was lean and milky-white in colour. Patricia awoke with a start, slapped Drummond and leapt out of bed.

'Don't do that!' Good snapped.

'Jesus fucking Christ!' Steve swore. 'You are my bleedin' girlfriend, what's wrong with you?'

'I don't want to have sex!' Patricia regurgitated her favourite line yet again.

'You said you'd let me screw you on your birthday!' Drummond belched.

'Well, it isn't my birthday, is it!'

'It's not far away!'

'I know that and I'm sure you'll enjoy loving me all the more as a result of being made to wait.'

'Do you really want to remain a virgin until you're thirty?' Steve jibed.

'Yes, I do,' Good choked on the words as though they were puke.

Patricia slipped into a dressing gown and then

padded along to the kitchen where she made a pot of tea. Good wanted to avoid any further arguments on the subject of sex. If there were to be any recriminations, they could wait until her birthday, when Patricia would lie back and let Steve do whatever it was that men did. With a bit of luck, it would be over and done with in five minutes.

Realising that he wasn't going to get any nookie, Drummond got up, washed and dressed. He toyed with the idea of chucking his girlfriend, she'd given him a right bloody run around. But it seemed silly to chuck Good when getting into her knickers was simply a question of waiting until the appointed night.

'Here you are,' Good said, handing her boyfriend a cuppa, 'get that inside you.'

Steve flopped into a chair, switched on the TV news and slurped at the brew. The headlines were dominated by the deteriorating economic situation and various industrial disputes. However, what really caught Drummond's attention was a short item detailing police raids on the homes of Hackney anarchists. There was footage of the Mets kicking in the door of Steve's Amhurst Road squat and a handcuffed Butcher being bundled into a police van. Clearly, it would be foolish for Drummond to go home, he'd have to sort something else out.

Swift Nick Carter sat in front of the word processor he'd acquired during the course of a burglary in Norfolk Square, Hove. Sussex generally, and Portslade in particular, did not offer the distractions that London had once provided for this sophisticated prole. Nick was bored, after his initial burst of enthusiasm for the production of polemics, he was suffering from writer's block. Perhaps this wasn't surprising considering that Carter had written approximately two hundred thousand words in just ten days. Bombing the Anglo-Saxon Movement HQ and a spate of burglaries had kept Nick's adrenaline levels sufficiently high to maintain this frantic creative pace, until now at any rate!

Carter tapped the space bar on his computer keyboard and then erased the result of this pointless operation. The Amstrad's screen was as blank as when he'd sat down in front of the machine twenty minutes earlier. Nick got up and made himself a cup of coffee, then typed out the words FUCK NATIONALISM in capital letters. Nick was beginning to regret the deal he'd made with Mike Armilus. Carter had to produce a critique of a new Spartacist Workers Group tract on Palestine. The work in question was down-the-line leftist drivel about national liberation, just another call for class collaboration from a cabal of shameless reactionaries who failed miserably in their attempts to come across as progressive. Nick was so incensed by this garbage that his anger prevented him from giving written expression to his contempt.

Carter swigged a mouthful of coffee, then tapped out the following words: The Working-Class Has No Country! Nick looked at what he'd written and concluded his efforts were pathetic. He pressed a few keys, abandoning the minuscule document and then closed down the computer. He'd wasted the best part of forty minutes on this rubbish, how depressing!

Having stood up and moved across to the hi-fi, Carter loaded a CD into the deck. It was a compilation called *Copulation Blues*. Nick loved jazz, particularly early stuff just banged out on a Joanna with a choice selection of obscene lyrics bellowsed over the top. Of course, the arty-farties had ruined the music with their intellectualisations. Carter couldn't abide contemporary jazz. Nevertheless, no one could deny the vitality of old recordings from the twenties, thirties and forties, before the music had been sanitised by eggheads who sought their kicks at concerts rather than in the dance hall and the brothel. Nick was tapping his foot and ruminating in this fashion when Tina came home unexpectedly.

'I got the fuckin' sack, didn't I,' Tina cursed.

'Why?'

'The bleedin' Industrial League,' Lea disgorged the sentence as if she was suffering from a dose of the shits, 'it's got to be that! I've had trouble getting work before because of them.'

'If that's the case, how come that firm hired you in the first place?'

'The personnel manager was away on a two-week holiday when they took me on,' Tina flared, 'they were desperate for an extra typist. The personnel manager has gotta be the contact man with the Industrial League. He's back now and must have had me checked out. I was simply called into the bastard's office, told to leave immediately and not come back. I was on trial for a month, so there ain't nothing I can do about it!'

'That stinks,' the words plopped out of Nick's mouth like two hard little turds.

'At least we'll be getting dosh off Mike Armilus in exchange for your writing.' Lea was trying not to sound despondent.

'The only snag,' Carter sneered, 'is he won't give us the readies until we've provided him with a critique of a bloody SWG pamphlet.'

'So what's the problem?' Tina catcalled. 'You should be able to write a piece like that in a couple of hours.'

'I've tried! I've tried!' Nick farted the phrase through clenched teeth. 'But I've got writer's block.'

'You're pathetic!' Lea snorted.

'If you're so bloody clever,' Carter growled, 'why don't you produce the critique?'

'Okay,' Tina said, rising to the challenge, 'I'll write it. Where's the brochure we're doing the demolition job on?'

Nick handed her the text and then sat down to drown his sorrows in the rest of the *Copulation Blues* CD. It took Lea twenty minutes to read the booklet. Then she loaded up the word processor, changed the disk, created a new file and quickly set to work:

'The cause of the Palestinians' vulnerability to exploitation and unemployment isn't their stateless-ness, but their status as a distinct and visible underclass in Israel and Israeli-occupied territories. Zionism hasn't just disenfranchised Palestinians, it has actually created the Palestinian working-class, by turning a population of small farmers into a pool of under-employed wage-labour in the space of forty years. The creation of Israel was the creation of a modern capitalist state. It began in the 1930s, when Zionist settlers began systematically buying out rich Palestinian and Turkish landowners (many of whom lived far enough away not to care about the erosion of their 'homeland') and the political transformation of Palestine into the new state of Israel was sanctioned by the United Nations in 1948. Accelerated economic growth meant the expropriation of the Palestinian peasantry, a process which is still going on in the occupied territories. That's what's meant by 'making the desert bloom'. Palestinians were faced with a choice: either they stayed and worked for the new landlord, or they went into exile. This 'progress' was sustained by the unifying force of Zionism, which set the seal on a pact of collaboration between all classes of Israeli citizens. Underwritten by the military and economic sponsorship of the US bloc, Israeli nationalism meant the near-genocide of the Palestinian Arab peasantry and the bedouin tribes . . .'

Nick was standing behind Tina, reading what she was typing. Lea found this somewhat distracting but decided to ignore it, at least for the time being.

' . . . The point is that Zionism would have remained a popular lost cause to this day, regardless of the suffering of European Jews in the 1930s and '40s, if the 'allied' powers had not found a use for it in their plan for constructing the post-war capitalist order. This plan transformed the sentimental dream of a Jewish homeland into the vicious reality of triumphant Zionism . . .'

Carter wandered through to the kitchen and put

on the kettle. When he came back, Tina was still tapping away.

'... Despite nationalist rhetoric, the homeland which the Palestinians lost can never be reconstructed – any more than modern Israel is a reconstruction of biblical Judea. In any case, it is hard to imagine educated Palestinians, living in the cities of Saudi Arabia or Kuwait, wanting to return to some rented small-holding owned by an absentee landlord (even if he was a Palestinian). Israel has obliterated the homelands of the 1930s. In their place it has established new townships, agricultural settlements and militarised zones. The Arab villages are still there, but – even in the West Bank – they have rapidly become workers' dormitories, serving the new industrial centres ...'

'Cup of tea?' Nick enquired.

'Yeah,' Lea replied.

Carter disappeared into the kitchen. Tina kept typing.

'... What makes ideologies like Zionism and Loyalism so much more obnoxious than Palestinian Nationalism and Irish Republicanism is the fact that they defend and strengthen the practice of existing national ruling classes. But the core of all nationalist ideologies is the same, and its function is always the same: to mobilise the working-class in defence of the interests of its political masters, whether they are in or out of power ...'

'Here you are,' Carter said as he placed a cuppa in front of Tina. She picked up the mug, sipped at the brew, put it down and returned to the task in hand without speaking.

'. . . Leftism embraces nationalist ideology when it appears to coincide with its own ambitions of power. When the losers start to get the upper hand, "contradictions" may appear . . .'

Nick sat down, put a cuppa to his lips and swallowed a mouthful of tea.

'. . . To us the meaning of nationalism should be clear, whatever its guise, nationalism means patriotic death. It means the suffocation of class struggle and the postponement of revolution – the only hope the working-class has of putting an end to the misery of capitalism, which colonises all our lives wherever we are. The working-class must take back, not just its squalid ghettos and miserable patches of desert, but the whole world. The working-class has no country, no homeland to return to, as long as every territory and every area of its life is carved up into spheres of capitalist interest. Nothing less than world revolution will alter that condition . . .'

Tina lifted her hands from the keyboard, raised her cuppa to her mouth and sipped at it. She put the mug down, read through the last few sentences she'd written and began typing again.

'. . . If the consequences for the working-class of recently successful left-nationalist campaigns is not enough to convince you that National Liberation ideology, far from being an "inseparable" part of revolutionary struggle in some parts of the world, has in fact – in each and every instance – proved to be a deadly mystification, then a look at the present role of social-nationalist organisations will probably not be enough to end the argument. But it's worth a try. Inevitably, the leaders and cadres of these organisations behave as a proto-ruling class the minute they manage to "liberate" a piece of territory from the "yoke of the imperialist oppressor". In the early 1970s, for instance, the IRA's enthusiastic policing of the "no-go" areas it established in Bogside and other communities gave some Catholics in the six counties of Northern Ireland a taste of full-blooded Republican rule, proving itself to be a capable defender of private property and public morals by its summary methods of dealing with wayward youths, vandals and petty criminals . . .'

Carter was standing behind Lea again, reading the words on the computer screen.

'I think you should break that into two paragraphs,' Nick suggested helpfully. 'End the first one with: "But it's worth a try". It'll read much better that way.'

'Is that all you've got to say?' Tina chided. 'What do you think of the text?'

'It's fuckin' great!' Carter admitted. 'Where did you learn all this stuff?'

'I have been reading all your writing since we met!' Lea shot back. 'I'm not thick you know, and in any case, it doesn't take long to grasp your line on class politics!'

Nick was impressed. He'd always gone for smart birds, couldn't stand people who lacked brains. Nevertheless, he'd definitely underestimated Tina's intelligence. He wondered if that was grounds for accusations of misogyny.

The Church of Valerie Solanas was just beginning to sense its own strength. Early operations had consisted mainly of luring male acquaintances to isolated locations where they could be tortured and finally put out of their misery. Many of the men who'd been beaten, strangled, clubbed, stabbed, flayed and shot, were former boyfriends of Church of Valerie Solanas activists with political affiliations to far-Right organisations. From these bozos, Vicki Douglas had pieced together the story of the destruction of the White Seed of Christ. She'd also learnt that three of Narcissus Brooke's former activists were still hoping to fulfil the wishes of their deceased leader by impregnating themselves with the sperm of one Nick Carter – the idea being that they'd save his genes for that monstrous abstraction, the White Race. Vicki was determined to thwart this project because she considered it an insult to femail supremacy.

Douglas knew that the elimination of individual men was simply a warm-up for the purge that would follow. The first target of any size selected by the Church of Valerie Solanas was a public meeting of the newly-formed Chelmsford Class Justice group. In a room above a pub near the town centre, three former members of the Workers League, a lone refugee from the Spartacist Workers Group, two punks, a skinhead and a ted were being addressed by Tiny from London Class Justice. The subject under discussion was 'Building the Movement and Selling the Paper'.

Tiny had escaped arrest during the police raids in Stoke Newington, he'd spent the previous evening with his family in Colchester, just a stone's throw from Chelmsford. Tiny was glad he'd decided to make the once-in-a-blue-moon visit to his folks. He'd seen the TV reports of the police clamp-down on anarchists, and had he been at home when they took place, it was a virtual certainty that the meeting would have lacked an experienced Class Justice militant to address it.

'So you see,' Tiny was explaining, 'if each of you here could get six newsagents to sell ten copies of Class Justice, then we'd be getting rid of an extra 480 copies of the paper in Chelmsford alone! Add in street sales and branch subscriptions and the overall sales figures could reach eight hundred. With a bit of hard work perhaps you'd even hit the symbolic one thousand mark in your branch alone. If you multiply that across the country, then you can see that we really do have the basis for a popular mass movement which will eventually overthrow the government.'

'Can I do the newsagents in the town centre?' one of the punks put in.

'You'll have to arrange that with your comrades,' Tiny replied diplomatically.

'I squat in the town centre,' the punk persisted, 'so it really wouldn't be convenient for me to do newsagents in outlying areas such as Great Baddow . . .'

The discussion floundered as Vicki Douglas led fifteen Church of Valerie Solanas militants into the room. They looked magnificent in combat greens, black berets and boots. Every foot soldier of the matriarchal revolution was armed to the teeth with guns, daggers and clubs.

'Hello boys,' the tone of Vicki's voice was

insulting, 'we've come to kill you. However, while your fate is sealed, it's up to you whether you die painlessly from a bullet in the head, or are slowly tortured to death. What I want is information. I understand that there are three wimmin offering every male anarchist they encounter a blow job, I wanna know whether any of you have seen them and where they can be located.'

'FUCK YOU!' the skinhead exploded as he leapt from his seat and charged at Douglas. 'These colours don't run, so don't give me any shit about Chelmsford not being bombed during the war!'

Before he'd managed to lay so much as a finger on Vicki Douglas, the kid was cut down in a hail of gunfire. Stray bullets killed two of the former Trots and the teddy boy, while one of the punks slumped back in his chair seriously wounded.

'That's what happens to pricks who disobey me,' Douglas barked. 'Now answer my question before I tear your fuckin' heads off! I wanna know where to find those wimmin who are offerin' anarchists blow jobs.'

'They were in the Tanners Hall, on Stoke Newington High Street, yesterday lunchtime,' Tiny volunteered.

'That's better,' Vicki purred, 'and since you've shown me a certain amount of respect, I'm gonna give you a chance to save your worthless skin. Get on your knees and lick my boots.'

'I'll lick your clit if you like,' Tiny offered, which as far as he was concerned, would have been the ultimate sacrifice since this punk went for arses and was morbidly afraid of cunt.

'Dolt!' Douglas brooded. 'How dare you insult me! I wouldn't let a turd like you anywhere near my genetic treasures! Janet and Sharon, debag the bastard and pin him against the wall.'

The two foot soldiers did as they were told. Vicki took a pistol from its holster and shot off one of Tiny's balls. The punk fainted. Douglas then shot the Class Justice activist through the head. Janet and Sharon released their grip on what was now a corpse. Tiny slumped to the floor, dead.

'One of you bozos gets to live because I want the world to know about the ruthless efficiency of the matriarchal movement. Mohawk,' Vicki exhaled while simultaneously pointing at the uninjured punk, 'tell me that you are a turd, a lowly abject turd.'

'I am a turd,' the boy said with feeling, 'a lowly abject turd!'

'Very good,' Douglas growled, 'you may go.'

The kid quit the room split seconds after being told his life would be spared. Those members of the anti-sex who still drew breath were shot through the head and the SCUM Commando then made a dignified getaway. Douglas considered the whole operation to have been a brilliant success. The information she'd gathered indicated that it was high time the Church of Valerie Solanas made a foray into Stoke Newington!

✣ EIGHT ✣

STEVE DRUMMOND HAD been lying low for a couple of days. Patricia Good was pleased to have his company but had become somewhat annoyed at being continually pestered for sex. Steve felt he was losing touch with the anarchist scene, besides, he was sick of Kensington. With luck, the heat from the cops would be cooling off and it would be safe for him to make the return trip to Hackney. Drummond didn't risk a visit to Amhurst Road. If the pigs had anywhere under surveillance, it would be his own pad. Instead, Steve took a bus to Clapton Pond and then strode briskly to Cotesbach Road. Mike Armilus was getting ready to leave the house when he heard the loud knock at the front door. Armilus squinted through the spy-hole, saw that Drummond was standing on the doorstep and ushered him into the house.

'Be quick about whatever you've got to say,' Mike blistered, 'I'm on my way out.'

'You've gotta let me stay 'ere!' Steve whinged.

'The cops are after me, I can't go back to me own pad coz it's probably being watched!'

'Keep your 'air on!' Armilus shot back. 'I know 'ow you feel. After all, I've already been arrested and beaten to within an inch of my life.'

'So is it okay to stay 'ere?' Drummond persisted.

'Use your bleedin' brain, boy!' Mike instructed. 'As far as we know, this place is safe, right! But supposing the cops got wind of the fact that we were both living here and raided us? It would be a dreadful blow to the revolutionary movement! It'd be silly for you to stay 'ere when there's so many other options!'

'Like what?' Steve demanded.

'Like getting one of my activists who isn't known to the cops to put you up,' Armilus made it clear that there was no point arguing with his decision.

Within a few minutes, Steve and Mike had come to an agreement. Armilus was on his way out to meet up with some of his followers, they had an action planned for that very afternoon. Drummond would tag along, so that he could ask around to see if anyone would put him up. Mike took Steve to the pad Bogroll Bates rented on Hackney's Well Street. It was a decent gaff and cheap to boot. The nihilist wrecking crew had assembled there.

'Look,' Bogroll put in after Mike explained Steve's housing situation, 'I know how to sort this out. Steve can have my pad, if I can have your old flat in Kennington.'

'Christ!' Armilus gagged. 'Why didn't I think of something along those lines?'

'Coz you ain't got my brains!' Bogroll flayed with a grin.

'Fuck you!' Mike mock scolded his comrade. 'I'm still your leader!'

'*Arm-il-us, Arm-il-us!*' the assembled nihilists harmonised.

'So is it all settled?' Drummond asked. 'Am I to stay 'ere?'

'Yeah,' Bates assured him and then dipping his hand into a pocket continued, 'here's a set of keys. I'll be back later today, to collect some of me gear.'

The nihilists filed down the hall, across the street and into a Ford transit van, leaving Steve alone in his new home. Armilus and Bates sat next to the driver, the rest of the crew were crammed into the back of the vehicle. It didn't take them long to get to King's Cross. The van was parked in Battle Bridge Road, a back street behind the mainline station. The Kent Union headquarters was just a few minutes walk away. A middle-aged Jute nationalist was minding the building. The Union HQ received few visitors during the week and this self-styled 'Son Of Wat Tyler' was bent over a drawing-board, totally absorbed in the task of producing a graphic guide to burning down holiday homes.

'Long live proletarian internationalism!' the nihilists raged as they stormed into the building. 'Down with patriotism! Down with all fatherlands! Down with would-be rulers who hope to trick the masses with lies about national liberation!'

As the Jute nationalist looked up, a fist thudded into his mouth. There was the satisfying crunch of splintering bone and the bastard staggered backwards spitting out gouts of blood and the occasional piece of broken tooth. A few kicks and cracked ribs later, the cunt was unconscious. The demolition of the Kent Union HQ was accomplished with both speed and fury. Chairs and windows were broken, files destroyed, plumbing and electrical fittings trashed.

When Cromwell landed in Eire, the English were exporting Republicanism and the Irish owned the land, now it is the other way around. In stark contrast, Jute Nationalism was little more than the pipe-dream of cranks. Nevertheless, it was still worth attacking the Kent Union to pose once again a question that had to be decisively resolved. Rendered as a slogan this issue can be summed up in the three words NATION OR CLASS? Proletarians across the globe had to choose one or the other of two irreconcilable systems: Polysexual Transnationalism or Statist Reaction? The Nihilist Alliance stood for progress and the destruction of the old world, therefore its stance on patriotism was both hardline and practical, whenever the hydra-headed monster of nationalism made a bid for power, it was to be mercilessly crushed!

Elsewhere, the creed of nationalism – as represented by Adam White's No Future Party – was encountering equally serious difficulties. The logistical problems of going underground had been far greater than White anticipated. For a day or two there'd been a holiday atmosphere among the stormtroopers who'd retreated into the Scottish highlands. Indeed, what could be more satisfying to ten race-conscious

Nordics than camping out in the hills of their European homeland with nothing but an all-weather tent between them and the stars that twinkle in the night sky? In theory, the NF activists were sentimentally attached to the romantic image of living on the land with their swastika banners fluttering in a cruel northern breeze; but in practice, the nationalists found it hard to endure the privations of life under canvas after years of TV dinners, double-glazing and central heating.

'I wish it would stop raining,' Alan Grant sighed.

'Shut up!' Ted Thornett snapped.

'It's been raining for two bloody days,' Grant persisted.

'At least the midges don't come out when it's raining,' Thornett countered.

'Pack it in!' Tony Healy put in. 'Why don't both of you pack it in. I'm fuckin' sick of your bickering!'

'I'm bored,' Grant complained. 'There's nothing to do out here. At least if I was in London I could beat up an ethnic! I'm sick of it all, I really am, I . . .'

His diatribe was interrupted by Gerry Cliffe, who'd opened the tent flap and pushed his way into their midst. Water dripped from Cliffe, it was pissing down and he'd been soaked in the few seconds it took to travel across the camp-site.

'Fuckin' 'ell, Gerry,' Grant remonstrated, 'you're drippin' water all over me!'

'Oh, shut up!' the others blathered in unison.

'What's goin' on in the other tent?' Tony Healy enquired.

'They're playing strip-poker,' Cliffe replied.

'Fuckin' queers!' Healy swore.

'Come off it, Tony!' Cliffe chided, 'you've been with loads of rent boys in your time.'

'So what?' Healy tried to shrug off the jibe. 'The point is I've never let anyone up my arsehole, not even when I was a nipper. That's what makes me normal and those other fuckers bent!'

'I'm bored,' Grant whimpered.

'We know you're bored,' Thornett gusted, 'we're all fuckin' bored. It's really boring here.'

'What's White got planned for this afternoon?' Healy asked.

'Nothing, sweet F.A.,' Cliffe prated. 'Some fuckin' Führer he's turned out to be. The cunt got us all to come out here as the nucleus of a nationalist guerrilla force but he clearly doesn't have a clue about how to proceed with the business of military action!'

'Well, I'm sick of it,' Grant said vehemently, 'I'm going back to London. I'm packing up my gear and I'll be off.'

'I'm going too!' Thornett added decisively.

'Count me in as well,' Healy offered.

'Hold on boys, hold on!' Cliffe protested. 'This needs a bit more planning. White won't let us go, just like that. We know too much about his plan to build a nationalist army, not to mention the fact that we could locate this base! We can't just leave, that would be suicide, before going we'll have to launch a surprise attack on White and those men who still support him.'

'Smart thinking!' the others intoned together.

It didn't take long to sort out a plan. The fascist deserters donned their waterproofs and skulked out into the rain. They poured paraffin over the tent in which their comrades had progressed from playing strip-poker to butt-fucking. Using Zippo lighters, each of the four plotters simultaneously set fire to a section of the tent. Split seconds later, the canvas was blazing. When White attempted to escape the flames, Healy shot him in the head. Gunfire was then directed into the blaze. No one else emerged from the tent as Cliffe and his comrades watched it burn to the ground. Six men were dead, victims of bullets, flames and fumes. When Nazi thugs can find no external target, they direct their violence against each other! This is why even the most successful National Socialist regime is necessarily unstable, it must expand or collapse.

It took K. L. Callan, the most radical of contemporary social theorists, to play Marx to Baudrillard's Hegel and stand postmodern theory on its feet. Thanks to Callan, it is now generally recognised that what is simulated tends to become real. Brown's jumpy behaviour after the fire bomb attack on the Industrial League HQ had aroused his employer's suspicions and they'd taken the unusual step of hiring a team of private detectives to investigate their own security man.

Life was not progressing smoothly for Brown. He'd had no luck in his attempts to get his sister to leave her husband. After reason had failed to win Paula to the view that she was married to a dirty and evil man, Dave had approached Martin Smith – head of the SWG – with an offer of valuable information in exchange for help in framing Bates as a dangerous terrorist and sex criminal. Smith had refused to participate in this scheme, he'd lost so many members to Class Justice that he simply couldn't afford to write off a dedicated activist in return for documents that would allegedly reveal a network of moles within his organisation. In any case, if the infiltration was anywhere near as extensive as Brown suggested, a purge would destroy what remained of the SWG.

Brown was becoming increasingly careless. He no longer made any attempt to evade the tails who'd materialised as a result of his own paranoia. He'd already been photographed leaving the SWG HQ. His next fuck-up was to inadvertently visit Steve Drummond. Dave had resolved to murder both Bogroll Bates and his own brother-in-law, he could see no other way out of his predicament. Brown didn't recognise the bloke who answered what was, as far as the Industrial League was concerned, Bogroll's last known address.

'Is Nigel in?' Dave enquired.

Drummond was immediately suspicious. He suspected the geezer doing the asking was trying to pass himself off as one of Bogroll's friends. Steve didn't know for sure that Nigel was Bogroll's first name, everyone knew him by his handle, and so anyone calling him something else had fink written all over them. Drummond stared blankly at Brown.

'I wanna see Nigel Bates,' Dave persisted.

'Never 'eard of 'im!' Steve lied.

'But he lives here!' Brown remonstrated.

'I dunno what you're talking about,' Drummond

was about to slam the front door in the security expert's face.

'Hold on!' Dave squeaked as he wedged a foot between the door and the frame.

'Why should I?' Steve rounded.

'Because I'll pay you for any information you've got regarding the whereabouts of the bloke I'm after,' Brown's delivery wasn't as smooth as it might have been, but this was a good recovery.

'Okay,' Drummond conceded, 'but we're doing this over a drink and you're buying!'

Steve led the security expert to the Falcon and Firkin. They were soon sitting in the beer garden nursing pints. With Victoria Park to the rear of the pub, and Well Street Common in front, the setting was about as rural as you can get in Hackney.

'Right,' Brown put in, 'we'll start with an easy question. When did you move into your flat?'

'What's it worth?' Drummond probed.

'A fiver,' Dave sighed, then pulled out a crisp note and handed it to the anarchist.

'This morning,' Steve said easily. Then Drummond caught a glimpse of something suspicious. 'Hold on a minute, this is a bleedin' set up. You're a fuckin' journalist. There's some geezers over there taking my picture!'

After jerking his thumb in the direction of Well Street Common, Steve disappeared into Victoria Park. Brown got up and walked over to the detectives who'd been tailing him. They just stood their ground, watching the suspect approach.

'What's this all about?' Dave demanded.

'That's rich, coming from a subversive and a

wrecker,' the taller of the men replied. 'You're finished Brown, we've been through the records, your brother-in-law is a communist, you altered his file. We've got documentary proof of your meetings with leading pinkos and anarchists!'

'That's nonsense!' Brown bristled. 'I've never had anything to do with communists, let alone anarchists!'

'Don't bullshit me!' the investigator hee-hawed. 'I just caught you in the middle of a tête-à-tête with Steve Drummond, the national leader of Class Justice. I'm going to my office now, to write a report. It'll be delivered to the Industrial League later this afternoon, and you can rest assured that you'll be sacked and blacklisted within minutes of it being read. You're a traitor, a Judas, you make me sick. If I was running this country, I'd have you and all your kind shot, this is a clear-cut case of entrism!'

Swift Nick Carter was becoming embarrassed by his inability to produce cracking copy for the Nihilist Alliance. He'd been sitting in front of his word processor for an hour and the computer screen was still blank. Nick felt he'd used up all his ideas and enthusiasm for creating texts. Now that Tina had lost her job, the money Mike Armilus paid for Nick's articles was their main source of income. Since Lea had demonstrated that she could produce the necessary verbiage with speed and precision, Carter had no option but to let his bird crank out the copy while his contribution simply consisted of signing the finished work. It was a humiliating situation for a revolutionary who'd long been proud of the many ways in which he'd resisted the dictates of Power.

Tina took Nick's place and was soon tapping away on the computer, knocking up an analysis of the current state of the straight left. It was plain to even the most partial observer that the Leninist parties were in a state of collapse. Their political survival was in the balance, and even if they didn't go under, it would be many years before there'd be even a remote possibility of their making a serious bid for power. It was equally clear that this created a vacuum, a great opportunity for anarcho-nihilism to break out of the ultra-left ghetto and transform itself into a historical force. For the first time in a hundred years, anti-statism was back on the political agenda! Nick knew this as well as Tina, he just wasn't able to formulate his thoughts in a way that would enable him to sit at the word processor and transform the insight into electronically coded text. It was depressing watching Lea perform work that, theoretically at least, he should have been able to handle without any real effort. Carter decided to take a walk in the hope that this would help clear the cobwebs from his mind. Before leaving the flat, the nihilist shaved off his beard. Safety be damned, he wasn't prepared to look like a wanker for the rest of his life.

Nick strode down Boundary Road towards the sea. He was lost in thought and didn't take in the nine skinheads who were jostling young mothers off the pavement. They all lived in Portslade and were known as the Olive Road Crew. They'd clocked Carter wandering around town on several occasions because his grown out crop, loafers and sta-pres made him stand out from the crowd. As a suedehead, Carter's hard and sharp sense of style was a first cousin to the Olive Road Crew's uniform of shaven heads, eighteen-hole DMs and army greens. Once Nick had shaved his beard, it was only natural that the boneheads introduce themselves to him.

'Alright mate?' Psycho addressed Carter. 'We're goin' into Brighton to fuck some students, why don't you come along?'

'Sure!' Nick agreed, since he didn't have anything better to do.

The Olive Road Crew introduced themselves as they marched up to the train station. As well as Psycho, there was Vince, Killer, Ned, Nutty, Spud, Willy, Tim and Rambo. They were working on a building-site down the road, when they'd heard on Southern Sound Radio that there was a big demonstration going on outside the art school in Brighton.

'Fuckin' students,' Rambo burped as they all got onto a train, 'why should I pay taxes so that they can ponce around making prats of themselves, while telling people like me we're thick because we didn't go to college!'

'You fuckin' pranny,' Ned chortled, 'you ain't got any cards, you don't pay no tax and you're signing on to boot!'

'I pay VAT!' Rambo objected. 'Anyway, I don't live at 'ome and ponce off me mum, so I need more dosh to meet my living expenses!'

'Shut up!' Spud interjected. 'Skinheads should stick together. The reason we're doing these students is coz they're our enemies. Give it a few years and they'll all be sitting behind big desks bossing ordinary people around, I HATE 'EM, I FUCKIN' HATE 'EM!'

'Makes me sick!' Killer added. 'Sick! Protesting about courses being cut, when loads of people are outta work. Our taxes could be better spent creating jobs. There's no point subsidising a bunch of loafers to sit around in a student bar talking about paintings by people whose names I can't even pronounce!'

The train pulled into Brighton station and the skinheads spilled onto the platform. They pushed past an inspector who rather timidly asked to see their tickets, there was no point in stopping coz they hadn't bothered to buy any. Then it was down Trafalgar Street and along the Old Stein. The art school loomed ahead of them. About a hundred and fifty long-haired youths had gathered on the steps of the college. Many were holding placards dished out to them by Trotskyists from Sussex University, who'd decided to inject a little political consciousness into the protests organised by the cretins from the art school. The Trot activists looked down upon those who were incapable of real brainwork and instead resorted to pissing about with pots of paint. Nevertheless, any dispute or demonstration was grist to their mill, an opportunity to sell papers, score recruits and screw fellow travellers for donations.

'Right,' Nick said, 'what we've gotta do is go for the leaders, the geezers sellin' the papers, they're the activists. Ignore the others, they'll probably just scatter as we charge.'

Carter had years of street-fighting experience on which to base this very solid analysis. There was panic among the students as the ten boot boys raced towards them. Car horns blared as two dozen teen-agers scattered across the road. Others scuttled into the college, while yet more simply stood rooted to the spot. For all their talk of revolutionary solidarity, the long-haired tossers had no idea about collective resistance to an external threat. Despite the huge weight of numbers on their side, the students had already lost the battle and those who had not made good their escape were shitting it.

POW! Skinhead fists and boots thudded into student faces and groins. ZOWIE! Several of the bastards staggered backwards spitting out gouts of blood and the occasional piece of broken tooth. KERRANG! The long-haired tossers were beaten senseless. Trotskyist newspapers wheeled across the street as posh activists were given a taste of prolet-arian justice!

'Students, students, Ha, Ha, Ha!' the Olive Road Crew bellowsed as they broke noses and cracked ribs.

Vince and Killer picked up a kid who'd been touting copies of *Revolutionary Worker*. The Trot was swung by his arms and his legs. Back and forth he went. Finally, the two skins released their grip on the youth. The kid shot across the road and landed in front of a lorry. After letting rip with an ear-piercing scream, the student fell silent as he was crushed under the wheels of the HGV. Things had gone further than Vince and Killer intended, they'd only wanted to rough the kid up, murder was the last thing on their minds.

There was a lot of paranoia going down in Stoke Newington. Steve Drummond had rung Butcher from a phone box and instructed him to chair the Class Justice meeting that night. It seemed likely that the event would be busted by the pigs and so Drummond didn't dare attend in person. Butcher, of course, complained that he'd already been beaten up by the cops and didn't want to suffer the same fate again. Steve countered this whinging with a forceful argument to the effect that since Butcher had already been charged with rioting and affray, it was unlikely that the cops would be hauling him in again prior to any court appearances.

Drummond's next move was to find a place to kip. It was bloody worrying that he'd been run down by journalists a couple of hours after moving into Well Street. Steve tramped the streets and knocked on various doors until he had one of those flashes of inspiration common to men of genius. Nuffin, a non-political skinhead mate of his from times long past, lived in Shakespeare Walk. His flat was ideally located to suit Drummond's purposes, a side-street, slap bang in the middle of Stoke New-ington. Nuffin was home and readily agreed to let Steve stay for a couple of weeks after hearing of the anarchist's plight.

It was a good thing that Steve Drummond was no longer wandering the streets because the entire membership of the Church of Valerie Solanas had made their way to Stoke Newington and were seeking retribution for the injustices they'd suffered under patriarchy. Vicki Douglas was on the war-path and men were the enemy. She'd taken the sisters on a voyage of intellectual discovery that had transformed them from neo-Nazis to femail supremacists. Vicki was pleased that the majority of the sisters had stuck by her through thick and thin. She was, however, somewhat puzzled by the loss of Tina Lea, who'd had the makings of an excellent cadre. The SCUM commander would have been outraged if she'd known the girl had shacked up with Swift Nick Carter.

Douglas banished all thoughts of Lea from her mind, instead she focused her attention on the most immediate menace – anarchism. Class Justice were a threat to the wimmin's movement because unlike the Leninists and the rest of the left, they'd yet to be fully exposed as patriarchal authoritarians. Vicki instructed Janet Skinner and Sharon Taylor to do the rounds of local pubs making contact with any free-wheeling chicks who might be interested in joining the movement. The rest of the gang were to join Douglas in attacking that evening's Class Justice meeting, Vicki had a hard time locating the pub in which the anarchists were hatching their patriarchal plots, and the proceedings were well under way before the Church of Valerie Solanas leader found her bearings.

Butcher was in full flow as he led the Class Justice meeting. He could have chaired it in his sleep, since there'd been so much talk of paper sales in the past that speaking on the subject was second nature to him.

'Now for the bad news,' he sighed and then paused, giving George Sanders, who was taking the minutes, time to catch up with what had just been said, 'it seems that certain members, not mentioning any names, but people who've been involved a long time and should be making more effort, have allowed the number of papers they're selling to remain static, or even to fall!'

'Look,' a kid who'd never been to a Class Justice meeting before hubbubed, 'can't we talk about something other than selling the paper? I've been 'ere for forty-five minutes and we ain't talked any politics yet! What about fuckin' the rich?'

'Building Class Justice through paper sales,' Dog put in, 'is the bread and butter of politics. Unless we can sustain the movement, there's no point in discussing specific issues because without an organisational form in which to resolve them, talking things over is just so much hot air!'

'Well expressed!' Butcher applauded. 'You see Class Justice is all about realistic working-class politics, we're not interested in intellectual bullshit or mindless discussions. What it's all about . . .'

Butcher was interrupted in mid-sentence as Vicki Douglas and thirteen of her matriarchal revolutionaries stormed into the room. It was a sight that would have made many a male masochist squirm in ecstatic delight. Unfortunately, none of those present at the Class Justice meeting were inclined towards this sexual bent, and so rather than being turned-on, they became fucked-off.

'What is this?' Butcher demanded.

'How dare you address me in that manner!'

Douglas pouted. As she shot the skinhead twice through the head, the matriarch added: 'Eat leaden death, you patronising bastard!'

George Sanders had come across Vicki's type before and knew better than to suggest that she was a borderline psychotic. He wanted to save his own skin and having read the *SCUM Manifesto* many years previously, knew by heart the only verbal formula likely to help him.

'I am a turd,' Sanders announced, 'a lowly abject turd!'

'You may go,' Douglas muttered benignly, 'and inform the world about the ruthless efficiency of the matriarchal movement.'

Vicki had intended to cross-examine the assembled anarchists about the chicks who were offering blow jobs in exchange for information on the whereabouts of Swift Nick Carter. But dealing with the pricks caused Douglas to blow her cool. Rather than extracting the information she was seeking from the Class Justice militants, Vicki simply ordered her troops to blow them away. The anarchists were mown down in a hail of gunfire. Moments later, armed cops burst into the room. They'd been planning to bust everyone attending the Class Justice meeting, but seeing the carnage, they opened fire on the femail supremacists, killing the lot of them.

✢ NINE ✢

THE FOUR-MAN RUMP of the No Future Party were not getting along very well. After murdering their comrades, they'd spent a tense evening and sleepless night at their camp-site. Only one bus a day passed through the area, heading west at noon and then returning two hours later to pick up anyone wanting to make contact with civilisation, in the shape of Inverness and a direct train service to London.

'When's this bus coming?' Alan Grant wanted to know.

'Can't you do anything but moan?' Tony Healy volleyed.

'It's late, it's more than thirty seconds late!' Grant persisted. 'That's appalling when you consider there's only one bus a day!'

'Shut up!' Ted Thornett and Tony Healy retorted in unison.

'If we had a National Socialist government,' Alan jabbered, 'all public transport would run on time!'

'I know,' Healy mooned, 'that's why I'm a Nazi, you dolt!'

'Here comes the bus,' Gerry Cliffe stated unnecessarily.

'Bloody hell!' Thornett groaned. 'The driver's a bleedin' ethnic!'

'Let's do 'im!' Grant suggested.

'Have any of you driven a bus before?' Cliffe challenged. 'Do you know the way to Inverness? Could you negotiate these country roads safely?'

'Okay,' Alan conceded, 'we'll set aside matters of doctrine for the time being, just so that we can get home. Maybe we can give the bastard a kicking once we get to Inverness.'

The four men sat in gloomy silence on the bus. There had only been one other passenger using the service when they climbed aboard the single decker, but as the vehicle trundled through the countryside, it was filled with hikers, campers and even the odd local. Sunshine poured into the bus but this did nothing to raise the spirits of the Nazi jackals. The disintegration of both their party, and the far-Right in general, meant that they'd experience great difficulties finding a new political home.

While other passengers were still filing out of the bus at Inverness, Grant lunged at the driver. The Nazi didn't realise that this particular soul brother was a karate black belt. The martial arts expert chopped his hand against the side of Grant's neck and the racist scumbag collapsed unconscious. Other drivers, hearing a commotion, rushed over to see what was going on. Grant's comrades, who'd been closing in on the soul brother, backed off.

'It's a serious offence assaulting a public transport

employee,' someone noted, 'I hope the bastard gets sent down.'

'There's a copper coming this way,' another bystander added, 'I wonder how he'll go about arresting an unconscious man?'

Gerry Cliffe was in two minds about what to do next. Thornett and Healy were already hurrying towards the train station. Cliffe pulled an SS dagger from his bag and stabbed Grant several times through the heart. There was shocked silence followed by screams from several members of the public as the psychotic Nazi hurried after his mates. A couple of blokes ran after Cliffe but quickly gave up chasing him. The Nazi legged it through the station and leapt onto a London train as it lurched forward. A minute later, he found Ted and Tony propping up the buffet bar.

'What took you so long?' Thornett railed.

'I had to stab Grant to death,' Cliffe panted, 'otherwise he might have told the cops about the camp-site massacre, you know what a blubber mouth he was. I can't stand a grass, so I had to kill the cunt.'

'You fuckin' idiot!' Healy whirred. 'Now the cops are bound to do a bit of serious investigating and it won't be hard for them to unearth the men we sent to Valhalla!'

Thornett and Healy grabbed Cliffe, lifted him above their heads and threw the bastard through the window of the speeding train. Gerry landed on a live rail and died instantly. Seconds later, six burly British Transport Police arrested the two remaining members of the No Future Party. It had been a bad day for National Socialism.

Martin Smith gazed despairingly into a cup of coffee. Despite every effort on his part to see off the forces of reaction, the Spartacist Workers Group was still losing members left, right and centre. Since the vast majority of the SWG's supporters had defected to Class Justice and other petit-bourgeois coteries, the group was now down to sixteen paid-up members. Smith briefly considered recruiting lumpens, then gloomily conceded to himself that amongst this constituency, his brand of highly disciplined politics wouldn't stand a snowball's chance in hell of successfully competing against the Nihilist Alliance.

Martin swallowed a mouthful of coffee and then scratched his balls. It had been a long time since he last had sex, too long! For many years, Smith had considered it a tactical necessity that he avoid both physical and emotional relationships with other sentient beings, so that he could devote all his energy to the communist cause. Now that the SWG was on the verge of collapse, Martin felt in desperate need of sexual release. Smith had come across clones cottaging in the Kennington Cross toilets on a number of occasions, and overcome by a desire to have his cock sucked, he decided to seek his kicks in this gay haunt.

Martin wasn't the only man with oral action on his mind. Dave Brown had received formal notice of his immediate dismissal as head of security at the Industrial League. Worse still, he'd been branded a Red mole and his former bosses had told him they'd see to it that he never worked again. Brown wanted revenge, but first he'd get his mouth around a juicy piece of meat.

'What the fuck are you doing here?' Smith twittered when he clocked the bloke he'd thrown out of his office a few days earlier.

'Cottaging,' Brown fenced.

'What's your kink?' Martin parried.

'I just love to suck cock!' Dave wheezed.

'In that case, give me a BJ, faggot!' Smith hummed as he threw the other man to the floor.

Brown nearly had an orgasm as he landed in a pool of piss. It occurred to the security expert that he was exhibiting the classic symptoms of a masochistic personality. What the fuck, he reflected, if humiliation turns me on, it must have something going for it! Dave got on his knees and lovingly undid Martin's flies, before taking three inches of erect cock from a pair of Marks and Sparks Y-fronts.

'Make me cum, cocksucker!' Smith beseeched the bottom.

Brown ran his tongue along the length, leaving a trail of saliva on the pink skin as his lips slid towards the base of the organ. He then proceeded to lick the sack containing Martin's perfectly spherical balls.

'Eat me up! Swallow me whole!' Smith squawked.

The Trotskyist yanked Dave's hair and using considerable force, made the cocksucker take his three inches in the mouth. Martin could feel love juice boiling inside his groin. Genetic codes were being scrambled and unscrambled across the muscular structure of his bulk. Once again, the almighty DNA had risen from the swamps of prehistory and seized control of its progeny – contemporary man!

'Zounds!' Smith exclaimed as love juice shot through his prick.

Brown didn't speak, he couldn't, he was too busy gagging on his partner's tool and simultaneously gulping down the liquid genetics that were being pumped into his throat. When it came to pleasure, Dave reflected, there was nothing to compare with the sheer ecstasy of sucking cock. For a few glorious moments, the security expert convinced himself that he should forget about his plans for revenge attacks on the Industrial League hierarchy, and instead set about plating every adult male resident in London.

Hyde Park was crawling with rich scumbags, the bastards had descended upon central London to flaunt their wealth in front of those whose poverty they perpetrated. Today the excuse was a classic car rally, tomorrow it would be a ball or some other equally nauseating event. Being idle, the posh cunts who attended these social functions could think of nothing better to do with their time than quaffing champagne in public.

Years ago, Class Justice had organised Bash The Rich marches. But the group had long since degenerated into a sect that was incapable of doing anything beyond attempting to raise the circulation of its paper. The torch of revolutionary populism had since been taken up by the Nihilist Alliance, and so it will not come as a surprise to the politically sussed that Mike Armilus was leading a merry band of proletarian insurgents into Hyde Park. They'd come to do battle with the rich bastards attending the classic car rally.

'The antis are here!' a womun howled as forty crop-headed proles descended upon the sea of well-polished metal and chrome.

'Skinheads! Skinheads!' the nihilists replied as they raised their arms in clenched-fist salutes.

Hammers, crowbars, lawyers' bodkins and other tools were whipped from pockets as the boot boys reached their target. There was the clang of metal against metal and the tinkle of splintering glass as the nihilists laid into Rollers, Bentleys and other valuable cars. Bodkins were stabbed into tyres, which deflated with remarkable speed. Bonnets were wrenched open and engines wrecked, radiators punctured with screwdrivers, wires cut and ripped out.

The owner of a Silver Shadow leapt into his car as a gang of skins set to work on it. Beyond cutting the brake cable, they'd not inflicted any serious damage. One of the boot boys lunged at the door but it was locked before the nihilist secured a grip on the handle. The windscreen was shattered as the posh bastard inside started the engine. The skins scattered as the car shot forward, rapidly gaining speed. The driver slammed his foot hard on the brakes as his motor careered towards a tree. Moments later there was an explosion and the car was engulfed by flames.

'No, no, no, no, no!' the distraught owner of an Armstrong-Sidley whined as he leapt in front of a crowbar that was rapidly descending upon his pride and joy. The implement crunched into the posh bastard's shoulder, shattering the bone and causing the bozo to wail like a whipped dog. The nihilist responsible for this injury proceeded to put the boot in, and having kicked his opponent unconscious, the skin laid into the antique motor.

Bogroll Bates was running between the cars, stuffing potatoes into the exhausts of those that had escaped the attention of his comrades, ensuring that they'd suffer at least a little damage once their owners got the motors running. Several lads were scrapping the message USE PUBLIC TRANSPORT YOU BLOATED SCUM into the paintwork of pre-war vehicles. Elsewhere, leather seating was being ripped and shredded, while hundreds of aristocratic menfolk trampled their wives and children underfoot as they sought to escape these proletarian avengers.

Dogged by false-consciousness, many of those who fled thought they could see a primitive violence in the behaviour of the nihilists. These pricks were incapable of comprehending the fact that they were representatives of a doomed and declining class, while the skinheads were the harbingers of a new society. The violence meted out by the boot boys was not primitive, it was an integral part of the material unfolding of history in the period of transition between humanism and nihilism. The skins were not Luddites, trying to reassert traditional craft values in the face of technological advance. Indeed, luxury cars, being little more than a mechanised imitation of the nobleman's horse and carriage, represent an ideological hang-over from the era of feudalism. They are an anachronism in our era of mass transportation and hence it is only natural that progressive social forces should play a key role in their destruction.

Cock-sucking is thirsty work and so after their steamy session in the Kennington Cross bogs, Martin Smith and Dave Brown decided to go for a drink. Having resolved their initial hostility, the two men got on famously and discovered that they had a lot in common. Even ideologically, despite having once inhabited opposite ends of the political spectrum, Smith and Brown realised that their opinions were converging. After a short discussion, it became clear that both were on the verge of embracing the so-called 'third way beyond capitalism and communism'.

'Trotskyism has been historically discredited,' Martin admitted candidly to his new pal. 'I was a fool for thinking I could ride to power on the back of that dead horse. What you've been saying to me makes a lot of sense. Clearly, I have to canvas for most of my support among what Marxists call the lumpen proletariat. However, if I do so from a leftist position, I'm bound to be outflanked by the Nihilist Alliance who'll undoubtedly put it about that I'm simply a Trot dressed up in libertarian clothing. Only by adopting a full-blooded National Socialist programme will I be able to wean the masses from their addiction to the dangerous fallacies of rootless cosmopolitanism. The nihilists are simply puppets, dupes of a worldwide conspiracy.'

'You're right!' Dave woofed. 'It's a sinister cabal of stateless Khazars who pull the strings!'

'They're not stateless!' Smith made the words sound as if they were being expatriated from his mouth. 'I've relied on funding from Muslim sources for years. The only reason I've been in receipt of that money is because of my strong anti-Zionist line, my total opposition, both theoretical and practical, to the bandit state of Israel! Now that necessity is forcing me to adopt the enlightened anti-Semitism of the anti-capitalist far-Right, I'm one hundred per cent certain I'll get the backing I need to bankroll a new party. Although my opposition to usury will go down well with the mullahs, we have to face the fact that they don't really give a shit about political ideology because they lord it over theocratic states. What they're interested in is the vehemence with which we attack the Khazars!'

'Don't forget,' Brown put in, 'that we'll be having a go at the Industrial League as well. If we're to gain a mass base, we've got to protect the people from exploitation by cartels and monopolies. What the masses want is strong corporate government so that they can realise their freedom and individuality in and through the State.'

'Don't worry about that,' Martin reassured his comrade, 'my days of making rhetorical attacks on abstract categories such as imperialism are over. And now that I've seen the error of my ways, I'm determined to do something about the Khazars. I think we both agree that bracing competition is a good thing, whereas finance capital is the creation of a decadent anti-race. Usury is an integral part of the worldwide conspiracy to destroy teutonic blood in a slithering chaos of mongrel nations.'

'Granted,' Dave put in, 'but let's not forget that the Industrial League is the organisational centre of this plot.'

'Only the firm hand of a National Socialist government can rescue our people from the clutches of the everlastingly bestial,' Smith felt his oratory gave him the edge over other cranks, although any objective observer would have considered it flatulent. 'But before such a force can seize power, there must be a pitiless exposure of the Industrial League's sinister activities by our party press. Once the people discover the League's anti-communist activities are simply a cover for protecting the interests of finance capital, they'll be baying for blood. The masses are being exploited on two fronts, both as producers and consumers. After we've exposed the corrupt nature of Khazar rule, the people will take to the streets to defend their race and nation!'

'That's not enough!' Dave bombasted. 'If I'm gonna help you set up this National Socialist Party, I wanna be able to organise armed squads to attack the Industrial League hierarchy!'

'Permission granted,' Martin conceded pompously. 'You can deploy our members against the League, but only on the condition that you also field them against the Nihilist Alliance and all the other parties controlled by the Khazars. The name of our glorious movement will be the National Socialist Party of New Labour, it will be etched in the hearts of the people forever!'

'It's a deal,' Brown shot back, 'let's get this show on the road, we must march forward to the first victories of New Labour!'

Inspector Newman rubbed his eyes before thumbing through the glossy ten by eight prints a second time. There could be no doubt about it, the man leading the gang of skinheads was the notorious Swift Nick Carter. This was a real break. The Hackney raids had produced plenty of suspects but no real leads, not that this was a problem, since Newman's men were busily faking evidence. However, the Home Office were putting an enormous amount of pressure on the Mets to arrest Carter. Blowing up the cenotaph was a crime against humanity and the politicians were baying for blood.

While giving a bunch of anarchists a good kicking in the privacy of London police cells did a great deal for Met moral, it failed to appease either Westminster or Whitehall. Now Carter had broken cover, things were moving and the inspector hoped he'd soon be able to show his superiors some results. Newman took another look at the photographs. Carter was years past his sexual sell-by date but the other boys were a sodomite's dream, fresh meat with rippling muscles, cropped hair and backsides that had been made for spanking. The skins looked young and rough, just the way the inspector liked 'em.

Newman pressed a button on his speed-dial phone, he heard the machine click through the pre-programmed digits and split seconds later, this sound was replaced by the ringing tone. He was through to SWG headquarters.

'Hello, this is the central office of the Spartacist

Workers Group. There's nobody here to answer your call right now. However, if you leave your phone number and a message after the tone, we'll get back to you as soon as possible . . . bleeeeeeep.'

'Martin, you son of a bitch,' the inspector boomed, 'it's your favourite detective! I know you haven't got a personal secretary, I guess what you did was get some femail militant to record that message. Anyway, I was phoning to say that Swift Nick has surfaced. He's been up to some mischief in Brighton. I'm gonna head down to the coast in about an hour, unless we're very lucky, I'll be there at least a couple of days. Don't mention this to anyone, I wanna keep it outta the press. Carter doesn't know we're onto him. I think there's a good chance of making an arrest. If you want any more details, phone me later today at Brighton Police Station. And make sure you tell me if you hear anything from your militants, I know you've been putting out feelers and you often pick up on things before my men hear the buzz on the street.'

George Sanders was standing outside Sainsbury's on Kingsland High Street with the latest issue of *Class Justice* clutched to his chest. He was attempting to build the party by selling the paper to the shoppers scuttling in and out of the supermarket. Sanders glared at the four Trots standing a few yards to his right. They, too, were making an unsuccessful bid to raise the circulation of their insufferably dull paper.

'Fight the cuts!' such hullabaloos are a serious cause of noise pollution in the borough of Hackney, and could be very frightening for kiddies. 'Build socialism!'

'Stop the speed-ups!' another agitated. 'Hit the bosses where it hurts, hit their profits!'

'Blimey,' a chirpy cockney chuckled, 'I started doing my shopping during the week because these Red bastards always get in your way on Saturdays. I'm gonna take my custom elsewhere if they've got nothing better to do with their time than block the street every bloody afternoon!'

'Get your 'air cut! 'Ave a barf!' another local whorled at the Trots.

'Fuckin' students,' a third vociferated. 'They should bring back National Service, that would keep these tossers off the street!'

George felt his chest swelling with pride. The locals were politically sussed. Although he'd only managed to sell three copies of *Class Justice* in the best part of two hours, he'd not heard a single disparaging remark made about anarchism, whereas there'd been plenty of Red-baiting!

'Bash the rich!' Sanders roared. 'If you want anarchy, get ready for justice, Class Justice and a law to end all laws!'

The three remaining disciples of the White Seed of Christ heard this cry and were attracted to it like moths to a flame or junkies to a fix. They'd been scouring Stoke Newington, Dalston and other parts of Hackney for anarchists who might provide them with information on the whereabouts of Swift Nick Carter.

'Hello big boy!' Eve Parry reverberated as she ran her hand over George Sanders' crotch. 'I'd just love to get your dick in my mouth!'

'Oooohhhh!' Liz Jones squealed as she felt George's arse. 'You're nice, let me have the first lick on your lollipop!'

'I give the best head in London!' Linda Cort announced as she stroked the anarchist's left arm. 'Don't waste your time on these amateurs, let me swallow you whole!'

Sanders couldn't believe his luck, this was the first time he'd ever had three gorgeous chicks arguing over who'd be the first to suck his cock. What's more, none of them seemed to recall that Eve Parry had given him a BJ in a pub toilet just the other day, and so he didn't really merit another dose of their interrogative oral action. It was almost too good to be true, but here they were, three live femails each of whom was desperate to get her mouth around his meat!

'I just love rebel dick!' Eve whispered as she felt George up. 'After you, the man I'd most like to give a blow job is Swift Nick Carter. It's been a long-term ambition of mine to give Carter head, I don't suppose you'd know where I could find him?'

'M... M... Maybe,' Sanders stammered, 'we should go back to my pad and talk about this in private.'

Unfortunately for George, the three remaining White Seed of Christ disciples weren't the only chicks prowling Hackney because a now deceased leader had assigned them a difficult task. Despite the fact that Vicki Douglas had been gunned down by the cops, Janet Skinner and Sharon Taylor remained true to the ideals that had been drummed into their heads by the founder of the Church of Valerie Solanas. They were determined to kill the bitches who'd been offering any and every male anarchist a plating. Such conduct was an affront to femail grooviness! And by chance, Janet and Sharon were passing Sainsbury's as the White Seed of Christ chicks seduced Sanders with their sexual banter.

'Death to cocksuckers!' Taylor raved as she whipped a blade from her jacket and charged at Eve Parry.

'Up the matriarchy!' Skinner raged as she took a Saturday Night Special from her handbag and blew out Linda Cort's brains.

Taylor plunged her dagger into Parry's heart. Skinner was about to take a pot shot at Liz Jones, when George Sanders charged at the femail supremacist. He knocked the wimmin's libber off balance and wrestled with her in an attempt to disarm this most dangerous of militants. Liz Jones disappeared into the crowd. Taylor removed her bloody blade from Parry's heart and rushed at Sanders. The knife plunged downwards, but as it did so, George and his opponent rolled over and the blade sank between Janet Skinner's shoulder blades.

'No, no, no, no, no!' Sharon incanted.

The fight attracted the attention of a couple of cops, one of whom raced across the road. The other was busy with his walkie talkie, calling up extra help.

'I'm arresting you for . . .' the first cop said as he grabbed Sharon Taylor.

Taylor spat in the bastard's eyes, she'd just killed her best friend in a horrific accident but that didn't matter if she successfully completed their mission. The bitch who'd got away must die! Until the cock-sucking lovely had been assassinated, Sharon would do everything in her power to avoid arrest. Taylor kicked the cop in the balls and the prick doubled up in pain. Split seconds later, she'd disappeared into the London crowd.

Steve Drummond was having trouble concentrating on the film despite superb acting by Ron O'Neal and a fantastic soundtrack featuring Curtis Mayfield. Steve had hoped taking in a blaxsploitation double with Patricia Good would help him forget his worries, at least for a few hours, but he was so caught up in the disastrous train of events that had overtaken Class Justice, that it was impossible to concentrate on the movie.

'Priest,' someone was saying on-screen.

Having had two Class Justice meetings busted up by a bunch of matriarchs made his outfit look pathetic. Worse still, it had been the cops, rather than Steve's merry band of anarchists, who'd wiped out the threat posed by the Church of Valerie Solanas.

'Thirty keys,' the words broke into Drummond's thoughts. Christ, Steve reflected, that's a hell of a lot of cocaine, Superfly. Then he turned again to more pressing matters. Class Justice had to prove that they were tough. The best way to do this was by attacking some other organisation. But who? In its early days, Class Justice had been notorious for the operations it mounted against Trotskyite and CND meetings. No one would be impressed by a repeat of this strategy, it was old-hat. Suddenly, Drummond knew what to do. He'd lead his followers in an all-out assault on the headquarters of the Brixton Black Separatists! It might take a bit of planning but Class Justice would prove itself more hardline than the Nihilist Alliance in its opposition to all forms of nationalism.

Steve knew that he'd hit upon the correct strategy to win public respect for Class Justice. He could have chosen to take on the Violent Party. That was an easy target, since the Third Positionists were incapable of fighting their way out of a paper bag. Others might have taken the easy option but not Steve, the Brixton Black Separatists had proven time and again that they were hard bastards, which made them the perfect target for Class Justice. Satisfied that he'd figured his way out of a tricky situation, Drummond's thoughts turned naturally enough towards sex. He placed his hand on Patricia's thigh and then pushed it under her skirt.

'Stop it!' Good reprimanded as she removed the offending palm from her leg and plonked it back down in her boyfriend's lap.

'This is crazy,' Steve whispered, 'you're my chick, I've got a bloody right to feel you up.'

'I've told you,' Patricia reproached, 'not to do it in a public place.'

'You've also stopped me from doing it when we're in bed!' Drummond complained.

'Can't you control yourself?' Good was reading the riot act. 'After all, I've promised to go all the way when I hit thirty and that's in a couple of days!'

Steve opened his mouth but before he had the

chance to say anything further, Patricia shoved several pieces of chocolate between his lips. Drummond realised that arguments were futile, instead he shut up and enjoyed the sweets. Good continued to feed him confectionery for the best part of five minutes. This and the thought of guaranteed nookie in a couple of days were of considerable consolation to the sex-starved anarchist.

'Have you got anything else to eat?' Steve asked when he realised that Patricia had ceased feeding him.

'You're so greedy!' Good giggled. Then added: 'I've got a packet of smarties in my bag, I can go and get some more sweets during the interval.'

'Great!' Drummond approved.

Patricia rummaged through her briefcase until she found the candies and then proceeded to pop them into her boyfriend's mouth.

❖ TEN ❖

INSPECTOR NEWMAN LOCKED himself into the toilet. After loosening his belt and undoing his flies, the cop pushed his pants down around his ankles. The inspector spat into the palm of his right hand and then smeared the gob over his erect penis. There were no glory holes in this police bog and so the rozzer was reduced to wanking himself off. As Newman massaged his length, he fantasised about the youths he'd been interrogating. Each of the Olive Road Crew possessed a mouth that had been made for blow jobs. The hayseeds who ran the local force had arrested this delinquent gang within hours of the inspector arriving in Brighton. Unfortunately, Swift Nick Carter had not been picked up during that first police swoop on Portslade.

Newman imagined that the kid who was nick-named Nutty had just swallowed his cock. In his mind's eye, the inspector was running his hands over the boy's cropped scalp. While the cop worked his love muscle with his right hand, he used the left to tug on his balls, all the while fantasising that the youth with the cruel smile was treating him to a BJ. Genetic codes were scrambled and unscrambled across Newman's bulk. The inspector was no longer in control of his own body, he'd succumbed to the Dictatorship of the DNA! Love juice boiled up from the cop's groin and splattered across the toilet.

Newman adjusted his clothing and then proceeded to wash his hands. It was a crying shame that the inspector's reputation as a perv had preceded his arrival in Sussex. The homophobic hayseeds had made it clear that they disapproved of officers who sought same-sex action with suspects. Indeed, Newman was told in so many words that the Olive Road Crew would be provided with round the clock protection from his sexual advances.

'How's it going?' the inspector asked as he walked back into the interrogation room.

'We've interviewed all of the lads now,' a detective replied, 'and each of them maintains that they ran into Swift Nick Carter on Boundary Road. They all claim never to have spoken to him before and that they don't know where he lives.'

'That's bullshit!' Newman dissented. 'Get one of the boys up from the cells. I'll make the cunt talk!'

A constable was despatched to fetch one of the suspects. Newman took a brass knuckle duster from a jacket pocket and slid it over the fingers of his right hand, then tightened the digits into a fist. The inspector and a local detective sat in silence as Killer was frog-marched into the room.

'Alright cunt!' Newman roared as he grabbed the youth by the throat and pushed him against a wall.

'Tell me where I can find Carter or else you're a dead skinhead!'

'I've already told you,' Killer replied, 'I don't know nothing about the bloke who helped us do the students, he was just some geezer we met in the street.'

'I don't believe you!' the inspector was in a bullish mood.

Then Newman raised his right fist and moments later there was the sickening crunch of splintering bone as the knuckle duster split the bonehead's face wide open. Further blows destroyed the youth's nose and most of his teeth. These were followed by a series of jabs to the stomach. When the boot boy doubled over, the cop kicked him upright, then crippled the kid with a particularly savage blow to the crotch. A karate chop to the back of the neck sent the suspect sprawling across the floor. Killer fell flat on his face, unable to break the fall because his arms had been handcuffed behind his back.

'Lighten up!' a detective cried. 'We don't want to kill the little bastard.'

'Take him back down to the cells,' the inspector huffed, 'and get a doctor to patch 'im up. Then I want a team of plainclothes men assigned to undercover work in Portslade. If the Olive Road Crew saw Swift Nick Carter on Boundary Road several times in the past month, it seems likely he's living in the area. And if he is, we'll come down on the cunt like a ton of bricks!'

Swift Nick Carter was depressed. It was a bloody embarrassment that Tina was knocking out copy as if there was no tomorrow, while he found himself unable to tap out so much as a coherent sentence on what was supposed to be a shared computer keyboard. Carter became extremely agitated whenever he saw his girlfriend working up a particularly cogent piece of political analysis and so to get out from under her feet, he now spent his days drifting around South Coast towns.

While Nick missed London, one thing he did appreciate about Sussex was the ease with which he was able to dodge train fares. He was forever going up and down between Portslade and Littlehampton without paying a penny. If he fancied a trip east, to say Hastings or Newhaven, bunking the train was somewhat trickier but certainly no great feat. Generally, Carter stuck to the coastal towns, although he had been inland to Lewes and Haywards Heath. Nick had just spent the best part of an hour in Worthing and now wanted to seek action elsewhere.

A train pulled into the railway station and was announced as the semi-fast service to London. Carter decided to hop it. Since Nick didn't fancy a visit to Haywards Heath or points north, he alighted at Hove and wandered down to the beach. Carter threw some pebbles into the sea, then made his way back up to the esplanade. It had started to rain and so he broke into a beach hut. Nick amused himself for a few minutes by turning over the contents of this home from home. He picked up an umbrella, it would keep him dry, there was no longer any need to shelter in this dingy shack. Carter removed the cap from a can of petrol and sprinkled the contents around the cabin. Opening the umbrella, he stepped out into the rain, then lit a match and threw it onto bedding that he'd primed with the fuel. The fire took hold immediately. Nick didn't look back as he walked away from the beach hut. He knew it was simply a matter of time before the shack burnt to the ground. While Carter greatly admired the antics of the innumerable teenage pyromaniacs who kept the home fires burning, he was well aware that the majority of those who were caught got done after hanging around to voyeuristically enjoy the forces of destruction they'd so skilfully set in motion.

Nick trudged up George Street and checked out a few of the shops. However, there was nothing he was inclined to steal. Carter wanted to go home. The South Coast was a great place to visit for a few days but it wasn't London, it lacked the polyglot millions who made the British capital a world centre of sexual energy. In the hot spots of the Smoke, where there was a frenzied mating of cultures, even the tourists could feel the excitement as new ways of living were born in the riots of colour that marked the passage of diverse crowds through ancient city streets. The gentle lapping of the English Channel on pebbled beaches was no substitute for the glorious spectacle of metropolitan life. Nick felt certain the stimulations of London would cure his writer's block within a matter of days. Considering all he'd done for the movement, Carter figured it couldn't possibly be too great an expense for Mike Armilus and the Nihilist Alliance to safehouse him in

Bloomsbury or Camden.

Steve Drummond had been going through the Class Justice membership and subscription lists. It didn't require any training in statistical analysis to figure out that there were a number of bulk subscribers to the paper who had not actually joined the movement. Steve resolved to visit all subscribers resident in London as part of a bid to get them more actively involved in the organisation.

The first address Drummond visited turned out to be a soap-dodger's squat in Victoria Park Road, Hackney. The occupants were bombed out of their heads on drugs. Visiting the house was an extremely unpleasant experience because it stank of rotting food and dog shit that had been left to fester in various hallways. Steve was ushered into the living room by a teenager who kept staggering into walls as he shakily negotiated his way around the terrace. A naked couple were attempting to 69 each other on a sofa that had been rescued from one too many skips.

'Spike can't get it up!' a spotty youth cackled while simultaneously pointing at his friend's limp dick as it flopped out of a scrawny girl's mouth.

'I'm 'ere to talk about Justice!' Drummond announced melodramatically. 'Class Justice!'

'AN – AR – CHY,' the spotty teenager bullshitted, 'gives me the right to piss on any straight who walks beneath my bedroom window!'

'Kill the bill!' another kid mouthed rhetorically.

'If you want anarchy,' a third chipped in, 'prepare for Justice, Class Justice, the law to end all laws!'

'Very good!' Steve was full of praise. 'You know the slogans, you take ten copies of every issue of the paper, so why don't you sign up with the movement!'

'No way!' the spotty youth replied. 'It's a rip-off. You take a pile of dosh from us and all we get in return is a poxy little card saying we're official members of Class Justice! Fuck authority!'

Then the kid turned his back on Drummond, slipped a death metal CD into his hi-fi, picked up a guitar and proceeded to hack away out of time with the recording. There was no way of holding a conversation over this racket and so, Steve split the scene.

The next address Drummond visited was in the City. Walking into a reception area, the anarchist was rather surprised to be confronted by a sign proclaiming: *ASSOCIATION OF CONSERVATIVE LAWYERS – LIFE, LIBERTY & PROPERTY.*

'May I help you?' a receptionist drooled.

'Yes,' Steve rattled, 'I'd like to see Mr T. Douglas-Muir.'

'Do you have an appointment?'

'No, just tell the man that Steve Drummond wants to see him.'

'I'll just buzz him,' the woman said. She then picked up a phone and punched out an internal number. 'Tim, there's a Steve Drummond here to see you . . . Okay.' After putting down the receiver, the receptionist looked up at Steve and informed him: 'You can go straight through, third door on the left.'

'Come in,' a male voice said in reply to Steve's knock. 'Mr Drummond?'

'Yeah,' Steve warranted as the two men shook hands.

'I'm Tim Douglas-Muir, what can I do for you?'

'Well Tim,' Drummond gushed, 'for a revolutionist you've got a very flash and convincing front! I've come 'ere today to ask you to join Class . . .'

'Wait a minute,' Muir interrupted. 'This is not a front, I run the Association of Conservative Lawyers, it's a genuine organisation. I'm certainly not a revolutionist, in fact, I'm a true blue Tory!'

'In . . . in . . . in . . . that case,' Steve stammered, 'why do you bulk order *Class Justice* from this address?'

'Your paper is considered a brilliant wheeze by many of the men who belong to my club,' Tim explained. 'All the chaps want their own copy and by putting in a bulk order we receive a considerable discount. The club isn't keen on members using its premises as an address from which to subscribe to revolutionary publications and so it was considered more convenient to put in an order from here.'

Mike Armilus staggered off the bus at Clapton Pond, he was carrying several cardboard boxes filled with pamphlets. The journey to Cotesbach Road was slow and laborious. Nevertheless, Mike made it without a rest. Having dumped the boxes in his hallway, Armilus walked through to the kitchen and made himself a cuppa. Mike really needed the lift he got from the brew because there were another three boxes to be picked up from the printers in Bow. Once he'd made the return trip, Armilus intended to spend the evening stuffing Swift Nick's shit-stirring pamphlets into envelopes, then attaching address labels and stamps so that the fuckers could be posted to more than five hundred Nazi activists whose details had been gleaned from a stolen mailing list.

Britain's crumbling fascist movement would be shaken to the core in two days' time when its leading activists received unsolicited copies of *For A Few Shekels More: The Ku Klux Klan Exposed!* and *National Socialism Is Jewish!* The Nazi leadership had been more or less destroyed and these two anonymous publications would create an atmosphere of suspicion among the jackbooted morons who were still advocating the Hitlerite creed of race-hate. As a result, any attempt at regroupment would prove extremely difficult. Nick Carter had done an excellent job when he knocked up the pamphlets. Without inside knowledge, no one would come close to guessing that these texts had been authored by an anarchist prankster. They were so virulently anti-Semitic that even Mike Armilus found it difficult to believe the pamphlets weren't the work of an ultra-rightist crackpot.

Mike downed the dregs of his cuppa and then marched back up to the bus stop at Clapton Pond. He stood out in a queue that consisted chiefly of pensioners and was clocked by Liz Jones, the last remaining disciple of the White Seed of Christ, as she walked along the Lower Clapton Road. Armilus looked familiar, Liz was certain she'd seen him hanging out with the anarchists in the Tanners Hall, and so she crossed the street and introduced herself.

'Hello, big boy,' Jones croaked, 'you're so horny it gives me an orgasm just to look at you. Why don't we go and sit by the pond and get to know each other.'

'Okay,' Mike assented.

Armilus started getting suspicious as soon as he'd parked his arse on a bench. As well as telling Mike how much she wanted to give him a BJ, Liz was slipping in questions about Swift Nick Carter. While Jones was a good deal better-looking than any cop Armilus had ever seen, he soon convinced himself that she was an agent of the state faking nympho-mania. As chance would have it, while Mike was figuring out how to extricate himself from this situ-ation, Sharon Taylor, the last Church of Valerie Solanas activist, came strolling down the Lower Clapton Road.

Jones was giving Armilus her undivided attention and didn't notice Taylor creeping up on them. When Sharon sprang at Liz, Mike knocked the blade from the assailant's hand, purely a reflex action. Split seconds later, Jones and Taylor were grappling with each other, clawing and biting as they rolled towards the pond. Armilus made the most of this oppor-tunity to escape from Liz, by running along to the S2 that had just pulled in at the bus stop.

'What are those two girls fighting for?' a pen-sioner asked Mike as they got onto the bus.

'You know what chicks are like,' Armilus boasted, 'they see a good-looking bloke and they'll kill each other to be the first to get into his pants!'

'It wasn't like that in my day,' the pensioner said

shaking his head, 'we considered ourselves lucky if a girl let us grope her in the back of the local cinema. You youngsters have it easy, no national service and plenty of blow jobs!'

Mike breathed a sigh of relief as the doors of the bus whooshed shut and the vehicle pulled out from the curb. Looking back through the window, he could see that Jones had got the better of her opponent, she was holding Taylor's head beneath the slimy water of Clapton Pond. The Valerie Solanas activist was no longer flailing her arms, Liz had killed the bitch. Jones rolled Taylor's body into the pond, weighed it down with a log so that it sank beneath the surface, and then made a hasty departure from the scene of the crime.

George Sanders was sick and tired of being pushed around by chicks with balls. This particular Class Justice militant had suffered considerable humiliation at the hands of the Church of Valerie Solanas and now felt the need to embark upon a campaign of revolutionary illegalism as a means of regaining his self-respect. Sanders, who'd been reading Sorel's *Reflections On Violence* and a biography of the Bonnot Gang, had fallen under the spell of inflammatory rhetoric. He wanted to emulate the antics of his anarchist heroes and rob banks. However, George didn't have the front to stage an armed hold-up, and so he opted for a less spectacular form of larceny.

Sanders had scanned the area for cops before approaching the bank on Kingsland High Street. He was sorely tempted to glance around him as he opened the night deposit box with a recently acquired set of skeleton keys. Somehow he managed to resist this almost overwhelming urge. George's hands were shaking and he kept reminding himself that it was essential to act naturally. As long as Sanders kept up the pretence that he was simply conducting a perfectly ordinary piece of business, it was highly unlikely that any passer-by would become suspicious and alert the Mets.

Although it took less than a minute to perform the task, for George it seemed like an eternity before he'd lined the night safe with a rubbish-bag. KEEP CALM, KEEP CALM, a voice inside Sanders' brain kept repeating. George turned around and walked along to Ridley Road. Padding into the 24-hour bakery and ordering two cream cheese bagels after embarking on a life of crime was a surreal experience. Sanders pinched himself and it was reassuring to feel a little stab of pain.

'Do you want them heated up?' the girl who was serving enquired.

'What?' Sanders winced, he'd heard the words but couldn't process their meaning.

'Do you want your bagels heated up?' the shop assistant asked again.

'Y . . . Y . . . Yes,' George stammered.

The girl popped the bagels in a microwave and then served another customer. A minute later, the shop assistant retrieved the snack. Sanders gave the girl a few coins and left the bakery clutching the bagels. George surveyed Kingsland High Street from the corner of Ridley Road, hyperventilating as a shop-keeper placed a day's takings in the night safe.

Sanders took one of the bagels from the paper bag and bit into it. Hot cream cheese oozed out of the snack and dribbled down the right leg of his sta-pres. By the time George finished the second bagel, another shopkeeper had deposited his takings and the sta-pres were in a right state, having been splatt-ered from top to bottom with cream cheese.

Sanders was in two minds about what to do next. He could have wandered up to the Tanners and got in a few hours' drinking before coming back to collect his swag from the night safe. While it seemed likely that a good deal more loot would find its way into the bin-liner as Sanders drank himself stupid, there was also the possibility that some petit-bour-geois element would spot the rubbish bag and alert the cops. On impulse, George strode up to the bank and retrieved his bin-liner. Inside were wads and wads of bank notes, more than a grand! Sanders had just pulled his first bank job and the proceeds would be used to underwrite the *Class Justice* paper. With a print run far greater than its fast-decreasing circu-lation, *CJ* was losing money hand over fist, but a few robberies would soon put the paper back in the black and keep the demands of the reborn anarchist movement on the contemporary political agenda.

Martin Smith and Dave Brown were enjoying a few rowdy pints in the Sun, a pub located in the Bethnal Green area of East London. They were ranting and raving at a group of teenagers who hung onto their every word. Martin had bought the youths drinks after they'd expressed an interest in joining his newly-founded National Socialist Party of New

Labour. Most of these teenagers had passed through one or more of the following organisations: the No Future Party, the Church of Adolf Hitler, or the Anglo-Saxon Movement. With the sudden demise of the British far-Right, these kids were looking for a political home. And they found Martin Smith's newly-adopted brand of Nordic racialism far more to their taste than the Khazar-loving ways of Nigel Devi's Violent Party. The pseudo-revolutionary rhetoric of the Third Position was a complete turn-off as far as these reactionary youngsters were concerned.

'Being patriotic may not be fashionable,' Smith discoursed, 'but it's essential for the defence of our race and nation! Patriotism is a matter of keeping our heads high and our wills strong, so that when ordinary British men and wimmin see columns of Nordic stormtroopers marching through the streets, they'll come flocking to our swastika banners!'

'Yeah,' Brown put in, 'this time things will be different, New Labour will deal with the back stabbers before it's too late. It'll be just like 1939, only better. All the traitors will be shot before we gain power because a glance back over past centuries teaches us wisdom. We have only one thing to regret, that the Teuton did not destroy with more thoroughness, wherever his victorious arm penetrated. As a consequence of his moderation, the so-called Latinising, that is, the fusion with the chaos of peoples, has robbed wide districts of the one quickening influence of pure blood and unbroken youthful vigour. At the same time, this mongrelisation has deprived our people of the rule of those who possessed the highest talents.'

Martin Smith was gloating over how easy it was to sway the minds of these boys. He'd been a fool to resist the Nazi doctrine for so long. Since the goal of politics was the attainment of power, the only question to be asked about the means was whether they were an efficient way of achieving the desired end. Given the ideological backwardness of the British proletariat and the essential passivity of the masses, the big lies of racism were better suited to the needs of ambitious politicians than an opportunist manipulation of dialectical materialism.

'And so you see,' Brown was ranting, 'the Khazars have been manipulating genuine patriots by channelling money through the Industrial League and into the Anglo-Saxon Movement!'

'That means,' a kid flinched, 'that I was a stooge of the bankers for the best part of two years!'

'You weren't the only one,' another teenager chipped in, 'we've all been conned by the Zionist puppet masters. But that's in the past, what we've got to do now is smash their power! Therefore, I propose we mount an attack on the Industrial League.'

'We'll all meet at Bethnal Green tube station tomorrow morning at nine,' Brown announced. 'I've a plan which will deal a death blow to the Industrial League.'

Martin Smith rubbed his crotch, then got up and walked across to the bog. Inside, one of the youths who'd just been recruited to the National Socialist Party of New Labour was taking a leak. Smith grabbed the boy by the shoulders and spun the youth around, before forcing him onto his knees.

'Peter James,' Smith brayed, 'I'm gonna piss all over your face, then I want you to suck my cock.'

'Ja wohl, mein Führer,' James only just succeeded in pronouncing the line correctly.

Martin fished his love muscle from his pants and moments later, a steaming discharge was sprayed across Peter's face. James succeeded in catching a little of the golden shower in his mouth but most of it soaked into his hair, T-shirt and jeans. Urine was still dribbling from Smith's plonker as the youngster took it in his mouth. Million-year-old genetic urges welled up through Martin's groin as Peter sucked and chewed on the love stick. Smith was no longer in control of his own body. DNA codes were scrambled and unscrambled across the muscular structure of his bulk. Peter thought the spunk that shot down his throat tasted like the sweetest of nectars. Then it was all over, they'd reached that peak from which man and man can never jointly return. Martin collapsed on the floor of the toilet, while the youngster adjusted his clothing and rejoined his mates.

Bogroll Bates led a squad of nihilists into the Roman Road. They were the real army of the night, not the dirty raincoat brigade but kids armed with catapults, hammers, glue, glass etching fluid and iron bars. Bates was about to treat Bow's premier shopping street to a summary demolition! Bogroll's political development had shot forward by leaps and bounds in the space of a few weeks. From complete ignorance, he'd developed into a fully autonomous subject days after discovering his blacklisting at the hands of the Industrial League. Bates didn't need Mike Armilus or Swift Nick Carter to tell him how to strike back at the system that oppressed them. He was their equal and possessed his own strategy for sabotaging the military-industrial-shopping complex he utterly despised.

The weather had turned nasty, which was just the way Bogroll and his nihilist wrecking crew liked it. Not only did the violent storm that was raging keep people off the streets, the strong winds covered the noise of windows being smashed. Bates strode up to Woolworth's, raised his sledgehammer and sent it slamming into a shutter that had been installed to protect a large plate glass window. A jolt from the impact travelled up Bogroll's arm and simultaneously the shutter buckled under the blow. There was the faint sound of glass tinkling and then the ringing of a burglar alarm. The shutter had been placed too close to the window and so both had been demolished in the attack.

Bates targeted another shop and a kid moved in behind him to glue the lock on the buckled grill. This would make the business of repair rather more difficult than if the manager had simply been confronted with a mangled shutter. The teenager squirted super glue into the Yale lock so that the key would no longer slot inside it. The activist also had a supply of small stones and bits of metal which enabled him to deal with mortice locks. A mortice had to be filled with rubble before being glued, if it was to be successfully sabotaged.

A third youth was armed with etching fluid that he'd watered down a little so that it would pour into a lemon-shaped squeezy bottle. Using this tool, he was busy inscribing the following message on the window of a trendy clothes shop: WHAT THE EYE COVETS, LET THE HAND GRASP IT! Another kid was using a Black Widow catapult and ball bearings to take out windows. Although the steel balls only made small holes in the glass, the proprietors of the shops thus hit would have no option but to replace the windows because the panes had been weakened and were likely to blow in at some point in the near future, with possible fatal consequences for anyone on the premises.

Other youths were using iron bars and tiller hammers to smash yet more glass. By hitting windows in one of the bottom corners, the job was done without making very much noise. Within five minutes of the nihilist wrecking crew arriving in the Roman Road, the street looked like it had been hit by a bomb. Having made good their work of destruction, Bates and his mates melted into the night, leaving behind them nothing but a trail of criminal damage that would distress many a shopkeeper the following morning.

✤ ELEVEN ✤

THE RECRUITS TO the newly-formed National Socialist Party of New Labour were collected from Bethnal Green tube station by Martin Smith and Dave Brown. The twelve patriots who'd volunteered for active service against the Industrial League were then led to a hired mini-van which was parked on a side street. The journey to Croydon was uneventful and the squad of Aryan soldiers passed the time by singing rousing songs about their race and nation. Brown's plan was simple, the Industrial League's annual general meeting was not scheduled to start until noon. By using a set of stolen keys and his considerable inside knowledge, Dave installed his men in the room that would house the AGM. The hierarchy of the Industrial League were to be picked off one by one as they entered the meeting. In the meantime, Martin Smith was to keep the troops entertained with an hour-long speech concerning their ethnic origins.

'Anyone who wishes to understand the English,' Smith murmured, 'must begin with the fact that we belong to the Teutonic Nation and come originally from Germany; a descent so honourable and happy that a just survey of the gloriousness of our Mother Nation shows that we could not have come from any other part of Europe. To the antiquity of the Teutonic House we owe the purity of our blood, the oldest and greatest in the world.'

'Wow,' the speech was blowing Peter James' mind.

'Sssshhhh!' another youth plainted.

'We are right to be proud of our German ancestry,' Martin continued, 'and the racial purity that we, as members of the noblest German tribe, have maintained. Such is the transcendent quality of our Mother Nation that she is undoubtedly the chief and most honourable country in the world. Of all those things that honour our land, we are the true inheritors and partakers, both as members of that body and children of that Mother, we being flesh of her flesh, bone of her bone, yes progeny of the most ancient of all tribes.'

Dave Brown was impressed by the power of Smith's oratory, particularly in view of the fact that his comrade had to speak in a stage whisper for fear of alerting their enemies to the fact that National Socialist Party of New Labour stormtroopers had secretly occupied part of the Industrial League's Croydon complex. Neither Brown nor the more youthful NSPNL cadre realised that Martin's speech was plagiarised from a text written by John Hare during the English Civil War. Had these reactionaries known that the dotty theories being elaborated by their leader were three hundred and fifty years past their sell-by date, they'd have been even more impressed.

'Our Progenitors,' Smith hectored, 'both man and maiden, who transplanted themselves from Germany, did not mix with the ancient inhabitants of this Country, as other colonies did with non-Germanic races, but totally expelling these submen, took sole possession of the Land, thereby preserving their blood, laws and language.'

Martin rambled on in this way for another half hour. He was about to conclude with a homily about sorting out the Khazars and delatinising British culture, when the door to the board room opened and in walked G. K. Masters, head of the Industrial League. One of the two NSPNL cadre who'd been guarding the door beat Masters over the head with an iron bar, causing the bastard to collapse like a bellows that had been punctured by a pin. G. K. was dragged to one side of the room and stabbed several times through the heart. This operation was repeated more than two dozen times, resulting in the assassination of the entire League hierarchy, as well as a cabinet minister and several captains of industry. Having accomplished their mission, the New Labour stormtroopers filed silently and unseen from the Industrial League's Croydon complex.

Swift Nick Carter pressed the off button on the remote control and killed the TV. Tina was tapping away on the word processor. Once Lea had knocked up yet another text for the Nihilist Alliance, she'd catch a train to London and deliver the copy direct to Mike Armilus. Nick was still suffering from writer's block, which he put down to his enforced absence from London. He wondered gloomily whether Mike had sussed that all the material he was now receiving had been authored by Tina.

'I'm bored,' Carter announced, 'I'm off out.'

'Will you come back before I go?' Lea asked.

'Dunno,' Nick replied, 'I'll probably go into Brighton, if there's nothing happening, I'll come straight back.'

'Don't bullshit me!' Tina joshed. 'You'll be hours pissing round the shops, you'll never get back before I leave.'

'Okay, okay,' Carter conceded and then kissed his girlfriend. 'Make sure Armilus agrees to safehousing us in London. If I have to stay here much longer I'm gonna go crazy.'

'Will do,' Lea promised.

Although Carter didn't realise it, Boundary Road was crawling with plainclothes cops. Working on the snippets of information he'd gleaned from the Olive Road Crew, Inspector Newman had ordered hundreds of men into the Portslade area. Nick was spotted by a detective as he made his way into the station. Word of Carter's movements went out over the police radio and the Sussex filth quickly got onto British Rail. The next Brighton train was halted at Fishersgate while the cops massed their forces.

'We apologise for the late running of the Brighton service, this is due to a passenger pulling the emergency cord at Fishersgate,' a BR employee fibbed.

The train came in five minutes late. Nick got into the front carriage. This was exactly what the filth had been hoping would happen. The train pulled part of the way out of the station, then halted. The end carriage had yet to clear the platform. The fifty cops who'd gathered on the corner of Boundary and Portland Roads made their way along the platform and then onto the train. Moments after the last plain-clothes detective had climbed aboard, the late running Brighton service began to gather speed for its journey east.

The cops made their way through the train, one man was sent into the carriage occupied by Carter and a handful of off-peak passengers. The cunt approaching Nick had filth written all over him. Carter pretended to be looking out of the window and when the cop pulled out a gun, ducked beneath the line of fire, while simultaneously lunging at his adversary. Nick got the bastard by the balls, the detective yelped and his revolver went off, killing an old lady who'd been knitting a romper suit for her great-grandson. The train sped through Aldrington, resulting in outraged comments from passengers who'd wanted to alight at this station. Carter kicked the cop who'd attempted to arrest him. Meanwhile, dozens of plainclothes detectives were pouring into the carriage. Nick leapt towards a door but before he had a chance to open it and leap from the speeding train, a cop had a gun in his back. Carter's days as a fugitive were over. Within a matter of seconds, the Sussex filth had slapped bracelets onto his wrists. Britain's Public Enemy Number One was under arrest.

Bogroll Bates had taken charge of the Nihilist Alliance wrecking crew and under his leadership, a small group of youths had succeeded in heaping destruction upon the heads of the myriad forces who were out to defend the values of the old world. Within the past hour, they'd razed two churches. Now it was the turn of one of the world's great secular religions to bear the brunt of the nihilist onslaught. First stop was the dole office on Hackney's Spurstowe Terrace, where a gaggle of Workers League activists were attempting to flog copies of their paper to unemployed youths.

'One, two, three, many Fourth Internationals!' the nihilists baited the Trotskyites as they laid into the bastards.

'Fascists!' a Workers League activist muttered.

Bogroll walloped the kid in the mush, there was the satisfying crunch of splintering bone and the would-be militant's legs crumpled beneath him. This particular toss-pot was no longer pretending to be a man, he'd been reduced to a twitching heap of flesh. His comrades stood with their mouths open, no one on either side moved for the best part of a minute. Then a visible wave of fear passed through each of the Marxist morons. Split seconds later, the nihilist wrecking crew swung back into action. POW! Fists and boots thudded into Trotskyite faces and groins. ZOWIE! Several of the bastards staggered backwards spitting out gouts of blood and the occasional piece of broken tooth. KERRANG! The bolshevist tossers were beaten senseless. Copies of *The Worker* wheeled across the street as posh activists were given a taste of proletarian justice!

'Permanent Revolution, Ha, Ha, Ha!' the nihilists roared as they broke noses and cracked ribs.

Kids were pouring out of the dole office to watch the fight. Beyond a bit of verbal abuse, none of them had given much expression to their feelings of resentment towards the politicos of both left and right, who week after week, year after year, attempted to exploit the plight of the unemployed. Suddenly, the dam of repressions that held them back from taking physical action against their enemies burst, and scores of jobless youths rallied to the side of the nihilists.

'Stick the boot in, kick to kill!' the cry went up from dozens of kids simultaneously.

Those who'd joined the fray were baying for blood and so the nihilists stepped back, allowing the locals to literally beat shit out of the Trots. While the target had been carefully chosen, the actual application of violence was completely indiscriminate – Workers League activists who'd blacked out were as savagely beaten as the handful of militants who were still conscious.

Having successfully accomplished this particular mission, the wrecking crew made its way back to a beaten-up Ford transit van. There was more work to be done! A further two targets were to be dealt with that afternoon – the Workers League printing press just off Well Street and a church in Spitalfields. However, none of the nihilists were complaining about this busy schedule, since there's nothing like wrecking machinery and burning down buildings to keep your spirits up! Bogroll Bates felt on top of the world, his only regret was that Mike Armilus wasn't around to enjoy the action with him. It was too bad that the Nihilist Alliance supremo was tied up with paperwork, he'd have got a real kick out of the confrontations that were going down all over East London.

Mike Armilus had spent the afternoon filing the orders that were pouring in for the publications he was offering through his Nihilist Book Service. The enterprise was a nice little earner and if business continued to boom, Armilus would soon be in a position to take on a full-time assistant. Then all he'd need to do was cash cheques and deal with the editorial side of the operation.

There was a fortune to be made from excerpting the juiciest passages of revolutionary literature and then publishing these as pamphlets with outrageous new titles. What the so-called radical reading public demanded was not intelligence or coherent theorising, but violence and sensationalism. The majority of those inhabiting the political fringe were prepared to pay through the nose to have extremist rhetoric served up to them in easily consumable chunks. Mike was meeting this need and the Nihilist Alliance basically existed as an advertisement for his lucrative publishing operation. However, with a little bit of luck and imagination, it might also prove itself capable of engineering a worldwide proletarian revolution with unlicensed pleasure as its only aim.

Armilus was left shaken after a radio news flash announced that Swift Nick Carter had been arrested by Sussex police. He took a can of Stella from his fridge and downed half the beer in a single gulp. Despite being chilled, the booze warmed Mike's belly and lifted his spirits. On reflection, the situation wasn't so bad, Carter would have plenty of time to write while he was banged up, and a court case would generate a lot of publicity. No doubt the vast army of media morons addicted to journalistic hyperbole would give Class Justice the credit for the rising tide of revolutionary violence associated with Swift Nick, but many of those who'd flock to CJ as a result of this coverage would soon tire of Steve Drummond's brand of bullshit and in time find their way to the Nihilist Alliance.

Texts by Sorel, Stirner and Necheyev were stuffed into an envelope as Armilus got back to work. It was amazing, the orders were coming from all over the country, this one was right out in the sticks! Mike had just picked up a Lafargue pamphlet, when there was a knock at the door.

'Alright Tina, come in,' Armilus was wondering about his chances of getting into Lea's knickers as he led her through to the kitchen.

'Here you are,' Tina said as she laid a folder on the kitchen table, 'some new texts.'

'Great,' Armilus swaggered. 'Now fill me in on Nick's arrest.'

'What?' Lea lamented.

'There was a news flash on the radio a little while back saying Sussex cops had arrested Carter. Didn't you know about it?'

'Oh, no, no, no, no!' Tina sobbed before bursting into tears.

'Come on, it isn't that bad,' Mike observed, then he paused for a long time. 'At least he wasn't murdered by a police marksman.'

'What are you gonna do about it?' Lea rasped.

'I dunno, 'ere 'ave a beer,' Armilus purred as he took two cans of Stella from the fridge.

The two of them sat drinking in silence. Mike was wondering why wimmin were always so bloody emotional. Carter was a hard bastard, he could look after himself. Nevertheless, Armilus felt sorry for the chick. If he could just come up with some kind of plan for a jailbreak, no matter how hopeless, it would make Tina feel better. If it wasn't for the girl, once he'd got over the initial shock of Nick's arrest, Mike would have treated the incident as a once in a lifetime opportunity to get rich quick. Christ, he'd no reason to feel guilty about what had happened, not after safe-housing Carter in his Kennington flat and then providing the fugitive with a regular income in exchange for the odd piece of prose!

Inspector Newman was gleeful. He'd won! The anarchist menace was smashed. Swift Nick Carter was strapped to a chair in the interview room down-stairs. Now that he'd got Carter in his clutches, he was going to make the bastard suffer. The inspector had been gentle during the initial interview but having filled his belly with the greasy muck served in the police canteen, he felt really vicious. Newman downed the dregs of his tea, got up and strode to the soundproofed interview room.

'Alright cunt,' the inspector walloped Carter in the guts as his badgering continued along the same repetitive lines he'd been following for several hours, 'are you gonna sign a confession or do you wanna play rough?'

'I've got...' Nick coughed, still trying to catch

the wind that had been knocked out of him. 'I've got nothing to say until I've seen a lawyer.'

'Lawyer!' Newman cackled as he slipped a brass knuckle duster over his right hand, 'unless you sign a confession immediately, the only person you'll be seeing is a fuckin' doctor.'

'I wanna see a lawyer and make me statutory phone . . .' Carter never got to complete the sentence because Newman smashed a clenched fist into his mouth. There was the sickening crunch of splintering bone and split seconds later, Nick was spitting out gouts of blood and the remains of three teeth.

'Maybe I was wrong,' the cop conceded. 'I guess you'll be seeing a lot more than a doctor, there'll be dentists, nurses and surgeons as well.'

'Yeah,' Carter was still defiant, 'and it's you who'll be seeing the lawyers. You'll never make these charges stick, I'm innocent! Once I get legal aid, I'll sue you for everything you've got. Just think of what you're gonna get done for, wrongful arrest, false imprisonment, assault. You'll be declared bankrupt and lose everything, from your home right down to your poxy job!'

'You can act as tough as you like,' Newman swanked, 'but by the time you leave here you'll have licked my arse and kissed my boots. I've come across your type before, borderline psychotics who fancy themselves as hard men, but there's never been a fucker I couldn't break. You don't frighten me, you slithering piece of shit. I'm no sadist but I'm gonna teach you the meaning of pain.'

'There's nothing you can teach me,' Nick baited

his tormentor, 'so bring me a telephone and get me a lawyer!'

'Forget about lawyers!' the inspector snickered. 'You've got a life term written all over you. So don't wind me up with bullshit about your innocence. I'm a career cop and all I care about is convictions. I'm sussed see, I've framed a thousand men in my time. Christ, if at the end of every investigation I've ever conducted it was the guilty party who got put away, I'd still be a bleedin' constable. There's only a limited number of criminals in our society and if all of them were banged up there'd be no call for a police force. Us career cops encourage crime by framing the innocent, that leaves the real villains free to scare the taxpayer and parliament into supporting Police Federation demands for improved pay, conditions and resources.'

'You're mad,' Carter heckled the would-be thespian, who was clearly playing to the gallery of constables loafing against the walls of the room, 'you're fuckin' mad!'

'Of course I'm mad,' Newman prided himself on this point, 'I'm mad at scum like you who ruin the lives of decent people. I'm so bloody mad I'm gonna boil up this kettle and then pour the contents all over you. That is, unless you agree to sign a confession immediately.'

'I wanna see a lawyer,' Nick growled.

This remark caused the inspector to lose whatever control he still retained over his temper. He laid into Carter with his knuckle duster, beating the suspect repeatedly about the head. After five minutes of this treatment, Swift Nick blacked out. Newman cursed, he'd have to wait until Carter woke up before dousing the cunt with boiling water. If he pulled this trick while Swift Nick was still unconscious, it was unlikely to have the desired effect.

The nineteen men and wimmin going about their business at the Workers League Printing Plant were taken by surprise when a Nihilist Alliance commando burst into their premises. Although the wrecking crew was outnumbered, it had surprise on its side and won an easy victory by cracking open several Trotskyite skulls. After Bogroll Bates smashed a new and very expensive process camera, weeping men were comforted by their femail colleagues as the witless leftists were thrown into the dark room. The door to this make-shift prison was then slammed shut and locked, leaving the bolsheviks free to raise hell in their windowless cell.

'We're doomed!' someone expounded. 'Doomed! We're all gonna die! There's not enough air in here, I'm suffocating!'

'Shut up,' a second voice retorted, 'it's your screaming that's using up all the oxygen!'

'Stop it, both of you,' a third voice put in. 'There's plenty of air in here, we've just got to keep calm and collect our wits.'

'What about the injured?' someone else cried, 'what can we do for them?'

'We'll have to have a meeting of the co-op to work out the correct course of action under present circumstances. Whose gonna take the minutes?'

Bogroll ignored the conversation going on between the imprisoned Trots. It didn't last very long. They were soon fighting amongst themselves, engaged in a ferocious war of all against all, as the rules that had governed their collective activities for so long shattered under the hammer blow delivered by the Nihilist Alliance.

The Workers League Printing Plant was a capital-intensive operation. There was a four-colour per-fecter press and a couple of A2 machines. All top quality, precision built, German imports. Just having them installed cost a small fortune, and paying off the bank loans on the gear was still a good many years away. Upstairs, in the design studio, there was an assortment of the latest Xerox machines, DTP and photo-setting equipment. Bates was unable to calculate the value of the hardware, but he could see at a glance that the software being run on these computers was worth at least six figures.

Downstairs, youths were laying into the Heidel-berg presses and plate-making equipment with crowbars and sledgehammers. Beds and blankets were being smashed under this onslaught, the machinery buckled and bent beyond all recognition. Upstairs, Bogroll was methodical in his own work of destruction. He unplugged all the hardware before laying into it. Then, computer monitors were smashed against walls, hard disks hurled to the floor and keyboards broken over the nihilist's knee. A few hammer blows put two photocopiers perma-nently out of action. Then drawing boards and floppy disks were pulverised, followed shortly after-wards by telephones and a fax machine!

'Ha, ha, ha, ha,' Bates cackled as he made his way downstairs, his work of destruction done.

The premises looked as if they'd been hit by a bomb. The wrecking crew had lived up to its name. It would be months before any more radical toilet paper rolled off the Workers League presses, and that was assuming the plant was covered by an extremely comprehensive insurance policy. If not, the operation would be closed down for good!

Upon hearing the news of Nick Carter's arrest, Liz Jones began formulating a plan to deal with this turn of events. It was something of a blow to her self-esteem to learn that she'd spent so much time trawling London while her quarry had been holed up in Sussex. Now that Swift Nick had been apprehended, the authorities would undoubtedly transport him to a London prison within the next twenty-four hours. All Liz had to do was work out whether Carter was more likely to be incarcerated in Brixton, Wandsworth or wherever, and then organise a means of gaining access to him. Since this was easier said than done, Jones decided to get on the case immediately and within a matter of minutes, the last surviving disciple of the White Seed of Christ had boarded a bus bound for Brixton Hill.

Shortly after arriving at the prison, Liz spotted a screw who'd just knocked off work. He was about forty years old and had bulges in all the right places plus a few more to boot. Years of working for the so-called prison service had left the bastard looking like a caricature of a human being. There could be no doubt about it, a bozo like this would not find it easy to pull birds and as a consequence, he had to be terminally sex starved. This was exactly what

Jones had been looking for and so she followed the prick down Brixton Hill.

'Excuse me!' Liz shouted as she ran after the screw, 'I've just moved to London and I'm looking for places where I could have fun. Have you got any suggestions?'

'I don't know,' the guard apologised, 'I don't go out very much myself but I know a pub where we could have a quiet drink together.'

'Oooh,' Jones squealed as she fingered a button on the prison officer's tunic, 'I just love a man in uniform, why don't we buy a four-pack and go straight back to your place? Just looking at you makes me feel so good! I want you to fuck me stupid!'

'My name's Brian Byford,' quite unconsciously the screw tugged his forelock, 'and there's an off-licence very close to my bedsit.'

'I'm Liz Jones,' the last disciple of the White Seed of Christ informed him.

After that, the two of them walked in silence. At the offie, Byford's hands shook as he forked out for a four-pack and a bottle of whisky. Then it was back to the screw's digs. Brian sat on the edge of his single bed and swigged at the whisky, while Jones reclined in a solitary chair.

'Your job must be ever so frightening,' Liz said, then paused as she took a swig of beer. 'I wouldn't like to be responsible for keeping all those dangerous criminals under control!'

'You develop a sixth-sense about how to deal with scum,' Brian sounded like a supplicant addressing an oriental potentate, 'the criminal eventually learns respect for prison officers because we're there to impose discipline. It's our job to help the offender understand that only in obedience to the law can they realise their true humanity.'

'But what about someone like Swift Nick Carter!' Jones pressed. 'How on earth do you deal with an anarchist?'

'One day at a time,' Byford put in, 'starting tomorrow, because that's when the bastard's being transferred to Brixton.'

'Do you think I could meet him?' Liz enquired. 'I've never understood evil and spending a bit of time with a mad bomber might help me get my head around the issue.'

'I'd be putting my job on the line sneaking you into the prison!' Brian squealed. 'But if you're willing to give me a blow job, I'll think about it.'

Jones didn't bother replying, she simply kneeled in front of the screw, undid his flies and took out his prick. Byford gulped down another mouthful of whisky. Liz kissed his smegma-encrusted love muscle. Moments later, the prison guard shot his load.

'That's the best orgasm I've had in years!' Brian groaned. 'It sure as hell beats wanking myself off. I haven't been serviced by a woman since 1975!'

Bogroll Bates and his wrecking crew couldn't believe their luck. A party of Anglican vicars had gathered on Commercial Street when they arrived in Spital-fields to burn down the local church. This presented them with yet another opportunity to demonstrate that as nihilists they were opposed to all forms of bigotry. Fists and boots smashed into the assembled clerics and quickly reduced the sky-pilots to blood garnished blobs of flesh heaving senselessly on the pavement.

Then Bates gave the word and Molotov cocktails were hurled into the church. Within seconds, the building had been transformed into a blazing inferno. Renovating what would soon be no more than a smouldering ruin would keep the God Squad occupied for a few months, and hopefully give wives and kids time in which to escape from a patriarchal nightmare. With luck, those who broke free would link up with other rebels so that together they could smash a system which foisted religious divisions on an underclass that had no need of Protestantism, Islam or Popery!

'Burn, baby, burn!' the nihilists caroused as they leapt into their Ford transit van and made a clean getaway.

Steve Drummond had been working hard all day. The artwork for the latest issue of *Class Justice* had been delivered to the printers late that afternoon. IGM Services had just won the *CJ* contract by promising to print overnight. This meant that thanks to Steve's hard work, the paper would be bang up to date when the first copies were distributed in the morning. Drummond didn't actually know who was responsible for the massacre at the Industrial League complex in Croydon. Nevertheless, he'd held the front page so that it could be used to celebrate this act of derring-do. Inside was a short piece about the arrest of Nick Carter, another last-minute addition.

Steve had ordered all members of the Class Justice organisation to report to the national HQ – i.e. The Tanners Arms – in London. He was massing his forces so that tomorrow they could launch an all-out attack on the Lambeth stronghold of the Brixton Black Separatists. A decisive victory was necessary to erase the blots on CJ's once untarnished reputation as a violent street force. Since the Church of Valerie Solanas had been wiped out by the cops, some other political gang had to pay for the loss of both standing and members Class Justice had suffered at the hands of the ultra-feminists. The South London followers of Marcus Garvey, with their reputation as hard men, provided CJ with a first-rate target.

Having spent all day immersed in anarchist ideology, politics was now the last thing on Drummond's mind. It was Patricia Good's thirtieth birthday and as soon as the former convent girl got home from work, Steve intended to do something about her virginity. Drummond had let himself into Good's pad, her parents were away again, and he rushed to the front door as soon as he heard his girlfriend's key turning in the lock.

'Happy birthday, darling!' Steve thrummed as he threw his arms around Patricia's neck.

'Mmmm, it's . . .' Good said before her incomplete sentence was transformed into a passionate kiss.

Then Drummond dragged the chick into her bedroom. It was a long time since he'd last had sex, too long! But Patricia had promised that today he'd get his evil way. Steve threw off his clothes, Good drew the curtains.

'Can't we have the light on?' Drummond enquired.

'No,' Patricia stated emphatically.

She took her clothes off and then climbed into bed. Steve placed his hand on Good's pubic thatch but she brushed it away. At least she's not wearing any knickers, Drummond reflected. Patricia knew she'd promised to screw Steve tonight, it was the first time she'd ever taken her knickers off before going to bed with a man. Good didn't want to have sex, she was frightened. However, she'd promised to accommodate Drummond's base lusts and was afraid that if she failed to make the ultimate sacrifice, then she'd lose her man. Steve put his hand back on Patricia's pubic thatch, she brushed it away again.

'For Chrissakes,' Drummond cussed, 'how the fuck am I gonna get you juiced up if you won't let me touch you?'

'Just screw me!' Good bayed, 'Get on with it!'

Steve mounted his girlfriend, thrust his erect prick at her pubic mound – but all to no avail because she wasn't ready to receive him.

Patricia started crying, Drummond was hurting her. Steve rolled over, put his hand on Good's pubes only to have it brushed away again.

'I can't do it,' Patricia sobbed.

Steve got up and began to dress.

'There's a Mars Bar in my handbag, why don't you eat it?' Good managed to pant between her tears.

Drummond ignored the suggestion. The bitch had

been leading him on for weeks, there was no point in having an argument about sex, he simply finished dressing and left.

✤ TWELVE ✤

PETER JAMES WAS simply one of many Nazi activists who woke to discover that something very nasty had been delivered by the Royal Mail. The two pamphlets were wrapped in a plain brown envelope and bore no return address. Authorship of both texts was credited to 'A British Patriot' and beyond this, there was no indication of who was responsible for their production. Being a dyed-in-the-wool nationalist, James felt obliged to make a thorough study of these works because they bore the titles *For A Few Shekels More: The Ku Klux Klan Exposed* and *National Socialism Is Jewish!*

James made himself a cup of tea and burnt some toast before sitting down to read the texts. Peter spluttered as he followed the arguments set out by the anonymous author. The two works were literally dynamite! James was unfamiliar with much of the material but in the light of what he already knew about the Learned Elders of Zion, it seemed to make sense. After he'd finished both pamphlets, Peter was convinced that by rallying under the banner of

National Socialism, he and many other patriots had been conned into assisting the Zionist cause. However, since James liked to think of himself as intellectually sophisticated, he decided to check out a few facts before committing himself to the views put forward by the author of *National Socialism Is Jewish!*

Peter took a central line tube to Chancery Lane and from there walked to Holborn library. Although he was now convinced that Nazism was simply a tool in the armoury of Zionist conspirators, James was rather sceptical about the claims the author of *National Socialism Is Jewish!* made for the Trojan origins of the British people. Several passages from a twelfth-century work by Geoffrey of Monmouth entitled *History of the Kings of Britain* were cited as evidence to back up this assertion and Peter was astounded to discover that the book actually existed! Clearly, the anonymous patriot who'd penned the pamphlet knew his stuff. The geezer in question had fought his way through a hundred years of media black-outs and lies to discover truths that had evaded the investigations of every other member of the British nationalist community, the vast majority of whom still suffered from the delusion that their ancestors were of Teutonic stock!

There was no need for further research, despite their anonymity, James now had absolute faith in the historical accuracy of the two pamphlets. Indeed, the fact that the texts had been circulated by a nameless patriot was an indication of their authenticity, because if the author had signed the works, he'd have become an easy target for Zionist murder squads.

It was obvious to Peter that he'd have to leave the National Socialist Party of New Labour because it was simply a front for the interests of rootless cosmopolitans. However, there were far trickier questions to be resolved. For example, was it the duty of committed patriots to go to the police and expose Dave Brown, Martin Smith and the faceless men behind them as the criminal clique responsible for the attack on the Industrial League's Croydon complex? James had participated in the action after being tricked into believing he was striking a blow for his race and nation. Now he knew the truth! The hidden hand of Zionism had been at work exploiting the healthy sentiments of race-conscious patriots to implicate them in a mass murder that served who knew what ends!

If Peter went to the cops he'd be risking a lengthy jail sentence! This would be a heavy price to pay simply to wreck a Zionist front organisation. James figured he could do more for his country as a free man than if he languished year after year in a dank prison cell. It was practical considerations such as this that gave him the idea of telling the filth he was prepared to testify in court in exchange for immunity from prosecution.

Inspector Newman considered torturing Swift Nick Carter a tedious business. Although his victim occasionally blacked out from the pain, the bastard refused to beg for mercy and clearly had no intention of signing a written statement. In itself, this did not present the inspector with any major problems, since the Mets had more than enough evidence to get Carter sent down without resorting to a faked confession or other more unorthodox techniques. However, the situation irked Newman because in his book, every police interrogation was a battle of wills in which the odds were heavily stacked against the suspect. The inspector felt cheated whenever he failed to win an easy victory over an opponent. Any fool could hospitalise a man who'd been handcuffed to a police chair, but crushing the criminal's spirit was a feat that only the cream of the cops could achieve on a regular basis.

'Listen Carter,' Newman snivelled, 'I don't like you.'

'I'd never 'ave guessed!' Swift Nick liked his sarcasm deadpan.

'Shut up!' as he slammed a fist into the suspect's mouth, the inspector felt the black depths of despair swallowing him up. 'Shut up and listen to what I'm gonna tell you. I've spent a long time on your case, missed a night's sleep because you've refused to make a statement, that probably makes you feel pretty big. However, let me warn you, I can spend a lot more time on this investigation. You won't feel so fuckin' clever in three weeks when I'm still on your case. So why don't you just make life easy for yourself and admit that you blew up the cenotaph?'

'I'm not saying anything until I've seen a lawyer!' Carter spat through split lips.

'This is your last chance,' Newman's warning sounded hollow, 'I'm fuckin' knackered and I'm off to get some kip unless you change your mind about making a confession. I could give you a kicking now but I'd rather leave you conscious and able to think about what's gonna happen next. If you fail to sign a statement within the next couple of minutes, you'll be sent straight up to London and I'll see you there some time this evening. There'll be a few medical boys with me, ready to shoot you full of all sorts of crap. The doctors will be advising me on how to maximise the pain we inflict without allowing you the luxury of blacking out. It's brutal, really brutal, much nastier than anything I can do with my fists and the odd kettle of boiling water. Think about it, these boffins are experts in medical torture, their whole lives are dedicated to teaching scum like you the meaning of pain!'

'You're full of shit,' Swift Nick smirked, 'And I ain't interested in no pathological dickhead's concentration camp fantasies. Now listen to this cop, I want a lawyer and a phone. The law says I'm entitled to these things and once I get them, it won't take me long to organise my release!'

'Cunt!' the inspector howled. 'You fuckin' cunt! I ain't jokin' when I say I can lay on top-flight medical torture! Why won't you treat my threats with the seriousness they deserve?'

Then Newman jumped up from his chair and set about giving Carter a good kicking. A regulation police shoe was slammed repeatedly into the suspect's groin. Swift Nick blacked out instantly. Nevertheless, the inspector proceeded to kick Carter and the regulation police chair to which the nihilist was strapped around the interrogation room. After several minutes of frenzied activity, Newman collapsed in a crumpled heap and burst into tears. It took a full hour before the inspector had regained sufficient composure to issue orders for Swift Nick's transfer to Brixton Prison.

Bogroll Bates led a squad of masked nihilists down Parkway and onto Camden High Street. The crew was armed with baseball bats, flick knives and Molotov cocktails. Wimmin screamed and men trampled toddlers underfoot as weekday shoppers attempted to escape a savage beating at the hands of this proletarian crew. However, working-class chicks in high heels, stockings and short skirts were spared. The nihilists were hunting bohemians, upper class trendies and dorks in suits.

'Here, have a hundred quid and my credit cards,' a businessman said as he held out his wallet.

Bogroll accepted the swag and then swung his baseball bat against the bozo's head. There was the sickening crunch of splintering bone and split seconds later, the middle-aged suit was lying in a pool of his own blood. Bates found himself another victim, a forty-year-old womun with upper class bitch written all over her face.

Other nihilists were throwing petrol bombs, a Molotov had shattered the windscreen of a Mercedes and inside the managing director of a well-known multinational was being burnt alive. An art dealer, at the wheel of a BMW, was so angered by this that he swung his Nazi slot machine onto the pavement and attempted to run down three of the masked marauders. This trio jumped out of the way and all their would-be assailant succeeded in doing was killing a young mother and her two-month-old baby. His motor then smashed into a shop window. Customers and sales assistants were showered with glass and suffered innumerable cuts. The art dealer was dragged from his car and beaten senseless by angry shoppers.

Unemployed youths were streaming out of back alleys so that they could participate in the nihilists' orgy of destruction. It was at this point that the organised looting began. A man in a wheelchair who asked for a cigarette was handed two dozen packets of Silk Cut. Goods were being passed down human chains and stacked up on the pavement so that anyone who fancied a new video or TV set could help themselves to commodities they couldn't afford to buy.

The trouble had spread from the High Street into Parkway, up towards Kentish Town and Chalk Farm. Within minutes of the disturbance erupting, the tube station had been closed. Traffic was at a standstill and the whole area was in pandemonium. Bates surveyed the scene with a sense of deep satisfaction. For years he'd suffered helplessly while an unfair blacklisting by the Industrial League prevented him from finding work. Now he'd discovered communal action and was beginning to sense his own power. Camden had been transformed into a riot zone and all it took was a word passed between Bogroll and his nihilist mates.

Bates laid into a Woolworth's window with his baseball bat. A cashier screamed as the plate glass shattered. The staff ran to the back of the shop. Pubescent customers began stuffing sweets and other goodies into their pockets. Bogroll gathered his troops around him and led them down to Delancey Street, where they all jumped into a stolen transit van. Minutes later, they'd made a clean getaway. It was a pity that the odd opportunist looter would be nicked, but this hardly mattered when one considered that the instigators of the disturbance were still free to riot another day.

Swift Nick Carter was only vaguely aware of being bundled into a police van. Despite the fact that Inspector Newman had kicked and punched the suspect senseless, the Sussex filth were taking no chances with this notorious malcontent. Carter was being escorted to London by a score of armed police. He would be handcuffed to at least one officer at all times. Two marked and two unmarked squad cars plus four motorcyclists made up the rest of the convoy. The brave men undertaking this duty saw themselves as a thin blue line between the British people and the very real danger of Swift Nick being sprung by a gang of fanatics who adhered to his anti-social creed.

The Black Maria pulled out into the street and Nick could hear the roar of traffic as the convoy threaded its way out of Brighton. Although several other prisoners were being transported to London, there were no muttered oaths as they caught their last glimpses of the seaside resort. For their own safety, the others were being transported in a vehicle that would wend its way up to the Smoke a couple of hours later. Carter was considered too important and dangerous a prisoner to be moved with ordinary felons.

Nick was in excellent physical shape and made a speedy recovery from nearly twenty-four hours of non-stop torture at the hands of Inspector James Newman. However, it was a long time before Carter actually opened his eyes and drank in the rolling South Downs. Despite his deep-rooted commitment to urban life, Nick's mind was anything but closed to the beauties of nature. He was perfectly capable of enjoying a vista of fields and forests from the comfort of a train or motor car. There was nothing wrong with the country, Carter simply detested the hayseeds who lived in it.

'Oh, so sleeping beauty awakes!' a cop who'd been handcuffed to Swift Nick jested.

'Undo the bracelets!' Carter ordered, 'I wanna stretch out.'

'Not a chance son,' the constable, who was at least a decade younger than Nick, falsely imagined there was gravity in his voice. 'You're a dangerous man and I'm here to prevent you being a menace to society.'

'Liberal,' Carter mocked.

The fields metamorphosed into the suburbs. Despite being the prisoner of a viciously repressive state, Swift Nick felt a stirring in his heart as the convoy sped through Croydon. He was returning to London and that was where he belonged. The rows of terraced houses seemed to wink at him. The Victorian ghosts that haunted both city and suburbs were whispering to Carter, telling him he'd never succeed in chasing them away. Nick wanted the ride to go on forever. As long as he travelled an arterial route that led to the heart of the city, he was free. Back alleys beckoned with tales of mystery and romance but the overall balance of the local psychogeography pulled the lonely wanderer north with promises of a place where all roads met in an urban Valhalla. Carter longed for a glimpse of the Thames and an hour spent among the dirty streets of Soho.

The convoy crawled through Streatham, for a brief moment Swift Nick was convinced it would become trapped in the ever-multiplying volume of traffic. Then there was a blast of police sirens and cars pulled aside to let the van past. Carter stared at girls in short skirts and young mothers pushing buggies down the street. He really needed a bit of what they'd got. Nick scanned the road for signs of anything that might put a stop to the relentless efficiency of the convey as it snaked its way towards Brixton Hill. The few remaining minutes this side of those grim gates meant so much to the nihilist.

All too soon the Black Maria shuddered to a halt. Carter watched as the warders stood back to let the van in. He saw the malevolent grins on their faces and in those split seconds, the connection between freedom and necessity was severed forever. Nevertheless, Nick swore silently to himself that the bastards would never break his spirit. He would rather die than let men deformed by the statist ideology grind him down.

Martin Smith was not a happy man. He'd been receiving the calls since before nine that morning.

Smith had unplugged the phone because he was sick of hearing about that notorious forgery entitled *National Socialism Is Jewish!* Every bloody patriot in the country seemed to have been mailed a copy of this malicious smear. As a consequence, the tiny National Socialist Party of New Labour was losing members left, right and centre. It was a black day indeed for Britain because the wreckers had succeeded in destroying the one organisation with the potential to save the country and reconquer every last inch of its lost empire. Several abusive callers had even made death threats after accusing Martin of being a front wheel. This was going too far! Although Smith had only recently rediscovered the patriotic ideals that had lain dormant within him since his childhood, even during his years as a Trotskyite militant he'd been a vehement anti-Zionist!

'Who is responsible for this outrage?' Martin lambasted as he waved a copy of *National Socialism Is Jewish!* in the air. 'We must arm ourselves and kill those responsible for spreading these lies!'

'Mein Führer,' Dave Brown whispered, 'before we can eliminate the bastards, we must first discover who they are.'

'I fuckin' know that,' Smith imprecated, 'so stop hectoring me with these petty details!'

'Mein Führer,' Brown ventured a second time, 'let me service your genetic wand. It will make you feel better.'

'On your knees, peasant!' Martin blistered. 'I want you to swallow me whole.'

Dave didn't need any further encouragement. There were two things he really loved in life, his country and sucking cock. Brown undid Smith's flies and fished out the top's love muscle. He fingered the fuck stick and watched with delight as it swelled out to its full length. Dave then ran his tongue along the meat, before playfully nipping at the tip with his teeth.

'Once I take control of the country,' Martin scorched, 'I'll organise a crew of teenage body-guards. These boys will be my motorcycle escort as I ride into Westminster in an open-topped car. The crowds will cheer as I play with the hair of the physically perfect specimen of Aryan manhood seated beside me.'

Brown didn't reply, he was too busy slavering over Smith's dick. In any case, his own fantasies were very different from his friend's visions of pomp and ceremony. Dave imagined that he was out on the mudflats of prehistory. Brown was the first amphibian to rut with its mate in the slime that was neither dry land nor swelling sea. Beyond him lay terra incognito, a world that had yet to be won for the fuck and its progeny. Mile upon mile of swampland ripe for colonisation by those who'd escaped the ocean and were looking for a place in the sun. The amphibian would blaze a trail leading directly to a future cum culture. This fluid discourse would endure forever since it was designed to satisfy all the needs of eroticised male flesh bonded together several million years before the birth of history.

'Oh, baby, baby!' Martin castigated. 'Do it to me!'

Then the wannabe Führer spoke no more, he simply moaned and groaned because million-year-old genetic codes were being scrambled and unscrambled across the surface of his bulk. The almighty DNA had seized control of Smith's cortex as endorphins were pumped through his brain. Brown had already tasted the pre-cum and now Martin's genetic wealth was spurting into the cock-sucker's mouth. Dave swallowed the cum and it tasted like the sweetest of nectars. Smith clenched and unclenched his fists. He felt like a New Man, he had been reborn! Gradually, the spasms of pleasure subsided and the two men fell to the floor, where they collapsed into each other's arms. For a few minutes it was possible to forget the work that lay ahead of them, although they'd soon return to the task of rebuilding their movement in the face of the blows being delivered by the anonymous author of *National Socialism Is Jewish!* Sex was their pas-sionate secret because being Nazi bastards, both men viewed their relationship as a love that dared not speak its name.

Once the prison gates swung shut, Swift Nick Carter was hauled out of the Black Maria and frog-marched to the governor's office. Here he was confronted by a man in his mid-fifties whose personality had been severely warped by a life spent in the prison service and a strong belief in the Christian faith. The boss screw was bent over some papers as Nick was bundled into the room. There were several minutes of silence before the governor looked up from his desk and proceeded to deal with Carter.

'Right,' the boss screw announced, 'I'm Governor Williams and while you're here I expect you to conduct yourself in an orderly manner. You have yet to be found guilty of any crime by a court of law but since it is only a matter of time before you receive a life sentence, I don't want you to bleat on at me about getting privileges.'

'Is that it?' Carter asked. 'I'm tired and I'd like to go to bed.'

'You've got a bad attitude, terrorist!' Williams lashed as he got up from behind his desk.

The two screws restraining Nick tightened their grip on him. The governor clenched his fists and moments later, was pummelling them into the nihilist's stomach. Carter would have doubled up in pain if the screws hadn't been holding him upright. The beating continued until Williams began wheezing. The governor had been so angered by Nick's words that he'd over-exerted himself and was now struggling to catch his breath.

The warders manhandling Carter stamped on the nihilist's feet, then threw him against a wall and began beating the prisoner about the head. After Nick slid to the floor, he was given a good kicking. Eventually, Carter blacked out. When he came to, Swift Nick found himself lying on a bed in a small cell. The nihilist stretched out on the thin mattress. He was bruised all over and movement was painful. Nevertheless, having swung his legs over the edge of the bed, Carter staggered to his feet. Through a small window protected by bars, Nick could see an exercise yard several floors beneath him.

There was nothing to do and so Carter lay back down on the bed. If he'd had a pen and paper, the nihilist would have started work on his autobiography. Despite the circumstances surrounding his return, simply being in London had cured Nick of his writer's block. There was so much of his life that he wanted to record. The nihilist's early childhood wasn't of much interest, his life hadn't really begun until he'd hit puberty. By that time, he was well into thieving, fighting and outrageous acts of vandalism. The first volume of his memoirs would deal with his deviant behaviour between the ages of twelve and sixteen, when he began venting his anger on the rich bastards who exploited his class. He'd write the book in the language of a schoolboy, it would be raw and alive. There'd be no direct references to specific ideologies, just a lot of violence and long rants against the rich. That way, no casual reader would be prepared for the next volume, which was to explore Carter's immersion in the politics of the Gay Liberation Front.

Nick's commitment to gay activism had eventually been supplanted by his devotion to the anarchist cause. He'd led Class Justice through it's heroic period and once that was over, the nihilist had discovered he liked fucking chicks. But now Carter was banged up, it seemed likely he'd be having blokes again on a regular basis. Male or femail, it didn't make a lot of difference, Nick simply wanted to rub his love stick between walls of human flesh.

Mike Armilus kept his contact with rank-and-file members of the Nihilist Alliance down to a bare minimum. Bogroll Bates organised the movement's supporters on a day to day basis. Armilus was only to be seen on ceremonial occasions or when he led the troops during major street clashes. He was a mystical leader who inspired a fanatical devotion among the two hundred fully paid-up members of his organisation. To meet Armilus was a privilege, and that was why Mike maintained a carefully cultivated distance between himself and the vast bulk of the membership.

Public meetings were an opportunity for pageantry, colour and controversy. The *East London Anarcho-Nihilist Solidarity Rally* being held in a small hall near Bethnal Green tube station was no exception. The platform was draped with black flags and movement banners, while the walls had been plastered with posters. Several members of the Alliance had already spoken and Bogroll was conducting a Dutch auction before Armilus took to the platform to make the final speech of the night.

'Alright, alright!' Bates implored. 'You all know it costs money to smash the state, so how many of you out there are gonna donate a hundred knicker to the cause?'

'I will!' someone shouted from the back of the hall.

There were cheers as the money was passed through the crowd and up to the platform. Several other individuals made identical contributions after seeing the enthusiasm with which such behaviour was greeted. Then Bogroll called for £75 donations and found even more members willing to cough up this sum to wild applause from their comrades. After this, it was a case of asking for £50, then £40 and so on until the sum requested had been reduced to £5. In this way, a couple of grand was very successfully solicited before a collection tin was passed around for smaller donations.

'*Arm-il-us, Arm-il-us!*' the cry went up from a hundred hardline nihilists who were really looking forward to hearing their leader speak.

Most of the anarchists who'd attended the rally out of curiosity found themselves caught up in the excitement. The literature table was doing a roaring trade, while the massed ranks of anarcho-nihilists were stamping their feet in time to the Fourth Movement of Beethoven's *Ninth Symphony*. At last, Mike Armilus took to the stage and was immediately greeted by rapturous applause. The leader raised his arms above his head and the clapping died down as he lowered them again.

'Comrades!' Mike's voice thrashed around the hall, making the word sound like an insult. 'We're about to witness a massive explosion of class anger that will make the 1990 Poll Tax Riots look like a tea party!'

There were cheers from the crowd, Mike's eyes seemed to seek out each member of his audience individually and suck them in like a welcoming cunt. Everything Armilus knew about public speaking, he'd learnt from pre-war gangster movies. Revolutionary leaders had to exploit the gang mentality of the masses, insurrection was to be organised around an image of unbeatable strength.

'The rich want us grovelling to them like feudal serfs, grateful that we don't live in Rwanda. They want us hidden away on council estates listening to Oasis, Blur and Menswear,' Armilus raised his voice many more decibels as he completed the sentence,

'BUT WE'VE GOT NEWS FOR THESE PARA-SITES, WE'RE GONNA DESTROY THEIR SYSTEM OF PROFITS AND PRIVILEGE!'

There was more frenzied applause and the few anarchists who still suffered from nagging doubts about committing themselves to nihilism were quickly won over to the cause. Mike's voice thundered through the hall, delivering judgement on the rich and their lackeys. Abuse was heaped upon cops and social workers, stockbrokers and school teachers, debutantes and bankers. The speech was crude but effective. It's emotional impact was more important than the somewhat limited content. The assembled crowd were able to fuse with each other through the medium of Mike Armilus and thereby gain a sense of their own power. And while the previously non-aligned were successfully converted to nihilism, adherents of the creed had their beliefs reinforced.

'We have no demands to make of the ruling class,' Armilus exuded strength, conviction and above all fanatical dedication, 'there are no concessions they can make to get rid of us, when we march into posh areas, our banners will read simply BEHOLD YOUR FUTURE EXECUTIONERS.'

The conclusion of the speech was greeted with rapturous applause, as nihilists leapt from their seats to scream 'hurrah'. After a ten-minute standing ovation, Mike held out a banner so that every last member of the audience could ritually touch the black flag of nihilism. Basing proletarian politics on reasoned argument was a waste of time. The working-class would fail in its historic mission if it fought the bourgeoisie on the enemy's terms.

Steve Drummond was in a fine mood. The lead story in the latest issue of *Class Justice* was going down very well. All fifteen fully paid-up members of the group had spent the day selling the paper and they'd succeeded in flogging over five hundred copies in London. Steve personally supplied all the shops in the Smoke that sold the paper, as well as the national distributors who would have *Class Justice* on sale across the country by tomorrow morning. While the rest of the left was pointedly ignoring the working-class offensive against the Industrial League complex in Croydon, Class Justice was proud to gloat over a body count that made World War II pale in comparison.

Drummond was also pleased that he'd finally given Patricia Good the boot. He'd let the bitch lead him on for too long. Now he was free to get his leg over chicks who didn't object to a spot of bedroom athletics. It had been a long time since Steve last had sex, too long. However, since he'd bulges in all the right places, the Führer of British Anarchism had no difficulty in convincing himself that it was simply a matter of time before he bagged a leggy nympho-maniac. Likewise, it would only be a couple of hours before Class Justice regained their reputation as hardened street fighters by trashing a bunch of right-wing loonies.

Drummond had discovered that the nationalist bastards who made up the membership of the Brixton Black Separatists were having one of their monthly strategy meetings that very evening and everything would be wound up in time for the brothers to catch last orders at their local. Therefore, Steve led his troops down to Railton Road just before 10 p.m. The Class Warriors split into two groups, each lurking to one side of the black nationalists' headquarters. Even with the entire Redhill Branch present, Steve's following was not strong enough to launch an all-out attack on the building occupied by the separatists. It was far safer to ambush the nationalist scum as they left their HQ.

The Class Justice crew didn't have to wait long, minutes after they'd taken up their positions, ten separatists ambled into the street. Sticking to a strategy worked out in advance, the Class Warriors waited until the nationalists had moved away from the entrance to their building. Split seconds later, the reactionaries were charged by the two squads of anarchists, who laid into them with knives and clubs.

For several minutes, the anarchists had the upper hand, but for all his careful planning, Steve Drummond had overlooked a very basic point. Hearing the sound of fighting, soul brothers were pouring into the street. Had they known what Class Justice were about, many of them would have been sympathetic to the aims of the group. Unfortunately, they were completely oblivious to the fact that a clash of ideologies was in progress, a ferocious battle between anarcho-revolutionaries and reactionary nationalists. To the soul brothers, it looked like a bunch of white racists were hell bent on causing trouble in Brixton. As many of the area's finest rushed into the fray, Class Justice were soon on the receiving end of a bloody good pasting.

POW! Fists and boots thudded into anarchist faces and groins. ZOWIE! Several class struggle militants staggered backwards spitting out gouts of blood and the occasional piece of broken tooth. KERRANG! The revolutionaries were beaten senseless. Only Steve Drummond and George Sanders had been quick-witted enough to evade a kicking. As soon as the fighting began, they'd realised there was a major flaw in their plan, and so these fast-thinking strategists legged it over a fence.

237

✤ THIRTEEN ✤

BRIAN BYFORD WAS woken by Liz Jones, who'd thrown back the bed sheets and was treating him to yet another blow job. The screw could feel love juice boiling up through his groin and split seconds later, the liquid genetics spurted inside Liz's mouth. Jones then French-kissed Byford. The screw could taste his own spunk on the girl's lips.

'Oh baby,' Byford croaked, 'you make me feel so good. What a way to wake up!'

'I couldn't resist your morning glory,' Jones moaned. 'Your stiff cock was poking against my bum and so I just had to put my lips around it!'

'It's years since I last had a spontaneous erection,' Brian confessed, 'all the oral action I've been getting off you must be rejuvenating my sexual drives. I've lost count of the number of times you've sucked me off but I've still to go up your cunt, and that's what I really want!'

'I've told you darling,' Liz flirted, 'I've got thrush, so you'll just have to wait a few days until it's cleared up.'

'Okay, doll, okay!' Byford was desperate to prove he was still virile. 'Just don't hold out on me unnecessarily, it's been a long time since I last had any pussy!'

'Listen,' Jones said in an attempt to change the subject, 'you remember I told you that I work as a journalist?'

'Yes,' Brian affirmed.

'And you recall letting it slip that Swift Nick Carter is being held in Brixton nick?'

'Hey,' Byford remonstrated, 'that's supposed to be a secret, so don't go blabbin' about it to any of your media friends!'

'I'd have to be crazy to do that,' Liz retorted. 'There's no way I'm gonna throw away the biggest break of my career.'

'I don't like the sound of this!' Brian looked like he was about to weep.

'Don't be a killjoy!' Jones was good at putting herself across as sultry. 'All you've gotta do is sneak me into the prison so that I can get an exclusive interview with Carter. We'll then be in a position to make a packet selling the story to one of the national papers.'

'Hold on bitch!' Byford sounded like he'd got a bone caught in his throat. 'You're asking me to put my job on the line. The governor would sack me if he found out I'd sneaked a journalist into the prison.'

'So what?' Liz knew she held the trump card. 'If we can pull this off, you won't need your poxy job. We're talking telephone numbers here, there'll be more than enough dosh for you to retire on.'

'Really?' the screw was letting the little imagination he had run wild.

'It's easy,' Jones said with great conviction, 'all you've gotta do is get me into Carter's cell for a few hours and make sure we're not disturbed. Then I'll get the nationals bidding for a serialised version of the story. After that, we can make a further killing by turning my interview into a book!'

'How do you know Carter will talk to you?' Brian pressed.

'Look,' Liz knew how to elicit the response she wanted, 'everybody likes to see their name in the papers, especially anarchist scum! Anyway, we'll sweeten him up before I make my approach. I'll give you some drugs to pass onto him, saying they're from a friend who hopes to pay him a visit. You're to be nice to him too, tell the bozo that we're on his side!'

'Yeah!' Byford grinned. 'We're keeping the cunt in solitary, he's gotta be grateful to anyone who offers him the hand of friendship. I'll butter the bastard up, ask him if there's anything he wants, maybe even allow him a chat with one of the other lags!'

'That's better!' Jones cooed as she patted the screw on the head. 'We're gonna be rich! Just give it a couple of weeks and we'll be rollin' in filthy lucre!'

Liz was actually thinking how pleased she'd be to dump the bore who was lying next to her. Byford disgusted her, he'd no sense of the spiritual values that had raised his race to greatness. The only things that interested this particular prison officer were money and sex, in that order! Jones had been keeping a careful record of her periods and knew that if she could get Carter to fuck her within the next two days, she'd definitely become pregnant. Zionist conspirators might have succeeded in wrecking the White Seed of Christ, but through Liz Jones and her future children, its ideals would live on!

Despite having missed an enormous amount of sleep, Inspector Newman was in high spirits. Not only was Swift Nick Carter safely locked up in Brixton Prison, thanks to Peter James coming forward with information, he'd arrested every last member of the gang responsible for the attack on the Industrial League's Croydon complex. Interrogation was an easy task because each and every National Socialist Party of New Labour militant was willing to grass up their comrades in the hope of obtaining a lighter sentence.

'You've disappointed me, Martin,' the cop was quite consciously anathematising his former friend. 'You provided the Mets with a lot of useful information when you were a Marxist, so why did you have to spoil everything by becoming a Nazi and resorting to terrorist tactics.'

'I've never been a Nazi or a Marxist,' Smith insisted. 'I just wanted to do my bit for Queen and Country by infiltrating those extremist groups that threaten the very fabric of our democratic society. The terrorist tactics used by the National Socialist Party of New Labour were all Dave Brown's idea, I simply went along on the Croydon mission in the hope of saving a few lives. Unfortunately, things got completely out of hand and I was unable to prevent the homicidal behaviour of the Nazi maniacs whose terrorist tactics I'd hoped to expose!'

'But Martin,' Newman was relishing the conversation, 'you founded the National Socialist Party of New Labour! And I've got signed statements from every last one of your former members saying that it was you and Dave Brown who murdered the men butchered in the Croydon massacre.'

'That's not true!' Smith blurted. 'I wouldn't lie to . . .'

The sentence was cut short by the inspector's fist landing with a sickening crunch in the suspect's mouth. Moments later, Newman booted his former friend in the balls. Martin tried to double up but he was tied securely to a chair. The cop then slipped a knuckle duster over his right fist and beat Smith repeatedly in the stomach.

'Jesus H. Christ!' the inspector blasphemed, 'you're a complete fuckin' cunt and I can see right through you! Don't try to bullshit me! I want you to sign a confession immediately, if you don't, I'll tear you apart with my bare hands!'

Fearing for his life, Martin felt he had no choice but to append his signature to the sheet that was shoved in front of him. Smith was no Swift Nick Carter, despite years of political activism, he lacked the strength of character to resist Newman's bullying tactics.

Fully satisfied with his ability to achieve quick results, the inspector had Martin carried back down to the cells and ordered that Dave Brown be brought to the interrogation room for further questioning. In the meantime, Newman nipped along to the police canteen for a quick cuppa. When he returned, the inspector found the Industrial League's former security expert strapped to a chair with blood pouring from his mouth.

'Did my men mistreat you?' the cop enquired.

'Yes they did!' Dave whinged. 'They beat me up and told me I was a murderous bastard who should be clubbed to death. It isn't fair, I've never hurt anybody. The National Socialist Party of New Labour told me they'd kidnapped my sister and that she'd be killed if I didn't lead them into the Industrial League's Croydon complex. How was I to know they were going to kill anybody? Once the slaughter began there was nothing I could do, my hands were tied behind my back and there was a gun trained on me throughout this terrible ordeal!'

'You know something?' Newman said as he brought his face right up against Brown's countenance. 'You're full of shit and I'm going to congratulate the men who worked you over for doing a good job!'

The Industrial League's former security expert wet himself. Newman looked at the suspect's crotch, his face a mask of disgust as a circle of urine darkened the prisoner's slacks. The cop turned around and picked up a can of petrol that had been left on the floor. He undid the cap and doused Brown with this highly inflammable fluid. Newman then took a few steps backwards and lit a cigarette.

'Okay,' the inspector boomed, 'either you make

an immediate confession or else I'll throw my fag at you.'

'I'll do anything,' the suspect whimpered. 'Anything! Please don't set fire to me!'

'Keep your hair on!' Newman said laconically as he waved the cigarette in the air and moved towards Brown in a bid to apply further psychological pressure to the snivelling coward.

Unfortunately, the inspector applied a little too much pressure and a piece of fag ash landed on the suspect's petroleum-soaked clothes. Newman leapt backwards, suffering no more than singed eyebrows.

'I don't believe this is happening to me!' was Brown's threnody as he burst into flames.

A most regrettable accident, the inspector reflected as he watched the pretty orange flames die down and pieces of the suspect's charred corpse flaked to the floor. It wouldn't have happened if I hadn't missed so much sleep. Newman decided that he'd better go and write up a report. Afterwards he'd catch some kip. Once he was properly rested, he'd tie up the loose ends remaining on this case. Then he could head over to Brixton and give Swift Nick Carter another kicking.

Swift Nick was waiting for some acid to hit. His luck seemed to have turned, he'd been given the drugs by a screw called Brian Byford. He'd also been offered the chance to fraternise with a Jute Republican who, like Nick, was being held in solitary. The screw had told Carter that the ordinary lags did not like paedophiles, serial killers or terrorists, and would murder this class of prisoner given half a chance. Therefore, the number of prisoners with whom he'd be able to socialise was extremely limited.

Swift Nick turned down the opportunity to meet the Kent nationalist, explaining to Byford that the Jute Republican Army were a bunch of gangsters who leeched off the working-class. As Carter switched on, his thoughts turned away from the sectarian scumbags who'd ruined the lives of so many ordinary wo/men. Naturally enough, Nick's acid-armed consciousness was chiefly concerned with whatever prospects he had of fighting his way to freedom. Looking at the outer wall of his cell, Carter observed the bricks burst into flame. Split seconds later, the fire died down, having burnt with sufficient intensity to leave behind a hole that was large enough to step through. As Nick bounded out of his cell, he saw two flaming arrows cross in the sky. Moments later, a star rose to the north, on which the crucified forms of monarchs, popes, presidents and a host of reactionary ideologists were clearly visible.

Carter ambled down Brixton Hill and at the bottom climbed into a golden chariot. He raced through the mean streets of South London, running down cops and traffic wardens. On and on Nick rushed, over the Thames and into Westminster. There'd been a time when Carter dreamt of burning down the Houses of Parliament and every other example of monumental architecture to be found within a thirty-mile radius of Soho. Now he realised that these buildings, which the ruling class wanted the world to view as symbols of their wealth and power, provided both bourgeois and proletarian with a constant reminder of how far everyday life was lagging behind what was possible. Instead of being cooped up inside endless Victorian terraces, the London mob ought to be living out their lives in the capital's many mansions and palaces. Everyone should inhabit a dwelling that was sufficiently fabulous to arouse the envy of contemporary royalty!

The golden chariot was swept into the sky. Swift Nick gazed down upon the city as the working-class streamed out of tower blocks and terraces to take possession of churches and cathedrals. Lightning flashed from Carter's finger tips and a row of two-up two-downs in Kennington burst into flame. Within the space of a few minutes, Nick had reduced terraces located as far apart as East Ham and Acton to smouldering ruins. The streets in which workers had once lived were now avenues of fire and the Victorian squalor that had blighted this celestial city since the middle of the nineteenth century had become a thing of dim memory.

There was nothing occult about Swift Nick's hallucinations, they were the utterly predictable results of an acid trip, and at that very moment, another member of the Nihilist Alliance was engaged in a mission that demonstrated the practical results of similar thought processes when they are allowed to proceed unshackled by the prison system. Bogroll Bates had taken a bus to the Bow Flyover and then walked the short distance to what had once been the Bryant and May Factory, scene of the famous 1888 match girls' strike. The building had since been renamed the Bow Quarter and converted into yuppie flats.

Bates pushed a stolen credit card into the crack between a door frame and a Yale lock, thereby gaining entry to some posh bastard's drum. The owner had forgotten to secure the mortice when he'd left for work that morning, this made life easy for Bogroll, there'd been no need to break a window and then climb through it! The nihilist pulled a flick knife from his pocket and quickly set to work slashing the thick carpet into which his feet had sunk. Bates was efficient and methodical, he'd soon shredded the fitted number.

In the living room, Bogroll smashed a marble fireplace, slashed a leather three-piece suite and inflicted irreparable damage on several original works of art. Bates didn't care for painting or sculpture, folk crafts were an anachronism in an age dominated by VCRs and virtual reality! The Nihilist Alliance was fighting for a world of ever-growing ecstasy and that was why Bogroll felt obliged to trash this posh flat. Ordinary living standards had to be raised way beyond those enjoyed by the affluent in this benighted era, until that happened, yuppie pads were a legitimate target upon which proletarians could vent their class anger.

Bates pulled a can of paint from his coat pocket and sprayed: 'THE MATCH GIRLS STRIKE BACK' on an internal wall. Moments later, he inscribed 'KRISHNAMURTI LIVES' above the fireplace he'd just destroyed. Bogroll was a right joker, there was nothing he respected, not even labour history and so he was more than happy to satirise the career of occult crank Annie Besant, who having played a leading role in the match girls' strike, went on to become head of the Theosophical Society. Besant was your typical upper class faddist, who over the course of a long life adhered to causes as diverse as Christian flagellation, militant atheism, socialism, spiritualism and Indian independence. While middle class lefties revered the memory of Besant, Shaw, the Webbs and their ilk, Bates felt nothing but contempt for these cunts. As far as he was concerned, it was the match girls who actually amounted to something. As a street-hardened proletarian, he knew instinctively that their posh benefactress wasn't worth a light.

Bogroll carved a CND symbol into an oak table and then smashed the glass of an aquarium. Water cascaded from the tank and spread across the carpet. Rare tropical fish were left gasping for breath. Bates grinned, their owner would be really upset when he came home and found his flash pets lying dead on the floor. Since the nihilist could think of nothing that would top this last act of vandalism, he decided to split. There would be plenty more opportunities to wreck yuppie cars and homes!

Mike Armilus figured it was high time he revoked his secret pact with Steve Drummond and the Class Justice group. The media and most of the left were unable to distinguish his own brand of revolutionary warfare from that practised by the wimps and wallies grouped around Drummond. There was a need for drastic action because Nihilist Alliance paper sellers were being insulted on the streets of London by morons who laboured under the misapprehension that they'd been part of the Class Justice crew creamed by Matt Dread and the Brixton Black Separatists in a late-night street fight. Of course, every name-caller received a summary kicking, but something more was required if the nihilists were to regain their reputation as dangerous nutters who could fight through to victory against the heaviest odds.

It was Steve Drummond's stupidity that had led to his men being trashed by the nationalist bastards. Armilus was not about to repeat the anarchist leader's mistakes. That was why he'd headed down to Brixton and proceeded to hand out a photocopied leaflet to every soul brother who'd accept one. The flyer exposed the links between the black nationalists and Nigel Devi's Violent Party. It also detailed the plans of black and white reactionaries to hold a joint meeting at the Separatists' Railton Road HQ in just over twenty-four hours' time. This provided Mike with the perfect opportunity to raise a multiracial task force capable of delivering a death blow to the nationalists and their bigoted ideology. To do this, he had to get the soul brothers on his side, or at least neutralise them, because if the local population misread the situation and rallied to the defence of nationalist reaction, there was no way the forces of progress could triumph over this political evil.

'Hey man,' a soul brother who'd just read Mike's flyer said as he extended his hand, 'this stuff is dynamite, there's a lot of people in Brixton very fucked off with the antics of the so-called Black Separatists.'

'We'll sort the bastards out tomorrow night,' Armilus was grinning as he shook hands with his new acquaintance.

'That's right,' the soul brother put in, 'the time has come to slay the fascist beast!'

'Glad we're in agreement,' Mike enthused, 'is there anything you don't like about what I'm saying?'

'What you say is great,' the soul brother affirmed. 'My only criticism would be that you've left too much out. For example, why don't you expose the nationalist monster for what it really is? Everyone round here knows that the so-called separatists use politics as an ideological cover for their criminal activities. Matt Dread is a gangster who's got all the local rackets stitched up. His hoods knee-capped one of my brothers because he was conducting a small-time dope dealing operation without their approval.'

'You're right,' Armilus admitted, 'I should've put stuff in about how fascism's just a more vicious way of organising the capitalist racket. I rushed the leaflet out, if I'd spent a bit more time on it, I'd have come up with something much better.'

'At least you're actively opposing the reactionaries and gangsters,' the soul brother allowed generously. 'I think your flyer's good enough to do the job of mobilising people against the nationalist menace. Making a detailed study of the beast can wait until the evil has been mercilessly crushed.'

This was simply the first of many similar conversations Mike had that afternoon. By the time he left

Brixton, Armilus was supremely confident of his ability to annihilate the nationalist creed.

George Sanders knew Class Justice were in a make or break situation and that Steve Drummond was relying on him to come up with the readies which would enable them to rebuild the organisation after the débâcle in Brixton. Following on from the success of his first bank job, Sanders had decided to pull another in affluent Islington. This time it was a night safe on Upper Street that was lined with a rubbish bag. Returning a few hours later, George was delighted to feel the weight of his bin-liner as he recovered it. As Sanders was reflecting that at least a dozen shop-keepers must have placed a day's takings in the night safe, a hand clasped his shoulder.

'You fuckin' tea leaf, I'm takin' you down the cop shop.'

George nearly wet himself, but within a matter of seconds, he'd regained his composure and tried to leg it. The stranger kept a firm grip on him. Sanders twisted around with the intention of punching the geezer out. When George took in the size of the bloke, who towered a good six inches above the scrawny anarchist and was built like a brick shithouse, he changed his mind. There's no point starting a fight you can't win!

'Look 'ere mate,' Sanders was trying to be diplomatic, 'be reasonable, I'm sure we can come to some mutually beneficial arrangement. There must be the best part of ten grand in this bag and I'd be more than happy to give you half of it.'

'Fuck you!' the stranger looked like he was ready

to give his interlocutor a drubbing. 'If there's that much money in there, I'm 'aving it all. Sod the fuckin' cops. But before I let you go, you've gotta tell me 'ow you get the night safe open.'

'Easy,' George replied, 'I've got a set of skeleton keys.'

The man mountain snatched the anarchist's bag of swag and his keys. He was about to shuffle off down the street when Sanders grabbed his arm.

'Let go of me, you prick!' the stranger roared.

'Don't be such a cunt,' George pleaded. 'You've taken everything I've got, give me back a tenner so I can console myself with a few drinks!'

'I'm a reasonable bloke,' the man mountain conceded, 'and since I've just learnt a grift off you, I'll teach you a con I've been pulling for a good few years.'

The stranger then pulled a book of raffle tickets from a coat pocket and handed them to Sanders, who immediately threw them onto the pavement.

'They aren't any fuckin' use to me!' George swore. 'Give me some bleedin' money.'

'What you do,' the stranger explained patiently, 'is go round the pubs saying you're doing a raffle for homeless children. Sell the tickets at a quid a shot and just pocket the dosh. You can make a couple of hundred quid in a night. No one ever tries to check up on you. It's easy.'

With those words, the man mountain was gone. Sanders picked up the book of raffle tickets, crossed the street and entered a pub. Five minutes later he padded out with thirty quid in his pocket. The stranger was right, it was easy money. George decided he didn't really have the front for pulling off bank jobs. In the future, he'd stick to simple cons like this one with the raffle tickets. Sanders was still pulling in the readies for Class Justice, the sums concerned might be smaller but there was less chance of getting caught. Even if George was nicked, he'd only be looking at a caution or a few hours' community service, nothing to worry about. If he'd stuck to bank jobs, he'd have been continually looking over his shoulder, worrying about some beak handing him a two to five-year stretch!

Steve Drummond could feel the weight of severe depression bearing down upon him. The Class Justice movement was floundering upon the rocks of disaster. After the bungled attack on the Brixton Black Separatists, Drummond had lost his entire membership with the sole exception of George Sanders. Even worse was the current issue of the organisation's paper which carried a front page story praising those proletarians who'd carried out the attack on the Industrial League's Croydon complex. Thanks to what the media were hailing as some very fancy police work, it was now well-known that this outrage had actually been the work of Nazi activists. Thousands of copies of the latest *Class Justice* had already been sold and Steve was having problems withdrawing the rest from various commercial distribution networks. Drummond had made some major political blunders at a time when his organisation was being eclipsed by the Nihilist Alliance and the anarchist leader was left wondering whether Class Justice would survive the resultant crisis.

On top of these political worries, Steve was frustrated by his inability to pull a bird who'd provide him with regular doses of genetic ecstasy. His relationship with Patricia Good had been nothing short of a nightmare. To have spent so long courting the Catholic bitch without actually getting his end away was highly embarrassing. Drummond wondered whether he should phone Patricia and offer to get back together with her if she'd give him a good shagging. Having toyed with the idea for several hours, Steve decided it was best to wait until the old bag came crawling back to him. That would put him in a stronger position for dictating the terms on which their affair could be revived!

As it happened, Drummond did not have to wait long before Good re-entered his life. As the Class Justice supremo set to work cooking up some cracking copy for the next issue of his organisation's newspaper, Patricia was heading for Stoke Newington. The Catholic girl wasn't sure where to find the light of her life but having tried the Tanners and then Amhurst Road, she finally tracked Steve down at George Sanders' pad.

'How did you know where to find me?' Drummond demanded when he answered Good's urgent knock at the door.

'A process of elimination,' Patricia replied, 'it's a standard method used by investigative journalists. Now let me in, I have to talk to you.'

'Okay,' Steve conceded.

Drummond and Good were silent as they walked through to the kitchen. Steve put the kettle on. Patricia was looking for words to express all the feelings that were welling up inside her. After what seemed like an eternity, it was Drummond who finally spoke.

'It's nice to see you, but why are you here?'

'I love you,' Good crooned.

'That's easy to say,' Steve was desperate to get his oats, 'but I want you to prove it to me. I need more than a platonic relationship. I want you to give me some physical loving too!'

'I've got a sweetie for you,' Patricia cooed as she pulled a Mars Bar from her handbag.

'Don't try to change the subject,' Drummond seethed. 'Let's hit the sack. George is out expropriating funds for the movement, he said he'd be late getting back and so no one is gonna disturb us.'

Steve took the Catholic girl by the hand and led her through to a bedroom. Good was still clutching the Mars Bar as she watched Drummond undress. Patricia let Steve paw her. She flinched when he removed her panties but did nothing to hinder the operation. Drummond kissed Good on the mouth and simultaneously massaged her left breast. Then Steve shifted his weight and the couple fell onto the bed. The anarchist tried to rub Patricia's clitoris with his finger.

'No!' Good yelled. 'No, no, no! If you have to make love to me, just stick your thing straight in and get it over with as quickly as possible!'

'I can't get it in,' Drummond explained, 'until you've juiced up. If you won't let me finger you, then you'll have to massage the love button yourself.'

'Okay, okay!' Patricia was desperate to please but morbidly afraid of sex. 'I'll do it.'

'That's better,' Steve gushed, 'keep rubbing your clit. Once the juice is really flowing, stick your finger inside your cunt.'

'I can't do that!' Good was distraught. 'It's dirty! I'll use the Mars Bar instead. I want you to unwrap the sweetie and hand it to me.'

The anarchist did as he was told and it wasn't long before Patricia was working the soft chocolate bar in and out of her twat. The Catholic girl was moaning softly but she was unable to loosen up completely and go with the flow of her desires. Years of papal repression had taken their toll on Patricia and not even Steve with his anarchist ideology was capable of breaking through to the ground zero of their common genetic heritage!

'You're doing well!' Drummond encouraged. 'Now take the Mars Bar out of your cunt and let me slip inside you!'

'No!' Good yelped as she pushed Steve away. 'I can't, I just can't do it! Why don't you eat the sweetie instead?'

Patricia held out the Mars Bar and Steve took it from her. It was covered in love juice and partially melted. Drummond figured that a mere taste of ecstasy was worse than the most vicious of repressions. He threw the sweetie against a wall before picking up his clothes and storming out of the room.

✤ FOURTEEN ✤

GANGS OF NIHILISTS were swarming out of Brixton tube station and fraternising with local youths. There was complete agreement between these two parties about the absolute necessity of slaying the nationalist beast. Animated conversations sprang up between groups of people who'd only just met each other. The time was repeatedly checked on hundreds of wrist watches. Everyone present was anxious to get stuck into the handful of racist morons whose meeting would very soon be trashed. The minutes ticked away and by seven o'clock, several thousand people had assembled outside Brixton tube station. At last, Mike Armilus gave the word and this barmy army marched on Railton Road.

Matt Dread and Nigel Devi had heard rumours that fanatical race-mixers were hell bent on attacking the joint meeting between the Brixton Black Separatists and the Violent Party. However, the nationalist leaders had dismissed these stories as the product of wishful thinking on the part of liberal toadies disappointed at the ease with which Dread had foiled the Class Justice assault on his HQ. As a result, the reactionaries had been rather lax about the security arrangements for their conference. It therefore came as something of a shock when they heard thousands of class-conscious proletarians chanting anti-fascist slogans outside the besieged nationalist meeting.

'Break out the guns,' Dread thundered. 'Snipe at the bastards from the upstairs windows and make sure you only shoot whites. I want the demonstrators divided on racial lines!'

'Hold on a minute!' Nigel Devi protested. 'I agree with you about dividing the lefties on racial lines but this is an Aryan country and therefore it's only ethnics who should be killed.'

'Crap,' Dread snapped. 'We were brought here against our will and we wanna go back to Africa, therefore it's gotta be whitey who gets shot. Anyway, you ain't got any guns, so it's up to me to decide who gets wasted!'

'Cunt!' Devi howled as he launched himself at Dread.

Thus, while the forces of progress smashed their way into the building, white nationalists fought black nationalists as each group of bigots desperately sought to prevent their opposite numbers from gaining access to a cupboard full of guns. By the time Mike Armilus led a band of teenage street fighters into the conference room, the nationalists had lost both the physical and the ideological battle.

POW! Black and white fists thudded into nationalist faces, while DM boots simultaneously smashed against exposed groins. ZOWIE! Several right-wingers staggered backwards spitting out gouts of blood and the occasional piece of broken tooth. KERRANG! The reactionary tossers were beaten senseless. Nationalist skulls were cracked open like so many eggs as the race-hate activists were given a taste of proletarian justice!

'Gangster! Gangster! We're gonna kill you for the shit you've pulled on our community. You'll never use nationalist politics as a cover for your criminal rackets again!' a group of soul brothers who'd surrounded Matt Dread thundered.

The nationalist leader was on the receiving end of a bloody good pasting. Führer Matt howled in rage as the boots rained against his prostrate body. He'd brought his arms up over his face but the steel toe-caps were still wreaking a terrible toll as they slammed into his flesh. The agony increased and Dread found himself looking down upon his tormentors as they literally kicked shit out of his mortal shell. Grids of white light bisected Dread's bulk. As the nationalist choked on his own blood, a dark vapour obscured the bastard's view of the silver cord that connected his spirit to his body. Blood welled up through Dread's mouth and pressure from the black cloud snapped the last few threads that bound him to this world.

The building was evacuated once the last black nationalist had been hanged by the guts of the last white reactionary. Immediately afterwards, the place was torched and as it burnt to the ground, rioting broke out in other parts of Brixton. The hydra-headed monster of nationalism had been defeated and there was now time for ebullient teenagers to have some fun. As shops were looted, Mike Armilus gathered his forces at the foot of Brixton Hill. He was preparing his followers for a second assault, a fight in which the nihilists would stand alone, unaided by feisty South London street kids.

While Mike Armilus was leading the forces of progress against nationalist reaction in Railton Road, Swift Nick Carter was marvelling at his luck. Liz Jones had just been ushered into his cell by Brian Byford and the two of them were now locked up together. Given the fact that Nick had been 'inside' for days, imprisoned without the benefits of femail company, there was now only one thing on his mind – SEX!

'I want you to fuck me senseless,' Jones buzzed once Byford was out of ear shot.

'No problem,' Carter assured her as he unzipped his flies and pulled out his cock. 'What about giving me a blow job before we get down to anything serious?'

'No, no, no!' after the débâcle with Byford, Liz was desperate for a good knobbing. 'I want you to go straight up my cunt! I want you to spunk up inside me! I want to have your baby!'

'There's a bit of a problem with your last wish,' Nick cackled. 'You see, I had a vasectomy years ago. I've always felt blokes should be more responsible about contraception and so I had myself snipped to prevent any chick getting knocked up on my account!'

'I don't believe it!' Jones felt as though she was the accursed of the gods. 'My mission to save your seed for Jesus, to protect the genetic heritage of the White Race, has been doomed to failure from the start! I've gone through so much shit to reach you and it was all for nothing!'

Then the last disciple of the White Seed of Christ killed herself by banging her head repeatedly against the wall. Carter didn't attempt to stop the girl from beating her brains into a bloody pulp, she was obviously a complete nutter and there was nothing he could do about her mental state. All things considered, she was probably better off dead. Unfortunately, the noise Jones had been making attracted Byford's attention.

'You've murdered my girlfriend!' the screw had clearly lost his frail grip on reality. 'Now I'm gonna kill you!'

When Byford unlocked the door to Nick's cell, the nihilist rushed at the warder. He soon got the better of the older man, who he kicked unconscious and then relieved of his keys. Within a matter of minutes, Carter had freed countless Category A prisoners. Fortunately, none of them recognised him, although he was challenged on more than one occasion.

'Are you that mad bomber?' a serial killer wanted to know.

'No, I'm a drugs dealer,' Nick lied.

'Let's take over the wing and demand to be given the cunt who blew up the cenotaph. I'm a patriot, I wanna kill that Nick Carter, 'ee don't deserve a trial. I'm gonna kill 'im an' the Jute bastard they've got banged up in 'ere!'

Troops were hurriedly called in to help deal with the disturbance at Brixton Prison. They arrived as

Mike Armilus was gathering his forces at the foot of Brixton Hill. The nihilists who marched on the prison did not expect to be met by soldiers armed with machine guns. They'd have been a match for the screws but against this heavily armed force the nihilists didn't stand a chance. Mike Armilus and Bogroll Bates were at the head of the revolutionary column, as a direct consequence of this, they were the first two victims of army gunfire. Dozens of nihilists were mown down by the soldiers, while those who'd managed to dodge the bullets, turned on their heels and fled.

Having had a taste of action, the squaddies marched into the prison and shot dead every inmate, including a great number who were securely locked in their cells. Swift Nick Carter was one of the many men summarily executed. Although the government ordered the inevitable inquiry into these deaths, the army was secretly assured that no charges would be brought against its men. The Prime Minister was pleased that his government had been spared the expense of dragging Swift Nick, and many another reprobate, through the courts.

❖ EPILOGUE ❖

STEVE DRUMMOND WAS sweating under the heat of the television lights. Nevertheless, he managed to hide his nervousness under an outward display of aggression. This was his first appearance on a national television chat show and it was guaranteed to boost the sales of the Class Justice book just issued by a major publishing firm. Simon O'Hara was an easy touch really, he didn't ask difficult political questions, he simply wanted to milk the interview for laughs and sensation.

'So tell me,' O'Hara was saying, 'what do you think of the people who rioted in Brixton last year?'

'They're working-class heroes, ain't they!' Drummond was shameless about stating the obvious.

'And what about Tina Lea, the woman police are seeking in connection with the murder of Inspector James Newman?'

'She's a personal friend of mine, ain't she!' Steve boasted defiantly, although having rowed with the girl he was destined never to speak to her again.

'Do you know where she is at the moment?' O'Hara persisted.

'No!' Drummond was emphatic. 'And even if I did, I wouldn't tell you. I know your brother works at Scotland Yard. He's on the Class Justice death list, you won't get anything out of me!'

There were a few more questions and then the show was over. Steve made his way to the bog. There was a big smile on his face as he pissed into a urinal. Things were going well for him, he'd built his organisation back up to a dozen members and publicly taken credit for a whole series of riots and murders that the authorities knew were nothing to do with Class Justice. While Drummond's organisation was not taken very seriously on the street, it got a lot of press coverage and in Steve's book, that was what really counted.

'You were super!' Simon O'Hara boomed as he minced across the toilet and then fingered Drummond's balls. 'Let me give you a blow job.'

'Okay,' the anarchist growled, 'but be quick about it.'

As the chat show host sucked on his plonker, Steve resolved to stick to gay sex in the future. Getting to shove his dick down some geezer's throat was easy, whereas his attempts at shafting Patricia Good had been a bloody disaster. When Drummond thought about it, he realised he'd never had a lot of luck with the birds. From now on, Steve vowed to concentrate on what he was good at, pulling blokes and facilitating media representations of revolt!

Also by Stewart Home
and published by Serpent's Tail

Slow Death

A gang of socially ambitious skinheads runs riot
through the London art world, plotting the rebirth
and violent demise of an elusive avant-garde art
movement. Taking genre fiction for a ride, *Slow
Death* uses obscenity, black humor and repetition
for the sake of ironic deconstruction. The sleazy
sex is always graphic and all traditional notions of
literary taste and depth are ditched in favor of a
transgressive aesthetic inspired by writers as diverse
as Homer, de Sade, Laus Theweleit, and '70s cult
writer Richard Allen.

'Home is a serious "wind-up" artist emerging from
a high-culture, oppositional tradition that started
with Dada and descended to the street in the 1970s
with punk. His main theme is that so-called
uncontrollable desire for sex (and maybe violence)
are in fact highly artificial constructed by social
convention in general, and by the modern state in
particular.'
—*New Statesman and Society*

'Speed-freak pose.'
—*Melody Maker*

'. . . The skinhead author whose sperm'n'blood-
sodden scribblings about the insane fringes of pop
culture make Will Self's writings read like the self-
indulgent dribblings of a sad middle-class Oxbridge
junkie trying to sound "hard".'
—*New Musical Express*

Come Before Christ and Murder Love

Ken Callan is running away but the past keeps catching up with him. That's the price he has to pay for using the occult to get his sexual kicks while manipulating everyone around him. Sometimes Callan claims to be the victim of a state-sponsored mind control programme, at others, the man in charge of the whole operation. The thing is, Callan has a thousand different identities, and a range of London apartments, disciples, lovers, and possibly murder victims to go with the lifestyle.

Come Before Christ and Murder Love is a tale of mental disorder, magick, London, food, thought control and human sacrifice. Stewart Home's outrageous new novel explores sex and the occult both as ideologies and ways of organizing 'knowledge'. Here, the traditional distictions between novelist and critic, truth and fiction, authors and their audience are visibly eroded.

'It's an exercise in futility to complain that Home's novels lack depth, characterization or complex plots: that is the whole point. The project operates within its contradictions, subverting the spirit of redundant industrial fiction, while honoring the form. . . . Home's language feeds on metropolitan restlessness, movement, lists of trains and buses, gigs in pubs, rucks outside phone kiosks, the epiphany of the grease caff.'
—Iain Sinclair, *London Review of Books*

Edited by Stewart Home

Mind Invaders
A reader in psychic warfare, cultural sabotage and semiotic terrorism

This collection comprehensively samples the resistance culture of recent years, featuring innumerable utopian protest groups dedicated to attacking the very foundations of 'Western Civilisation'.

In London, the Association of Autonomous Astronauts is expanding the terrain of social struggle, launching an independent proletarian space exploration programme. Future ventures shall include raves in space. In Italy, the Bologna Psychogeographical Association is helping to levitate government buildings and playing mind games with prime-time TV. Meanwhile their London counterparts are busy exposing the macabre occult practices of the British Royal Family, and Decadent Action plots to bring capitalism to its knees through a programme of exorbitant shopping sprees leading to hyper-inflation. Break out the champagne and canapés!

'Stewart Home curates the fistful of mercury that is the commonwealth of the "mind invader". Texts so crazy you have to trust them ... A dazzling anti-anthology.'
—*Iain Sinclair*

'In the 2090s *Mind Invaders* will be revered as the roots to the creative paranoia that has corroded our once mighty civilisation. Read this book and die.'
—*Bill Drummond, KLF*